Down and Dirty

ITALIAN STALLIONS, BOOK 1

MARI CARR

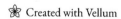

Down and Dirty

What happens when a down-on-her-luck single mom meets not one, but two sexy saviors? Roommates with twice the benefits.

Jess has one goal in life—protect her son. But when an overcrowded shelter puts her and Jasper out on the street in the dead of winter, she fears she's going to fail that mission. Help comes in the form of confirmed bachelors, Tony Moretti and Dr. Rhys Beaumont.

Tony and Rhys share the same motto—work hard, play harder. But when fate drops a homeless waitress and her young son on their doorstep, their wild and free lifestyle takes a sharp turn. Their desire to help her is only surpassed by their desire to claim her, share her, make her theirs.

When Tony and Rhys offer Jess a place to stay and security, there's no denying the chemistry between the three of them. All she has to do is let them in. But Jess isn't willing to get hurt again . . . no matter how persuasive, how determined, how deliciously possessive her new roommates are.

Chapter One

"I'm sorry, but we don't have any more room tonight."

"Yes, but—" Jess started.

"Lady, if I had room, I'd let you in. I'm not being a dick. I'm just telling you we're maxed out. Try the shelter down on..." The man glanced down at Jasper and hesitated. Then he went ahead and finished. "Forty-Eighth Street. They might have some room."

Jess could tell from the man's frustrated tone she wasn't the first person to beg to be allowed in tonight. She also knew there was no way in hell she was taking Jasper to the 48th Street shelter again. There were degrees of homeless shelters in Philly and she'd learned firsthand that 48th Street was one of the worst. While it was open to women only, that didn't mean it was particularly safe.

Last night, they'd listened to a mentally ill woman cry loudly for hours, while another woman—strung out on God only knew what—screamed obscenities at anyone who looked at her twice. Jess knew beyond a shadow of a doubt that she and Jasper would be safer taking their chances on the streets.

Instead of continuing to fight, she merely nodded, a feeling of utter defeat washing through her as she watched the man close the door to the shelter.

She remained outside the door for a few moments, her mind whirling over what the hell she was supposed to do now.

January is no time to learn how to be homeless, she thought wearily.

"Mommy. I'm cold."

Jess glanced down at her sweet little six-year-old and fought back the panic threatening to break through the cracks in her fake composure.

"I'm know, buddy. Let's, um..."

Let's what?

She was the mom. She was supposed to have the answers, but she was fresh out of options. She was tired, hungry, stressed out, freaked out, and running on fumes. She'd been racing toward this brick wall in a speeding car with no brakes for weeks now. Tonight, she'd finally slammed into it.

Game over.

"Let's walk back to Miss Debbie's and get the car."

Jasper, who was obviously experiencing the same exhaustion and hunger she was, did exactly what *she* felt like doing.

He whined.

Loudly.

And even stamped his feet, just to make sure he was driving his point home.

"I don't want to walk anymore. I'm too tired." The tears in his eyes were her undoing, and she swallowed the lump in her throat. She couldn't stand to see him cry, especially when none of this was his fault.

She took a deep breath and beat back her panic, her fear, her own tears. She couldn't let Jasper down, and she sure as hell couldn't let him see her fall apart.

She also couldn't blame him for refusing to walk on. She'd taken him on a ridiculous crisscross pattern around downtown

Philadelphia, in search of somewhere they could stay for the night.

Debbie, another waitress at the diner where Jess worked, lived ten blocks from here, and there was no way Jess could cajole Jasper into making that trek. It simply wasn't fair to ask it of him.

"Come on," she said, bending down. "I'll carry you. It won't take us long."

He lifted his arms and she hefted him up, positioning him on her hip securely. He was growing up so fast, getting bigger every day, and she realized her days of being able to carry her baby boy around were numbered.

"This way, we'll stay warmer too," she added, fighting hard to infuse her tone with some optimism, a difficult task, given the fact she wanted to scream the world down right now.

Jasper didn't respond, either with words or even a smile. Instead, he put his head on her shoulder and closed his eyes, which proved exactly how tired he was. Lately, Jasper had been proclaiming himself too big to be coddled or babied. The fact he was willing to be carried proved she'd pushed him way past his limits today.

The two of them made the trip back across town, plowing headlong into the biting, brutal January wind. Weather forecasters were predicting more snow in the next day or two. Jasper turned his face away from the strong gales, burying it in the crook of her neck and shoulder. Jess wished she could do the same. Her eyes stung, her nose ran, her cheeks were numb, and she shivered violently, even though she was bundled up in a hat, gloves, boots, and a coat. Granted, her coat and boots had seen better days, and the pointer finger on her right hand was sticking out of a hole in the glove.

Nothing had gone right today.

No, in truth, the shit had been hitting the fan ever since New Year's Day.

That was when she'd finally run out of ways to rob Peter to

pay Paul, and her landlord followed through on his months-long threat to evict them. Jess and Jasper had been couch-hopping since then, trying not to overstay their welcome with friends and even acquaintances, people who truly didn't have room for them to begin with. She'd used up every favor and then some in the past four weeks. So last night, for the first time, they'd resorted to sleeping in the shelter.

Though Jess wouldn't call what she did there sleeping. It was probably more accurate to say Jasper slept. She'd merely stayed in place, sitting in an uncomfortable chair, clinging to her son, praying no one did anything to hurt them while counting the hours until morning, when she could fight her way through another day. She'd managed to grab less than an hour of sleep, which had left her stumbling around in a fog all day, her brain struggling to function properly.

"I don't wanna stay with Miss Debbie. The bad man is there," Jasper murmured against her neck.

Jess wasn't intending to ask Debbie to take them in. They'd stayed at Debbie's house the majority of the first three weeks after losing their apartment, but a week ago, Debbie's husband had given the couch she and Jasper had been sharing to his just-out-of-jail brother, Mario.

Mario was bad fucking news, and there was no way Jess could stay at her friend's place while he was there. Not with the way he leered and made lewd sexual comments about all the vile things he wanted to do to her—in front of Jasper.

When Mario's hateful, threatening words confused and frightened her son, Jess had tried to explain, as gently as she could to her sweet, innocent little boy, that there were good people in the world, but there were also some bad ones as well.

Unfortunately, it felt like all she and Jasper had been encountering lately were the bad people, including not only Mario but also a junkie who'd tried to steal her bag on the street, the guy at the grocery store who'd embarrassed them when they didn't have enough money to buy the few measly things in their basket, and...

Jess sighed and mentally added Brenda, her *former* babysitter to the list. It was Brenda's fault they'd been too late to get in line for a bed at the shelter. Brenda was a stay-at-home mom of three rambunctious boys, and she'd agreed to take care of Jasper after school every day until Jess finished her shift at the diner.

That afternoon, Brenda had claimed her husband, Rodney, didn't want her to babysit Jasper anymore. Apparently, he didn't like having a houseful of loud kids when he got home from work. Then she informed Jess that Jasper had broken a lamp. Jasper said it was an accident and he was sorry, but Brenda was too pissed off to accept his apology.

Jess tried to explain that removing Jasper from the equation wasn't going to make Brenda's house suddenly quiet, but the woman wouldn't back down, claiming she was done taking care of "someone else's brat."

Then she demanded that Jess pay everything she owed her for babysitting, plus fifty dollars for a lamp Jess was certain hadn't cost more than twenty. It had taken every bit of the tip money she had in her purse to cover the debt—which meant in addition to having no place to stay tonight, she didn't even have cash to buy them food.

And now she only had two days to figure out childcare for Jasper after school on Monday.

She pushed that worry away until tomorrow. The more pressing problem was getting them through tonight.

Jess blew out a sigh of relief when they arrived at Debbie's. She considered going in for a moment and asking to stay, but then she recalled Mario's comments about her tight ass—and how he'd like to fuck it raw. So instead, she reached into her bag and pulled out her car keys.

Her car was the one thing she'd refused to relinquish when

facing eviction, even if the money she could've made off selling the hunk of junk would have paid a couple of bills initially.

She'd decided against it. For one thing, it really was a piece of shit, and she'd be lucky to get a few hundred bucks for it, nowhere near enough to allow them to rent a new apartment or keep the old one for more than a month or two. Plus, she needed the car to get to her weekend job as a housekeeper at a motel on the outskirts of Philadelphia.

If she was being honest with herself, she knew she was going to have to sell the car at some point. But as she considered the dire straits she and Jasper were in at the moment, she was glad to have the security blanket of a vehicle.

If she could just hold on to it until spring and better weather...

For now, she was able to park it for free at Debbie's. The only time she drove it was on the weekends, so it wasn't like she was wasting a ton of money on gas. The rest of the week, she and Jasper either took the bus, the subway, or walked everywhere.

"Come on, Jasper. Hop in." She opened the back door and secured Jasper into his booster seat, then she reached for a blanket she kept in the car and tucked it around him. Once he was settled, she bopped him on the nose with the finger sticking out of her glove. His scowl finally loosened, and he giggled.

"You're silly, Mommy."

She walked around to the driver's side and climbed behind the wheel, briefly sending up the same short prayer she always did when she turned the key.

"Please start."

Mercifully—and for the first time today—something went right and the engine turned over. She cranked the heat up on high, even though she knew it would be at least ten minutes before it stopped blowing out cold air. Right now, she was so fucking freezing, even the cool air felt like a blessing.

She pulled out of the parking lot with absolutely no clue

where she was going. All she knew was they were out of the frigid night air and off the streets.

"Are we going to get some dinner? I'm hungry."

Damn. Now that he was sitting down and out of the cold, it seemed Jasper had moved on to the next item on his list of needs.

Jess did a mental inventory of what she had in her gargantuan bag. Ever since losing their home, she was never without her oversized canvas tote, where she kept her wallet, a change of clothes for both her and Jasper, toiletries, and snacks.

"Let's find somewhere to park and I'll rustle something up for us." Jess glanced at her gas gauge and grimaced when she realized she only had a quarter of a tank. She'd resigned herself to the idea that they would have to sleep in the car, even though the thought terrified her. The streets of Philadelphia weren't somewhere she really wanted to be after dark, and there was no way she had enough gas to keep the car running all night.

She considered her empty wallet again.

No help there, she thought.

Wait. It wasn't completely empty.

She fumbled around inside the bag for her wallet while she waited at a stoplight. Once she found it, she withdrew the business card tucked inside and looked at the address. The place wasn't too far from here.

She turned left at the next stoplight, her course decided. When she pulled up in front of the building, she parallel parked on the street in the spot right outside the main entrance and put the car in park. She took a moment to study the large four-story brick building that was a perfect blend of old and new architecture. Connected to the other buildings on either side, it took up a large part of the block, boasting a corner spot.

She'd always been fond of American history, so when she'd first arrived in Philadelphia, she'd enjoyed walking around the city, studying houses and historical sites that had been around since the nineteenth century. It was clear this building was quite old, though it had been beautifully restored.

The tall, arched windows on the first floor were part of the original design, but the glass inside was new, crystal clear and shiny. The sign on the main entry indicated the two businesses —a doctor's office and a restoration company—that resided behind the dark brown wooden door. The front portico was impressive, grand and inviting, made even more so by the ornate lunette window above the door.

She assumed the businesses occupied the first and second floors, which were both dark, as it was well after work hours. However, there was lots of light coming from the top two floors, allowing her to easily see the third-story balcony that jutted out above a large bay window on the second floor. She found herself wondering about those top two floors, not because she was terribly fascinated in the layout of the building, but because she was curious about the people inside.

She'd lifted the business card several months earlier from a bulletin board her boss had hanging near the front door of the diner—his way of promoting local businesses. At the time, she hadn't been able to reason out why on earth she thought she'd ever need it. She sure as hell didn't have a home that needed renovation.

Jess had brushed it off initially as a foolish—and lonely— woman's silliness. The men who lived here—Tony Moretti, who owned the restoration company as well as the doctor, Rhys Beaumont—were regulars at the diner where she worked, so she'd seen them pretty much weekly ever since she'd started working there four years ago.

She'd overheard them talking about buying this building a couple of years earlier, describing their plans for renovating it to their weekly Wednesday lunch companions, a large group of men who were either relatives or friends. She'd been so enthralled by their intentions for the building, she'd eavesdropped more than was polite, refilling their water glasses far too often.

The men always sat in her section at the diner, and the other waitresses constantly expressed their jealousy over that fact. Tony, Rhys, and the other men were all handsome and funny, kind to her, and good tippers.

Those small tidbits—plus their names, occupations, and this address, thanks to the business card—were the sum total of Jess's knowledge about them. So coming here had been stupid as hell. Because apart from where she worked and her first name, the men didn't know *her* either, and there was no way she could knock on that grand, gorgeous door, and say, "Hey, remember me from the diner? Can my son and I crash on your couch tonight?"

She shook her head, feeling like a fool for thinking the words, and even more foolish for coming here.

Chalk up another stupid decision due to her lack of sleep.

Her mother had always accused her of having too much pride, but damn if it hadn't taken a beating this month. Regardless, she pushed away thoughts of the strangers inside the building, turning her attention to the more pressing matter.

Unfastening her seat belt, she twisted around so she could speak to Jasper.

"Are you up for a little adventure tonight?" she asked, trying to infuse as much excitement into her tone as possible.

Jasper gave her a curious look. "What?"

"We're camping," she said, aware the word alone would help sell her insane idea to her son.

As expected, he lit up like a Christmas tree, his eyes going wide. The two of them had spent a lot of time at the public library this month, as it gave them somewhere warm to kill a few hours so they wouldn't arrive at her friends' houses until just before bedtime. She'd been working hard not to overstay her welcome or be an unwanted burden.

Jasper's latest obsession was camping books. She couldn't

count how many times she'd read *Llama Llama Loves Camping* and *Curious George Goes Camping* to him the past few weeks.

"We are?!" he said, unhooking his seat belt to jump up and hug her.

She laughed at his enthusiasm, even though she knew what she was proposing was stupid, and even dangerous. "Yes, but our camping is going to be a little different from the books we've been reading because we're going city camping."

Jasper was squirming around, full of energy now. "What's that?"

"Well, since it's winter, we have to improvise. So we're going to build a backseat tent out of clothes. All our clothes."

God bless six-year-olds and their willingness to try anything.

"Okay!" he shouted, unable to contain himself.

"But first, camp food."

She did an internal eyeroll because, while she'd never camped, something told her peanut butter crackers weren't the normal fare when crowding around a campfire. Pulling half a sleeve of saltines and a nearly empty jar of peanut butter from her bag, she waved them in the air, as if displaying something really wonderful. "Since we don't have a camp stove or a fire, we'll have to eat something that doesn't need to be cooked."

Then she dug around in her bag again, withdrawing a plastic knife. When she'd been younger, she'd read the Harry Potter books voraciously. The tote she now carried reminded her of Hermione's charmed bag in the final book, the one with a magic extender that allowed her to carry tents, books, pots and pans, and countless other things. Jess's bag was the muggle equivalent, her version heavy as hell, containing very little that would actually help them.

Jess spread the peanut butter on the crackers, more thinly than she'd have liked, but she wanted to stretch it out. In the end, she was able to make five peanut butter cracker sandwiches. And despite her growling stomach, she gave them all to Jasper because he was a growing boy and she refused to take a single bite of food if she could keep him from going to sleep hungry tonight.

"You don't want one?" Jasper asked.

She shook her head. "Nope. I had a big lunch. I'm still too full. Couldn't eat another bite." It was just a little white lie, and enough to convince her son, who shoved the crackers in his mouth like he'd never eaten before. She'd noticed lately that Jasper attacked his food like it might be his last meal, shoveling it in far too quickly. She'd told him countless times to slow down, but the words fell on deaf ears.

The same vise-like pressure that had been slowly crushing her since she'd come home from work to find the eviction notice taped to their door pressed down hard, and she found it difficult to take in a deep breath of air.

Something was going to have to give, but she didn't have a clue what. She was terrified of going to social services. Her mother hadn't been the world's greatest. Before she finally managed to get sober for good, her mom had been a mean drunk who sometimes forgot to come home at night.

As a result, Jess had been shuffled in and out of the foster care system a handful of times when she wasn't much older than Jasper, and the experience had stuck with her in a negative way. There was no way in hell she would ever let Jasper experience the bone-shaking fear of sleeping in a houseful of strangers, some of whom hadn't been kind at all.

What if social services deemed her an unfit mom?

What if they took Jasper away from her?

The thought of spending a single night away from him made her physically ill.

But...would that be better for *him*?

Was she being selfish, keeping him with her because of her own feelings?

He was cold and hungry and tired, and that was *her* fault. She'd failed him, failed them both, but she didn't know what more she could do. She worked seven days a week, for minimum

wage and tips, and she hadn't taken a single day off for herself.
Though, she'd missed one day last spring, when Jasper fell down
at school and broke his arm. That was the day that had begun
their downhill descent, as she'd started drowning in doctor and
hospital bills, in addition to the rent and food and Jasper's ever-
growing feet, which seemed to need new shoes every time she
turned around.

God. She hated feeling so helpless.

Time to get a grip.

Jess tried to shake off the heavy feelings.

Again.

This was just a bad night at the end of a bad day. They were
going to get through tonight, and then tomorrow...she'd come
up with a real plan. There had to be a place for women and children in the same position she and Jasper were in. It was time she
stopped letting her fear of social services overwhelm her better
judgment. She couldn't keep waiting for a miracle that was
never coming. She was an adult, and it was time to act like one,
time to figure this shit out.

Tomorrow, she would put the time at the library to good
use, researching options for homeless women and children in
the city. And she would bite the bullet and seek help from social
services.

She stifled a yawn and blinked a few times, her eyes dry
from lack of sleep.

Jess turned off the car and got out to open the trunk. They
were on a well-lit, quiet street, away from the heavier traffic of
downtown. Her landlord had only given them thirty minutes to
vacate their apartment, so she'd been forced to quickly shove
everything she could into trash bags and lug them down to her
car. The trunk had become their closet since then.

She grabbed three huge, overstuffed bags, carrying them to
the back car door. Opening it, she put them onto the seat next
to Jasper, then returned to the trunk to pull out a blanket and

the comforter from the twin beds they'd had in their one-bedroom apartment.

Returning to the car, she quickly climbed back into the driver's seat, kneeling on it and facing backwards so she could "cocoon" Jasper in a mountain of clothing that she prayed would keep him warm enough. In addition to that, she figured she had enough gas to run the heater ten minutes every hour until dawn, and still have enough to get to the motel for work in the morning. Hopefully, all of that would get them through the freezing-cold night.

She pushed Jasper's booster seat onto the floor, then told him to add three more pairs of socks to his feet, something he found absolutely hilarious. She let his childlike laughter bolster her, help her to beat back the terror she felt, so that she could make him believe this truly was a great adventure instead of the actions of a desperate woman.

She threw another sweatshirt on over his head, then put his coat, hat, and gloves back on.

"Okay. Here." She twisted around the back of the driver's seat awkwardly, grabbing a pile of shirts. "Lay down on the seat and you can use these as your pillow."

Jasper followed her instructions, though she wasn't sure if it was exhaustion or excitement making him so compliant. Once he'd settled down comfortably, she picked up the comforter and tucked him in tightly. Thanks to the heater, the car was actually quite toasty—for now—but she knew it would be a different story when she was forced to turn the vehicle off to conserve gas.

He looked at her expectantly. After all, she had promised a tent.

"And now...for the rest." With a flourish, she picked up one of the bags of clothing and dumped it on Jasper, prompting loud peals of laughter from her young son.

"Mommy!" he said between giggles. "This isn't a tent."

She upended another bag of clothes on him, praying it would be enough to keep him warm throughout the night.

"What?" she asked, pretending to be confused. "This isn't a tent? Are you sure?"

His wide grin gave her a great view of the gap left behind from his loss of a front baby tooth. She could tell even by the dimness of the streetlamps that the other one was loose as hell and wouldn't be far behind.

"I'm sure," he insisted.

"Then I guess we're going to have to change the name of our structure," she said as she picked up the last bag and shook the clothing out on top of him. "This isn't a tent. It's a cocoon."

She knew he'd understand the word because they'd learned about caterpillars turning into butterflies in his class at school. He'd come home that day to share what had been a thrilling discovery with her. Jasper was an intelligent, inquisitive boy, who had a genuine love for learning. She hoped that never changed.

Once he was buried in a pile of clothing, she glanced at his still-happy face. "All good?" she asked, not allowing herself to ask what she really wanted to know, which was whether or not he was warm enough. She was afraid to point out her true purpose, in case he figured out this wasn't really a game.

He nodded.

"Good. So...let me get settled and I'll read you one of your library books."

Bedtime stories were their one constant. She'd read to him even when he was a baby and too young to understand, and the ritual had become even more important—not just to him but to her as well—as they found themselves sleeping in different strange places at night.

Jess quickly removed her own boots, adding two more pairs of socks. She added another T-shirt and a sweatshirt to her layer of clothing, then put her boots, gloves, hat, and coat back on.

Tucking the last remaining blanket over her, she picked up a book and turned off the car.

"Okay." She took a deep breath, holding the book up over her head, finding the perfect beam from a streetlight so that she could see the words. Jasper would probably struggle to see the pictures, but they'd read this story many times, that wouldn't matter. "There is a house, a napping house," she began.

As she read, she realized she didn't need to see the words any more than Jasper needed a view of the pictures. This book was one of their favorites, and as she began the singsong repetition, she looked less and less at the words and more at the illustrations, at the cozy bedroom, the warm bed, the safe home.

Jasper was asleep before she finished the story, but she kept reading it. When she reached the end, she closed the book, tucked the blanket around herself—aware it would do little to keep her warm—and shivered as she sent a wish out to the universe, not just for herself but for her son as well.

"Help us find a home," she whispered to the night air.

Chapter Two

"You ready for this, old man?" Tony taunted as they stepped out of the building, both of them instantly assaulted by air so cold it cut like a knife.

"Take it easy with that 'old man' shit," Rhys replied. "I've only got three years on you."

"Yeah, but while you're knocking on the door to forty, I'm still residing in my mid-thirties. Young, virile, and about to kick your ass on this run."

Rhys chuckled even as he shook his head. He and Tony Moretti had been roommates for two years, though their association had been much longer than that.

For the last eight years, the two of them had shared office space in this building, Rhys occupying the first floor with his medical practice, while Tony and his brothers ran Moretti Brothers Restorations from the office suites on the second floor. When their landlord told them he was planning to sell the building, both he and Tony had wanted to buy it.

What could have evolved into a nasty battle for real estate instead turned into one of the best business—and personal—decisions Rhys had ever made. The two of them had decided to invest in the large building together, renovating the top two floors into a living space.

After fifteen years of living alone, Rhys certainly hadn't intended to suddenly move in with a roommate, and it hadn't been his *or* Tony's plan to live where they worked.

When Tony first proposed they renovate the top two floors, the idea had been for them to create an upscale apartment that they would rent out, increasing the value of their purchase, while giving them some income to lower their monthly mortgage payment.

Then Tony and his brothers had built the most gorgeous living space Rhys had ever seen—and he'd realized he wanted the apartment to be his home. At the time, he'd owned a house in the suburbs of Philadelphia, but because he worked long hours, he was rarely there. He'd never made any connections to his neighbors, and the large, cookie-cutter house had never felt like a home, but instead more like a hotel suite. The king of takeout, he hadn't used the kitchen to do much more than make toast for breakfast. It had basically been a place to store his stuff and sleep at night.

However, just like with their shared desire to own the building, Tony had come to the same conclusion about the apartment, anxious to get out of the too-small apartment he'd been sharing with his brother Joey across town.

And once again...they'd found that middle ground, agreeing that the apartment was large enough—actually, too large—for the two of them. The transition to roommates had been smooth, and Rhys had no regrets. His commute to the office had shrunk from a twenty-five-minute drive to two flights of stairs.

"Fuck," Tony muttered, stopping mid-stretch. "It's cold as shit out here. What do you say we do the three-mile route today and the five-mile one tomorrow?"

Rhys was tempted to accept the suggestion, but he knew putting off the longer trek wouldn't work out to their benefit in the long run. "I checked the weather," Rhys said. "Tomorrow is going to be even colder."

"Fuck," Tony repeated. "Philadelphia winters suck."

They walked down the three steps that led to the sidewalk, did a couple more quick stretches, then turned north, ready to begin one of the three routes they'd established when they first started running together.

"Let's get this over with," Tony muttered, and Rhys began with a slow jog.

He'd only taken a few strides when something unusual caught his eye, and he paused, looking toward the street. He noticed Tony hadn't even started to run—his attention already drawn to the same vehicle parked by the curb, just outside their building.

"What the hell?" Tony mused, stepping toward the vehicle. The windows of the ancient Honda were slightly frosted, but still clear enough that they could make out a person sitting in the driver's side. The car wasn't running, and given the low temperatures, it seemed odd that someone would choose to remain in an unheated car.

He and Tony moved slowly, using caution as they approached the vehicle.

"It's a woman," Tony said.

Rhys had noticed the same. Though her features were obscured by the frost on the windshield, he was able to see the slight form of a dozing female, violently shivering. Because her eyes were closed, her head tilted awkwardly in an attempt to use the headrest as a pillow, she hadn't noticed them yet.

True to his take-charge nature, Tony crossed around the car to the driver's-side door and tapped on the window. The woman inside jerked in surprise as Rhys remained on the sidewalk, observing. Her face was now turned away from him, so all he could see was the back of her winter hat and dark hair beneath, curling over her shoulders.

"Jess?" he heard Tony say.

His curiosity piqued, Rhys walked around the car as he asked, "Jess who?"

"The waitress from the diner."

Rhys confirmed it was indeed the woman who typically waited on their table every Wednesday, when he and Tony met up with several other friends for lunch at Paulie's Diner. It was a tradition the two of them had started long before they'd ever moved in together, and one that stuck afterwards. Once a week, without fail, a large table of Moretti brothers, cousins, and their friends claimed a big table at Paulie's to indulge in whatever the special of the day was.

Tony knocked on the window, bellowing at her as only a Moretti man could do. While Rhys was known for his gentle bedside-manner tone, Tony was brasher, more demanding, more...Italian. "What the hell are you doing out here? It's freezing! Open the door."

Rhys's doctor instincts took over. "You're going to scare the hell out of her, Tony. Move over." He gave the waitress a smile. "It's Rhys and Tony, from the diner, Jess," he said. "I can see you're cold." She was shivering violently and hypothermia was a real concern. "We live in that building right there. Why don't you open the car door and come inside for a few minutes? You can warm up." They needed to get her inside sooner rather than later.

What on earth was their waitress doing parked outside on a cold winter's morning?

Given the amount of frost on the windshield, it was a safe bet she'd actually been here most of the night.

"I'm o-k-kay," she said through the closed window, though her chattering teeth and the weakness of her voice belied the reassurance. "I'll l-leave."

"That isn't what we asked you to do," Tony said gruffly. "Open the damn door."

Rhys sighed. "Let me handle this, Tony."

His friend considered the request for a moment before nodding his head just once. "Do it quick."

Rhys didn't take offense to the demand, used to Tony's gruff manner. "Jess. We're not going to hurt you. You know who we are. Please open the door."

She didn't move for a moment, and Rhys feared she'd refuse, start the car, and drive away.

Finally, with trembling hands, she reached for the door, unlocking it.

Tony opened it before she could, swinging it wide.

Jess flinched at the sudden gust of cold air.

"What are you doing out here?" he demanded, forgetting his agreement to let Rhys take over.

"That doesn't matter," Rhys interrupted when Jess's eyes darted around, clearly looking for an escape. She looked like a kitten cornered by two big dogs. "Come on, Jess, we need to get you ins—"

"Mommy, I'm cold."

Both he and Tony shifted their attention to the backseat as a small boy, who couldn't be more than five or six, emerged from a huge pile of clothing.

"Mommy?" he whispered, his gaze locked on Rhys and Tony.

Jess, despite her shivering, recognized her son's unease. "It's o-k-kay, J-Jasper," she said, unable to control her intense trembling, her voice weak, breathy.

Rhys's concern grew. They needed to move her inside—but he now understood her reticence was due to her desire to protect the little boy.

"Are they bad mans?" Jasper whispered, his eyes fearful.

"M-men," Jess instinctively corrected.

Rhys's chest tightened when he realized—inadvertently or not—they were genuinely scaring the little boy and his mother.

Mercifully, Jess intervened quickly. "And n-no, b-buddy.

Not at all. These men eat at the d-diner, where I work. They're n-nice."

Jasper studied them for a moment before a more pressing need than safety took over. "I'm cold," he repeated.

"I'll t-turn on the c-car so the heater..." Jess reached for the key, then froze, her gaze shifting to the dashboard before she closed her eyes wearily. "I, uh..." she started, but it didn't appear as if she was going to find her words.

Utter exhaustion had partnered with her extreme shivering, her face pale with dark circles under her eyes, her dry lips chapped. Rhys hated the look of numb defeat as she lowered her hand, not bothering to attempt to start the car. "I...it...um..."

"You out of gas?" Tony asked.

She nodded, the simple motion appearing to cause her pain, which was no wonder, considering the awkward angle she'd been attempting to sleep in.

"This conversation can continue inside where it's warm. Come on, Jess," Rhys said, reaching for her hands, intent on getting her into one of his exam rooms, where he could treat her.

She hesitated, as did Jasper, whose look of trepidation reappeared. "Mommy," he said, reaching for her, ready to cling to her like a life preserver.

"You like pancakes, Jasper?" Tony asked before either of the skittish pair could attempt to run. "Bacon?"

Jasper licked his lips, his hungry reaction the only response as he glanced at his mother, suddenly torn.

Rhys had to hand it to Tony. He'd found the best way to ease the boy into accepting their help. Of course, there wasn't a Moretti man in existence who didn't think with their stomach.

Tony knelt down, purposely making himself appear smaller —a futile act, given the man was well over six feet tall and about that broad. "I only ask because my aunt Berta is upstairs, and she makes the fluffiest, most delicious pancakes you've ever tasted. She drowns them in butter and maple syrup. Seems to me that might be something you'd like."

Tony's aunt Berta was likely still in bed asleep, but again, Tony was using everything in his arsenal to convince Jess she would be safe to come inside. She already seemed less hesitant with the knowledge another woman would be present.

The little boy's hunger won out. "I love pancakes," he said enthusiastically. "And bacon!"

Tony chuckled. "Come on. We need to get your mommy out of the cold air and some of those pancakes in your tummy."

Jasper's love for his mother took over when he turned his attention back to her, appearing to notice her distress for the first time. "Mommy. You're shaking."

"I'm o-k-kay, Jasper. I'm not sure... We c-can't impose...s-should g-go." Jess's inability to reason things out—like the fact she'd just admitted they were out of gas, so they weren't able to go *anywhere*—concerned Rhys. Hypothermia was dangerous if left untreated, and there was no way he was letting her leave until he made sure she was okay.

"No," Rhys said more firmly, ready to drag her out of the car if necessary in order to treat her. "You know I'm a doctor, Jess. You've clearly been out in the elements too long. I want to do a quick exam of you—and Jasper," he added, though it was clear the boy had been better insulated against the cold, indicated by his lack of shivering and the healthy pink hue of his cheeks. Jasper appeared to have escaped their night in the car relatively unscathed. The same couldn't be said for his mother.

While Jasper could be coerced by food, Jess's kryptonite was clearly her son. At the mention of examining him, she glanced back at Jasper. "Is h-he okay?" she asked, genuine concern—and fear—in her tone.

"Let's go inside and I'll have a look," Rhys said noncommittally. They needed to get her warm immediately. If she continued to refuse, Rhys was going to have to let Tony steamroll through the situation. He was sort of surprised by the level of patience his friend was currently showing. Tony wasn't the type to ask for something twice.

"F-fine," Jess said, turning around to reach for a huge bag on the passenger seat next to her and pulling the strap over her head. It took her several attempts to pull the car keys from the ignition. Rhys started to reach in to do it, but he didn't want to spook her. He figured the only reason Tony hadn't intervened was because he'd opened the back door and was attempting to extract Jasper from beneath a mountain of clothing. Jess had obviously used everything at her disposal to protect her son from the cold, at the expense of her own warmth and health.

Jasper bounced out, full of energy and enthusiasm, now that a big breakfast was on his morning agenda. Jess moved more slowly, wincing in pain when her feet touched the ground.

Rhys glanced at Tony, the two of them communicating without words. Jess wasn't going to be able to walk inside on her own.

Tony, who'd grasped Jasper's hand, handed the little boy over to Rhys, then bent down in front of Jess, who was clinging to her huge bag and attempting to rise without giving away how much pain she was in. Rhys wasn't sure if that was for their benefit or her son's. Given what he'd seen from her this morning, and the small things he'd observed about her at the diner, he decided it was probably both.

"I'm going to carry you," Tony said quietly. Jess started to shake her head, but he merely reached for her. "Nonnegotiable."

Rhys waited as Tony picked up Jess, juggling her in his strong arms and carrying her to the sidewalk. Then Rhys shut the driver's door, guiding Jasper in front of Tony and Jess so the two of them could open the front door to their building.

He started for one of the examination rooms, but Tony blew by him, carrying Jess to the stairs while glancing over his shoulder. "Get what you need. You can check her out in our apartment. Promised Jasper breakfast."

Rhys considered arguing, then decided against it. Given her violent trembling, he was fairly certain she was only in the first stage of hypothermia, her case mild. Otherwise, the shivering would have stopped, and she'd be fading in and out of consciousness.

He retrieved a stethoscope—which he looped around Jasper's neck, much to the boy's delight—heating compresses, ibuprofen, and a couple of thermometers. Then, the two of them followed in Tony's wake as he carried Jess up the two flights of stairs to their place.

Tony gently sat her on the couch. Jasper dropped Rhys's hand once they were in the living room, quickly darting across the space to sit next to his mother.

As Tony placed a warm fleece blanket around her shoulders, Rhys perched on the edge of the coffee table in front of her, activated a couple of the heating compresses, and slid them inside her coat.

Turning on one of the thermometers, he held it out. "I need to take your temperature."

Jess glanced down at Jasper. "What about h-him?"

"I'll get to him in a minute. You're the one I'm more worried about."

"B-but—" Jess started.

Tony dropped down on the couch, claiming the side opposite Jasper. "Put the thermometer in your mouth, Jess."

Rhys resisted the urge to smile when Jess shot Tony an annoyed look that gave him hope she wasn't in serious danger, health-wise.

Tony's demand worked when she turned back to Rhys and opened her mouth. She tried to hold the thermometer in herself, but her hand trembled too hard. Rhys gently took her hand away, holding it in his until the thermometer beeped. He withdrew it and glanced at the reading. "Ninety-five degrees. Not good but not terrible. I need to check you for frostbite," he said, as he pulled her gloves off, looking closely at her ice-cold fingers, which were red and chapped but didn't show any signs of severe frostbite. Then he recalled her inability to walk and reached for her foot, pulling one of her boots onto his lap to remove it.

"Tony, I need a tub of warm water and some more hot water bottles. Grab that heating pad from the linen closet too."

"On it." Tony rose, pulling his phone from the pocket of his Under Armour twister jacket. "I'll text Aunt Berta to bring up her electric blanket."

Around the same time they'd renovated this apartment, Tony's uncle Renzo had died of a massive heart attack, leaving behind his wife, Berta. The family had been worried about Berta—who'd never had any children of her own—living alone, so Tony had created a small apartment for her on the second floor, claiming Moretti Brothers Restorations didn't need so many offices. Berta had been delighted by the invitation to move closer to "her favorite nephew," a line she used when talking to every single one of the Moretti boys.

And while Berta had her own place on the floor below, they were more likely to find her tidying their apartment—claiming she didn't know how two such intelligent men were incapable of properly cleaning a bathroom—or in their kitchen, cooking them incredible, delicious meals. Those meals were the reason he and Tony were outside at the ass-crack of dawn to run, taking the risk of freezing their balls off. Aunt Berta—as she insisted everyone call her—had sort of become their unofficial third roommate over the past couple of years, as she, Tony, and Rhys formed a strange but working living arrangement.

Rhys unzipped Jess's boot, observing that it had seen better days. He grimaced when taking note of her attempts to keep herself warm with not one, not two, but three pairs of socks. He suspected she would have kept adding more if she could have gotten the boots over them.

Jess winced once her foot was finally free, the chill of her skin almost painful for Rhys to touch. "How does it feel?" he asked.

"It prickles. Like p-pins and n-needles," she responded.

"That's good."

"It is?"

He smiled. "Means we're looking at a case of frostnip, not full-blown frostbite. Trust me, this is better."

Looking over his shoulder, he called out for Tony. "Make sure the water in the tub is warm," he stressed. "Not hot."

"Got it," Tony yelled back from the bathroom.

"What about Jasper?"

Those were the first words Jess had spoken this morning that weren't labored, either by shallow breathing or trembling. She was beginning to warm up.

"Hang on, Miss Impatient," he said. "You have another foot." He removed the second boot and socks, checking it out as well. Like the other, there wasn't a sign of frostbite, but there was no question if she'd remained outside in that cold car for much longer, the damage would have been more severe.

Jasper had remained quiet during the examination, his wide eyes tinged with fear. Rhys offered him a comforting smile. "Your mommy is fine. She just got a little bit too cold. How are you feeling?"

"Hungry," the little boy answered honestly, and Rhys laughed. Even Jess managed a weak smile, clearly relieved to know Jasper wasn't suffering like she was.

Now that she was warming up, her energy was waning fast. Jess looked like she hadn't seen the inside of her eyelids in months. Her face was gaunt, pale, making the dark circles under her eyes all the more prominent.

Rhys was angry at himself for not noticing the subtle changes in her...but now that he considered it, she *had* lost weight in the past couple of months, and the tiredness that was now amplified by a thousand had been right there on her face the last few weeks when she'd waited on them as well.

"The clothes tent was w-warm enough?" she asked Jasper, who nodded.

"Yeah. I liked car camping, Mommy, but I don't want to do that again."

Jess shuddered, blinking rapidly several times. "I know."

Rhys noticed that she didn't offer any reassurances that they wouldn't have to—which told him exactly how bad Jess's situation was. Bur there wasn't time to delve into that. Priority number one was getting her warm.

Tony returned with the tub of water and a couple towels. He placed the tub on the floor, then slid it between Rhys and Jess. Rhys checked the temperature, nodding with approval. "This is probably going to sting, but it's the quickest way to bring your temperature back up. I assure you, this water isn't hot enough to burn. It's lukewarm at best."

Jess nodded wearily as Rhys lowered her feet into the water. She winced at the first contact, then closed her eyes, trying hard not to let them see her discomfort.

She stilled for a few moments, her breathing slower, steadier, and he let her acclimate to the water.

Tony lifted the hot water bottle in his hands. "Still need this?"

Rhys took it from him. "Yes. We'll wait a few minutes for her feet to warm up, then she can lay down and sleep with this against her chest."

Jess's eyes flew open. "I—we can't stay. I have work in a couple of hours."

Tony scowled. "I'm sure they can make do at the diner without you this morning, Jess."

She shook her head. "Not the diner. I work as a housekeeper on the weekends. At Crossings Motel, just on the outskirts of town."

"Rocco's place?" Tony asked, as Rhys chuckled. Their group of friends had a standing joke, referring to Tony as "the mayor" because they were convinced that he knew every single person in the city of Philadelphia. It was impossible to go out with Tony without him stopping to chat with no less than half a dozen people he knew from God only knows where.

"Yes. You know him?" Jess asked.

Tony nodded. "My dad's got a bunch of buddies who get together for a monthly poker game. Rocco's always there. The guy is shit at—" Tony paused as he remembered Jasper's presence, too late to clean up his language but making the attempt anyway. "He's crap at bluffing."

"What's bluffing?" Jasper asked.

"Lying about the cards," Tony explained.

Jasper was clearly still confused, but he didn't press for a better answer.

"I don't have time to sleep," Jess repeated. "I really need to get to work. I can't miss."

Tony looked ready to argue the point, but that would only serve to agitate Rhys's patient. "You said you have to be there in a couple hours?"

Jess nodded.

"Then you can lay down for one hour. Get some rest and warm up while Tony and I—"

Before he could finish, the door to their apartment opened, a female voice calling out. Jasper and Jess both jumped, but neither he nor Tony were alarmed when Aunt Berta hustled into the living room.

Tony's aunt Berta had free rein of the place, and no doubt the unusual, early morning call for an electric blanket had been the equivalent of throwing up the Bat Signal. She fussed over them like the most loving of mother hens, and while Tony pretended to be annoyed by it, Rhys felt nothing but gratitude for her efforts on their behalf. He worked extremely long hours, his work always coming first, so he appreciated Aunt Berta taking over the household chores, buying groceries, doing the laundry, preparing meals.

They'd tried to convince her that wasn't something they

expected from her, but Aunt Berta had confided in him shortly after moving in that they'd given her a purpose after losing her beloved husband, who'd been the previous recipient of all her attention. Aunt Berta was only happy if she had someone to take care of and, according to her, they were filling that need.

"What do we have here?" Aunt Berta said, her arms laden with three hot water bottles and an electric blanket. Her curious gaze landed on Jasper first, then morphed into one of genuine concern when she saw Jess huddled under the blanket, her feet in the water.

"Oh my heavens," she said, crossing the room to stand next to Tony. "Is everything alright?"

Tony took over the introductions. "Aunt Berta, this is Jess..." He paused. "I just realized I don't know your last name, Jess."

"It's Monroe," she replied.

"Jess Monroe," Tony continued. "And her son, Jasper. Jess is a waitress at Paulie's. She usually has the misfortune of having to wait on me and Rhys and the rest of the guys every Wednesday."

Jess laughed. "It's not a hardship. You're good tippers."

"I'd read him the riot act if he wasn't," Aunt Berta added. "I brought up the electric blanket."

It was obvious Aunt Berta was dying of curiosity about why a waitress from Paulie's, and her son, were in his and Tony's apartment this early in the morning, but she didn't ask. Rhys knew she'd corner one of them later for all the details.

"Thanks." Tony took the blanket and plugged it in. "Jess was just going to lay down for a while. Then we have some work to do in the kitchen. We promised this little man some of your award-winning pancakes."

"And bacon!" Jasper practically shouted.

"Jasper," Jess said, putting her hand on his knee.

Aunt Berta lit up. If there was something she loved more than anything else, it was feeding people. "Absolutely bacon.

There's no way I'd serve pancakes without it. Would you like to help me, Jasper?"

Jasper hopped up instantly, then seemed to reconsider. "Mommy," he said, "can I?"

"I'd welcome the help," Aunt Berta said when it became obvious Jess was resistant. Now that she was warmer, she was plotting to escape once more.

"Please?" Jasper pleaded.

Jess relented, obviously too tired to put up much of a fight. "Okay. But be on your best behavior. It's very nice of Miss Berta—"

"Aunt," Berta interjected. "You call me Aunt Berta, sweet pea," she said to Jasper, who seemed more excited about a new relative than the promised food.

"I'll be good, Aunt Berta," Jasper promised.

"I know you will. Now you come right on with me to the kitchen and we'll whip up a breakfast fit for a king."

Jasper practically bounced out of the room after taking Aunt Berta's hand.

"And now..." Rhys said, lifting Jess's feet from the water. After another quick, cursory exam, he dried them off and shifted the tub of water out of the way. "Lay down, Jess."

She looked as if she wanted to argue, but exhaustion was clearly winning the day. "Only for a few minutes," she said, shifting on the couch to lie on her side, facing them. She hadn't bothered to take off her coat, and he wondered if that was based on the fact that she was still cold or simply too tired to make the effort.

Tony took the electric blanket and spread it over her. "Warm enough?"

She nodded drowsily. "So warm. Just going to rest my eyes. Just a little while. I promise," she murmured, sleep claiming her quickly, her breathing slower, deeper.

Rhys knew a brief respite wasn't going to be nearly enough,

but he'd missed his opportunity to convince her to call in sick. She was already dead to the world.

He gently felt her forehead, relieved to discover she was warmer. She'd been very lucky—and he intended to make sure she realized just how much, before she left their apartment.

"Breakfast?" he whispered to Tony, who was staring at Jess with an expression somewhere between concern and frustration.

Tony nodded and followed him out of the living room.

Chapter Three

"She needs *hours* of sleep, not a damn catnap," Tony said to Rhys, just outside the doorway to the kitchen. He kept his voice low so that Aunt Berta and Jasper wouldn't hear him.

"I know, but I think we've already pushed the limit on what we can get her to agree to. She was reluctant to come in and be examined. I'm fairly certain there's no way we'll talk her into staying longer."

"Of course we can. We just take away her reason for leaving." Tony pulled out his phone.

"Who are you calling?" Rhys asked, but Tony ignored him, knowing perfectly well his friend wouldn't agree with what he was about to do.

He turned away from Rhys when Rocco answered on the third ring.

"Hey, Rocco," he said. "This is Tony Moretti."

He heard Rhys's heavy sigh behind him. "Jesus, Tony."

He didn't bother turning around to acknowledge his friend's disdain.

"Tony," Rocco said, his voice thick and raspy, a dead give-away that the old guy was a two-pack-a-day chain smoker and had been since birth. "How you doin'?"

"Doing good."

"Your dad tell you about my big win last month?" Rocco asked. "I cleaned up."

Tony chuckled. "He told me."

"You finally gonna get in on the game?"

"Hell no," Tony said. "You guys cheat."

Rocco laughed, the mirthful sound dissolving into a wet cough that had Tony wondering if he should suggest the old guy pay Rhys a visit for a checkup.

"Not me," Rocco declared after catching his breath. "But I wouldn't put it past Harvey Mitchell to hide an ace or three up his sleeve. Competitive bastard."

"Takes one to know one. Listen, Rocco," Tony said, getting to the reason for his call. "I'm calling about Jess Monroe. She works for you as a housekeeper."

"Jess? Is she okay?"

Tony took note of Rocco's sudden change in demeanor, the joking tone replaced by one of concern.

"Yeah, she's fine. She showed up here this morning," Tony fibbed, "to see Rhys. She's sick and needs some rest. I was wondering if you thought you could make do without her today."

"Oh sure, sure. Got a couple a gals I can call in to take the shift. Is Jasper sick too?"

"No. He's in the kitchen putting a dent in a stack of Aunt Berta's pancakes."

Rocco chuckled. "I bet he is. God bless that kid's appetite. Tell Jess to take it easy and if she's not better by tomorrow, just give me a call and I'll get someone to cover her again."

"Will do. And thanks, Rocco."

"No problem. Hope you reconsider joining us for this month's game—and bring your doctor friend. Be nice to have some new blood in the group."

"You're just looking for someone else to fleece."

Rocco laughed. "That too. Gets boring stealing your dad's money month after month. Give it some thought," he said before disconnecting.

When Tony finally faced his friend, he saw exactly what he expected.

Rhys was annoyed. "Seriously, Tony? You barely know this woman, yet you think it's okay to call in sick for her?"

"Rocco's motel rooms have exterior doors, not some fancy interior hallway. Which means Jess would be going right back out in the elements in a couple of hours. Would you recommend that as a doctor?"

"Of course not, but that's not our call to make."

Tony shrugged unapologetically. "Well, I made it my call."

Rhys's expression was just what Tony would have expected —resigned but unwilling to rock the boat or make a big issue of it.

Tony had lots of lifelong friends, guys he'd grown up with, played street hockey with, chased pretty girls with, and gotten drunk with.

Rhys wasn't on that list. The two of them had met eight years ago, when Rhys began renting the first floor of this building and converted it into a doctor's office. At the time, Tony had been working on the second floor with his dad and Uncle Renzo, learning the ropes of running Moretti Brothers Restorations. For the first couple of years, he and Rhys had been nothing more than acquaintances, exchanging a few pleasantries whenever their paths crossed.

One day, on a lark, Tony had invited Rhys to join him, his brothers, and friends for the Wednesday lunch get-together. And to his surprise, the workaholic doctor accepted.

Since then, Rhys had surpassed all the guys Tony had known forever, becoming his best friend in an opposites-attract sort of way.

Rhys was calm to Tony's hot-headed, careful to Tony's

impulsive, and where Rhys was driven by rational thought, Tony tended to act on pure emotion most of the time, led by gut feelings instead of his brain.

As such, he'd seen Jess shivering in that car and it flipped a switch inside him. He couldn't stand aside when someone was suffering, and though Jess put on a strong front, he could see the fear, the desperation lingering in her eyes.

He was going to help her whether she wanted him to or not.

"I wouldn't expect her to thank you for that call," Rhys said, proving exactly what Tony knew. Rhys had seen Tony's alpha male surface, and had—in his logical way—played the entire scenario through to the fallout. "Something tells me that once she's warmed up and gotten some sleep, her real personality will emerge. My money is on spitfire."

Tony smiled, hoping that was true. Over the years, Jess had become more at ease with their lunchtime gang, trading jokes and sometimes playful barbs. Ordinarily, she was always cheerful and friendly, and it wasn't a coincidence they always chose to sit in her section.

Jess was a great waitress, attentive without hovering, intelligent, funny...and if he was being really honest, gorgeous as hell. She wasn't hard on the eyes with her wavy chocolate-brown hair, bright blue eyes, high cheekbones, and petite but curvy figure.

He hadn't liked seeing her so beaten down this morning. And he realized there had been subtle changes in her appearance —weight loss and dark circles under her eyes—for several weeks now. He was kicking himself for not taking the time to ask if she was okay.

"She's looked tired at work," Tony mused.

"Yeah. I was thinking the same thing. I should have noticed. Should have asked if she was alright. I'm feeling like a pretty shitty doctor right now."

Tony waved those words away. "You're a good doctor. We don't know Jess outside of the diner, so how were we supposed to know the tiredness was more than just a bad night's sleep or the weight loss wasn't part of some diet?"

Rhys wasn't that easily convinced, but he didn't continue the argument. "She's going to be pissed when she wakes up."

"Yeah, well, she would have been late for work even if I hadn't called Rocco—because I don't intend to let her leave here today until we find out why she was sleeping in a car outside our building."

"Awesome," Rhys muttered. "So now you're adding kidnapping to your list of offenses."

Tony laughed. "Nothing quite that dire. Unless it becomes necessary, of course. Let's keep that option in reserve."

The sound of Jasper's laughter drifted from the kitchen, prompting both him and Rhys to smile. Jess had a seriously cute son.

"We better get in there," Tony said, "before the kid eats all our pancakes."

Rhys turned and led the way just as Aunt Berta placed another pancake on Jasper's plate.

The little boy looked up at their arrival, his cheeks protruding like a squirrel hoarding nuts.

"Aunt Berta can make pictures in her pancakes!" he said through his full mouth. "I got Mickey Mouse."

Rhys joined the boy at the table, while Tony stepped next to his aunt at the stove. "Can I get an Angelina Jolie one?" he joked.

Aunt Berta playfully smacked him on the arm. "You and Rhys are getting my standard circles."

"You're no fun," he teased, giving her a quick kiss on the cheek. "What can I help you with?"

"Nothing. I have everything well in hand. You go on over there and sit with Jasper and Rhys, and I'll have a stack ready for both of you in a jiffy."

As Tony approached the table, he watched as Rhys put his hand over Jasper's, stopping the boy from taking another bite.

"Slow down, Jasper. Chew what's in your mouth and swallow first. Otherwise, you're likely to choke," he cautioned.

Jasper nodded. "Okay," he said, the word muffled once more by his mouthful of pancakes.

"Here we are," Aunt Berta said as she placed two more plates on the table, one for him and one for Rhys. She turned back to the stove, then returned with another plate loaded down with crisp bacon.

Jasper's eyes widened. "Could I have a piece of bacon, please?"

Aunt Berta picked up a fork and speared three pieces to put on Jasper's plate. "You can have as many slices as you want."

"Really?" Jasper picked up the first piece, consuming it so fast, Tony wondered if he'd swallowed it whole.

"Now there's a good lad," Aunt Berta said, patting Jasper on the head. "Nice to see a boy enjoying his breakfast. Not picking at it like young Billy."

Billy was one of Tony's second cousins, and the finickiest kid he'd ever met. The family joked that Billy must have been switched at birth because if there was one thing the Morettis loved more than hockey, it was food.

"Is Mommy going to eat?" Jasper asked, eyeballing the bacon plate that was dwindling, now that he and Rhys had helped themselves to several slices.

"Your mom is asleep," Rhys said. "I don't think she got much rest last night."

Jasper put another bite of pancakes in his mouth, but this one was smaller. He appeared to have hit his limit on breakfast after four Mickey Mouse pancakes and three pieces of bacon. Tony wondered if it was a bad idea to let him stuff himself so full. While he had several cousins with kids about Jasper's age, he didn't spend a lot of time with them, and he certainly didn't pay much attention to their eating habits.

"She stayed up to turn the heat on when I got cold," Jasper explained.

"I see. Do you and your mommy spend the night in the car a lot?" Rhys asked.

Jasper shook his head. "No. Last night was the first time we went car camping."

"Where do you usually sleep?" Tony asked, aware they were more likely to get truthful answers from Jasper than Jess.

Jasper shrugged. "Depends. We used to sleep in our apartment until Mr. Robertson put a letter on our door and said we couldn't stay there anymore. Then we started sleeping on Miss Debbie's couch, but now we can't stay there on account of the bad man."

"Bad man?" Tony asked.

"He's Miss Debbie's brother-law," Jasper said, mislabeling the title. "He got out of jail and he's not very nice. He said some mean things to Mommy." He leaned forward and whispered, "Bad words. About her butt," before adding, "I...I didn't like him. He was scary." The slight tremble in his voice gave away his fear—and suddenly Tony understood Jasper's question in the car about whether or not he and Rhys were bad men.

"So you don't sleep there anymore?" Rhys asked.

Jasper shook his head. "No. We stayed with a couple more people, on their couches, but they said we couldn't keep doing that. And we couldn't ask to stay with Miss Brenda, on account she doesn't want to babysit me anymore. And we can't go back to that one shelter 'cause there was a mean woman there. Mommy said she took some drugs and they made her say a lot of bad words, just like the bad man who tried to steal Mommy's bag with all our stuff in it. She wouldn't give it to him and he knocked her down, and then some other guys came over and they made the bad man run away."

Tony felt sick as he listened to Jasper retell stories of things he was too young to have experienced. "You stay in the shelter a lot?"

"Just the one time. We tried to go to the nice one last night, but they didn't have any beds, so Mommy said we could go car camping. She made me a cocoon, like a butterfly, and put all our clothes on me. And we had camp food."

"Camp food?" Rhys asked.

"Peanut butter crackers. But Mommy didn't have any because she was still stuffed from lunch, couldn't eat another bite."

Under normal circumstances, Tony might have found humor in the small boy parroting back what were clearly his mother's words. As it was, he suspected Jess gave up her food to ensure Jasper wouldn't go to sleep hungry. Just as she'd made certain he would be warm at the expense of her own comfort. Those things would be admirable...if her actions hadn't been so damned dangerous.

He exchanged glances with Rhys, aware that his friend had come to the same conclusion. Jess and Jasper had absolutely no business staying in the homeless shelters.

"Sounds like you've had quite the adventure," Aunt Berta said carefully.

Tony had been aware of her quiet presence by the stove, knew she'd been hanging on Jasper's every word. He glanced in her direction, and it was as if he was looking in a mirror. He felt every bit of the determination he saw etched on his aunt's face. Aunt Berta had found a new cause—and it was Jess and Jasper.

He hated to break it to his aunt, but she was going to have to get in line behind him.

Then he mentally added Rhys's name to that list as well, when his roommate reached out to ruffle the boy's hair fondly. "We're glad we ran into you and your mommy."

Now that his stomach was full and he was warm, Jasper began squirming on the chair, uncertain what to do without his mother there to guide him.

"I have some crayons and coloring books down in my apartment," Aunt Berta said to Jasper. "I keep them there for when the great-nieces and nephews come to visit."

"What makes them great?" Jasper asked with genuine interest, prompting all three of the adults to laugh.

"So many things," Aunt Berta said in response. "How would you like to come color me a picture while your mommy sleeps?"

"Okay," Jasper said enthusiastically as he glanced at Rhys and Tony. "May I be excused?"

Rhys nodded. "Of course."

"Such lovely manners," Aunt Berta said, praising Jasper as he rose from his chair and accepted her proffered hand, the two of them leaving the kitchen, as if they were long-lost friends.

"Those two can't spend any more nights in the shelters." Tony wasn't sure how he was going to convince Jess to accept their help, but she sure as hell wasn't leaving until she did.

"I agree, but I don't know how she'd feel about accepting financial help from us. Seems to be quite a bit of pride in that little frame of hers." Rhys looked at his watch and cursed under his breath. "Unfortunately, I don't have time to brainstorm options with you. I have a couple of patients coming in this morning."

"You know...you could take Saturdays off occasionally."

Rhys grinned. "I'll do that. Just as soon as people stop getting sick over the weekend."

Tony shook his head, well aware his words were wasted on his workaholic roommate.

"I need to get downstairs. You good here?"

"Yeah. I'll be fine. I've got some paperwork to do. I'll hit the recliner in the living room with my laptop and watch over our patient, make sure she's okay."

Rhys nodded. "Text me when she wakes up."

"I will."

Rhys left the room as Tony remained at the kitchen table, lightly tapping his fork against the surface as he considered everything Jasper had told them.

Then he thought about Jess. He'd seen her nearly every

Wednesday for years as she waited on him and Rhys, as well as his brothers and cousins, but apart from her pretty face and cheerful demeanor, he'd known very little else about her.

Hell, he didn't even know she had a kid until this morning.

He hadn't truly noticed Jess Monroe before today. She was simply one of a hundred people who crossed his path during any given day, their interactions straightforward, simple, never going any deeper than what was on the surface.

However, now that he had seen her, learned about her life, discovered bits and pieces of who she was, he couldn't look away.

Wouldn't look away.

Because he wanted to know more.

Rising, he grabbed his laptop and quietly walked into the living room. Jess was still sound asleep, and he was relieved to see some color had returned to her cheeks. She was breathing slowly and steadily, getting the rest she desperately needed.

He refused to wake her up, and he didn't care if she gave him hell for it.

Jess was exactly where she needed to be for now.

Chapter Four

J ess sighed, her body lethargic and warm. She couldn't remember the last time she'd felt so peaceful and easy and relaxed.

Opening her eyes slowly, she blinked a few times, trying to focus her vision. She frowned when she became aware that she wasn't in her own bed.

No. She didn't have a bed or a house or...

Just like that, all her memories crashed down on her.

"Jasper!" she gasped, jerking straight upright, struggling to recall where she was.

"He's fine," a deep male voice said.

Her startled gaze darted that direction and she saw Tony Moretti, slowly lowering the leg rest of his recliner before placing his laptop on the table next to him.

"He's taking a nap in the guest room down the hall," he added, speaking to her while texting on his phone.

Jess's eyes flew around the room as she tried to force her fuzzy thoughts into focus. She and Jasper had spent the night outside in the car. Rhys and Tony had found them.

She rubbed her forehead. She'd been freezing cold and so fucking tired, she hadn't been able to think clearly. Tony had carried her inside—she flushed when she recalled that—and Rhys had given her a checkup.

The bright sunlight streaming through the window told her they were well into the morning hours.

"Shit," she said, standing quickly. "I'm late for work."

"No, you're not."

Jess glanced around the room in search of a clock but didn't see one. "What time is it?"

"Three."

"In the afternoon?!" she said loudly. "Oh my God." Then another piece fell into place. "You said you'd wake me up!"

"No, I didn't."

Jess didn't know if that was true or not. All she knew was, she'd lain under the warmest, softest blanket she'd ever felt and slept for...God...nine hours. On a stranger's couch.

And on top of that, there was a good chance she'd lost her job at the motel.

Ever since losing the apartment, Jess had worked hard at keeping her chin up, making sure she kept putting one foot in front of the other because she didn't have a choice. Jasper needed her to keep moving.

Now she wondered if she'd simply been fooling herself all this time, mistakenly believing she was strong, when really all she'd been was too tired and numb to see how miserably she was failing.

Well rested, she could suddenly see all too clearly how crappy her life was. It had all been going to shit slowly over the past seven months, and every time she thought she'd hit rock bottom, she found yet another level below it.

"I needed that mon—" she started, intent on arguing with him, raging at him for letting her sleep and lose a day's pay, even though it wasn't really Tony she was mad at. She was mad at herself. So instead, she cut herself off and muttered, "fuck it," before dropping back down on the couch wearily. "Fuck it all."

"I called Rocco, told him you were sick and wouldn't be in. You didn't lose your job, if that's what you're thinking."

She stared at Tony for a moment. "You called him?"

"You were in no condition to go to work, Jess."

She narrowed her eyes, her temper piquing again. "That wasn't your call to make." What she didn't add was that she was royally screwed without today's pay. Rocco paid her at the end of each workday in cash. Now she was sitting here with no money in her wallet and no gas in her car.

The universe was having a lot of fun at her expense.

Tony leaned forward, resting his elbows on his knees. "You were making the wrong decision, so I made the right one."

"Who the hell do you think you—"

"How's my patient?" Rhys asked, walking into the room and cutting her off mid-tirade.

"Fine," Jess said sullenly.

At the same time Tony responded, "Grumpy."

Rhys laughed. "I told you she wouldn't thank you for calling in sick for her."

"You were right," Jess said.

Rhys took a thermometer out of the breast pocket of his doctor's jacket and tapped Jess's lower lip with it, silently encouraging her to open up. She allowed him to put the thermometer under her tongue, the three of them waiting quietly until the thing beeped.

He pulled it out and looked at the readout. "Ninety-nine point six. Looks like the electric blanket did the trick. Maybe too well."

She shook off her anger, feeling bad about it. These men had done nothing but help her. "I feel much better." Reaching down, she tugged on her socks before reaching for one of her boots. The quick movement left her suddenly light-headed, and she wobbled briefly. Something neither man in the room missed.

"Jess," Rhys said, placing a steadying grip on her elbow. "Are you okay?"

"I'm fine. Just...moved too fast. Got dizzy."

"When was the last time you ate?" he asked, in that soft-spoken manner that had her convinced he was a wonderful doctor.

"Dinner last night," she lied.

Tony crossed his arms, scowling at her. "Jasper said you didn't have any of the peanut butter crackers because you were too full from lunch."

"I shouldn't have taught that kid how to talk," she joked, hoping it would lighten the sudden tension in the air.

Rhys gave her a kind smile. "Try telling us the truth this time."

"I had a sandwich before my lunch shift yesterday." After nine hours of deep, dreamless sleep, she felt too deliciously groggy to keep trying to match wits with these two.

"So you haven't had a thing to eat in over twenty-four hours. Come on." Tony crossed the room and reached out to her, and she placed her hand in his before she could consider her actions.

His hand was large, calloused—no doubt from construction work—and warm. Her stomach fluttered at his touch...and not just from hunger. She did an internal headshake at the fact something as simple as holding a man's hand could excite her. She'd obviously been alone for too long.

Tony tugged her gently from the couch, taking her coat off and tossing it down on the coffee table before reclaiming her hand.

"Where are we going?" she asked.

"Kitchen. You need food."

"No. That's not necessary." She was beholden enough to them and hated the idea of asking for anything more. "I've already overstayed my welcome," she said, even as she allowed

Tony to drag her to the kitchen, with Rhys following. "I'll go wake up Jasper and we'll get out of your hair."

"Nope. You're eating," Tony said, pulling out a chair at the kitchen table and pushing her into it. "Nonnegotiable."

"Has anyone ever told you you're a bossy son of a bitch?" she asked, looking over her shoulder at him and trying to still that flutter that wouldn't go away.

Rhys laughed loudly at her question as Tony leaned down, his breath hot in her ear as he whispered, "Every single person I've ever met."

Jess harrumphed. "Well, good. At least you're surrounded by honest people."

Tony chuckled, and she felt her cheeks flush at the deep rumble. "Morettis are honest to a fault. Always telling you shit you don't necessarily want to know."

Jess and the other waitresses at the diner had spent countless hours discussing Tony Moretti and his long, sexy, coffee-colored hair. Lately, one of the waitresses, Joy, had started a weekly pool, where the girls all took bets on whether he'd wear it down or up in a man bun. Jess had to admit she was a big fan of both styles. It was currently tied up, and her fingers itched to pull out the hair band and watch it fall over his shoulders.

"Ain't that the truth. So much honesty," Rhys muttered, and Jess's gaze traveled over to Dr. Beaumont.

Her co-workers didn't restrict themselves to mooning over just Tony. Rhys was also pretty swoon-worthy in a clean-cut, tall, dark, and handsome way. A few months ago, he'd mentioned to her at the diner he was taking part in No Shave November, and he clearly hadn't picked up a razor since. His beard was short and neatly trimmed and totally sexy.

Actually, Tony, Rhys, and *all* the guys they ate lunch with were equally hot, and more than a few of the girls at work had offered everything from home-baked cookies to free haircuts to setting her up with some cute male relative if Jess—whose section they sat in every Wednesday—would trade them tables.

Tony walked to the stove, bending down to pull a skillet out of the bottom drawer. "How do you feel about grilled cheese and tomato soup? Made some for Jasper earlier and he scarfed it down."

"I hope he wasn't too much of a bother," she said, suddenly sorry for being such a smart-ass. These men had spent the day watching her six-year-old while she slept as if she didn't have a care in the world.

"That kid? He's awesome," Tony said.

"He's polite and smart," Rhys added. "You should be very proud of him."

Jess wasn't sure why their praise caused her eyes to fill with tears. She blinked them away quickly, not wanting them to think she was a lunatic. Or any more of a lunatic than they probably already believed. "Thank you for taking care of him. And me," she added softly.

Rhys grinned. "You made our sleepy Saturday a lot more exciting. And got me out of a five-mile run. Win-win all around."

"Even so, I'm sure you had better things to do."

Tony flipped the sandwich, her mouth watering as the smell of melted cheese and butter filled the air. Her stomach growled loudly.

When the microwave beeped, Rhys rose and retrieved a bowl of tomato soup, placing it in front of her at the same time Tony delivered her sandwich.

"This is a fun turn of events," Tony mused. "It's usually you feeding us."

She picked up the sandwich and groaned in absolute delight when the first taste of gooey cheese hit her mouth. "Oh my God. This is so good."

She polished it off in five quick bites, aware she was scarfing down the sandwich exactly like Jasper would. But she couldn't stop. She was just so damn hungry. Once the sandwich was gone, she turned her attention to the soup.

"Glad you're enjoying your lunch. So...what are your plans for the rest of the day?" Tony asked.

Jess paused, spoon midway to her mouth. She considered her response as she put it back in the bowl. "I was going to figure out how far the closest gas station is from here. Jasper and I can walk for gas and—"

"I already filled your tank," Tony said. "Took care of that while you were sleeping."

"You what?" Jess was inundated by gratitude and panic at the same time. She was touched that he would go to that kind of trouble for her, while wondering how in the hell she could pay him back. She never filled her tank, instead giving it ten dollars of gas at a go. "How..."

"Your keys were on the coffee table." Tony grinned, and she tried to beat down the same arousal that struck every Wednesday when the handsome man gave her his order with that heart-stopping smile. "The tank's full. So you can mark that off your to-do list."

"I'll pay you back," she said. "Um...is Wednesday okay? I don't have any cash on me right now."

"You don't need to pay me back. It's on me."

She refused to accept that. "I'm paying you back."

Tony ignored her, pressing for more information. "So what else is on your agenda?"

She gave him a quizzical look, wondering why he was so interested in her plans. "I guess we'll hit the public library to return some books, hang out there until it's time to line up for the shelter."

Tony scowled. "I don't like the idea of you and Jasper staying in shelters, Jess."

"It's not that bad," she lied.

He and Rhys exchanged a look she couldn't begin to interpret. Until Rhys said, "If it's a case of money, let us loan you some. Just until you get back on your feet."

Jess was shaking her head before he'd finished the sentence. "No way. Absolutely not. I've got a plan." A very loose, not fully formed plan. "I'm going to do a little research in the library and..." She swallowed hard, trying to dislodge the lump that appeared whenever she thought about asking for help from social services.

"And?" Rhys prompted. "What's the plan?"

She was too ashamed to mention her fear of losing Jasper. Now that she'd had some sleep, she wondered if there was any merit to it. She wished she felt comfortable asking them their opinion.

Then she dismissed the thought. The city wouldn't take him away from her. She wouldn't let them.

"I'm going to call social services and ask for help. I should have done that earlier, but I thought I could pull us out of this hole quicker. When my friend offered to let us stay on her couch, I figured that would be enough. And then..."

"The bad man got out of jail," Tony filled in.

"Wow. Jasper really gave you the whole sordid tale, didn't he?"

"He did."

Jess ran her fingers through her hair, aware she had a serious case of bed head. "I'll make the call and hopefully they can help us immediately. If not, I figured out which shelters are safe enough. We'll stay in one of those."

Tony shook his head. "Stay here tonight."

She laughed incredulously. "Hell no."

"Why not?" Rhys asked, surprising her. She hadn't expected him to be on Team Tony regarding this. Given the fact he was in his doctor's coat, it was clear he was working. She couldn't imagine he'd want his waitress from the diner and her son under foot.

"Because..." There were too many possible responses to that question. "Because we've imposed enough."

Tony crossed his arms. "No, you haven't."

"You guys don't even know me that well. For all you know, I'm a thief here to rob you."

Rhys and Tony both laughed, as if she'd told a hilarious joke.

"We'll take our chances," Rhys replied.

Tony reached out and placed a comforting hand on her forearm, and her body tightened with an overpowering desire that felt almost foreign. It had been years since she'd felt serious lust, but there was no denying she was rolling in it right now.

"If you won't stay here for you, stay for Jasper. The kid is worn out from your ill-advised night in the car. Besides, Aunt Berta's making a pan of lasagna big enough to feed half the city. We need your help eating it, or it'll take us well into next week to finish the leftovers."

Rhys added his own fuel to the fire roaring inside her when he reached out to touch her hand. "The guest room is big enough for both of you and it has its own bathroom. You can lock the bedroom door if that's what you're worried about."

Rhys could have saved his breath. Jess might not know them well, but she was a good judge of character, and she knew without a shadow of a doubt these men wouldn't hurt her or her son.

"I'm not worried about that. I know you're good men."

"Good men. Bad men. You and Jasper seem to have two very simple, distinct categories," Tony mused.

Jess sighed. "Yeah. I guess we do. It seemed like the easiest way to explain some things..."

"Things?" Rhys prompted.

"Some things Jasper's seen and heard lately."

"Things about your ass?" Tony's question was laced with a fury that caught her off guard.

"My friend's brother-in-law made some...comments," she said, hating that Jasper was clearly still upset about them. Enough so that he'd mentioned it to Tony and Rhys.

Tony crossed his arms. "Were they *just* comments? Do I need to pay this guy a visit?"

Jess was secretly thrilled by the idea that Tony Moretti seemed more than determined to fight for her honor. She shook her head. "They were just comments, and I'm definitely keeping a wide berth between me and Jasper and that asshole."

"Exactly how long have you been homeless, Jess?" Rhys asked quietly.

She flinched inadvertently at the word *homeless* even though that was definitely what she was. It was a hard thing for that damned pride of hers to accept.

"Since January first. Jasper and I bummed places to stay with friends at first because I thought—hoped—I could find us a place to rent. But I should have known that was never going to work out for the long term. I couldn't keep asking friends to put us up, especially when they didn't have the room to begin with. So we stayed at a shelter night before last. It wasn't a great experience. I wound up sitting in a plastic chair all night. Jasper dozed on my lap while a strung-out woman kept screaming obscenities, so I asked around at work yesterday and got the name and address of a couple shelters that would be safer. I intended for us to stay at one of those last night. It's just that... yesterday, Jasper's babysitter quit on me, and she demanded that I pay her what I owed early. It cleaned me out financially and made us too late to get a bed anywhere, so we...well...you know what we did."

Tony frowned, but she raised her hand when he started to speak to cut off what she was certain was going to be a lecture.

"I know it was stupid."

"And dangerous," he added, proving she'd been right about the lecture. "If we hadn't found you when we did, Jess..."

She hadn't had time to consider that since waking up. She was sort of sorry she'd gotten so much mind-clearing sleep because when she was numb with exhaustion, she didn't have the brain capacity to face just how bad a decision she'd made. "I shouldn't have done it. I...I was tired and scared, and I did the wrong thing."

Rhys took her hand in his, squeezing it comfortingly, and the first thing she registered was how soft his touch was, how gentle, how kind *he* was. "People in desperate situations do desperate things. Promise us the next time you find yourself in such a position, you won't sit outside in a parked car. Knock on the damn door."

Jess gave him a wry grin. "I'm kind of hoping there isn't a next time."

"Me too," he said, his tone full of compassion.

"So it's settled," Tony said, rising and taking her empty plate while leaving the bowl. "You and Jasper are staying here tonight. Now finish your soup."

"I don't remember us settling anything," she said, though she wasn't about to continue the fight. The idea of staying in this warm, safe house with the promise of lasagna and a soft bed, and Tony and Rhys sleeping down the hall, was something she'd be a fool to resist. For one night, she'd give herself a break from reality.

Tomorrow, she'd venture back out into the cold, cruel world.

Tonight...she was taking the gift they were offering.

"Mommy!" she heard Jasper cry out.

She rose quickly, Tony and Rhys leading the way to the guest room. She gasped when she stepped inside one of the most beautiful bedrooms she'd ever seen. It was painted a pale dove gray and boasted tall ceilings with recessed lighting, and a huge bed with a thick, soft-looking duvet that had her itching to touch it. "This is your *guest* room?"

She didn't mean to ask the question aloud, but this bedroom was bigger than the entire shitty apartment she'd been evicted from.

She'd thought the building looked big from the outside, but it felt even larger inside.

"Yeah," Tony replied, stepping next to her. "Rhys and I renovated the top two floors when we bought the building. I have a fairly large family, so it's nice to have a room for them when they come to stay. My sister Layla, and her partners, Miguel and Finn, stay here when they come up from Baltimore for a visit."

Partners? Jess wondered what that meant, but it felt rude to ask.

Jasper was sitting up on the bed, rubbing his eyes, slowly shaking off his drowsiness. The large king-size bed seemed to swallow him. "Mommy?"

"I'm right here, buddy." She sank down next to him on the mattress, almost groaning aloud at how comfortable the bed felt. "Did you have a good nap?"

He nodded, then filled her in on his day's activities, which included everything from pancakes to coloring, to watching his favorite Disney movie, *Up*, to sleeping in the biggest bed he'd ever seen.

"And, Mommy, look," he said, pointing at the wall directly opposite the bed. "They have a movie screen in their bedroom!"

She would have laughed at Jasper's amazement if she hadn't been so taken aback by the big-screen TV occupying most of the wall. She'd been raised by a single mother who, when sober, worked two crappy jobs that gave them just enough money to exist in the "barely scraping by" column. She'd never seen true wealth up close and personal, but it seemed pretty clear neither Tony nor Rhys were hurting in the financial department.

In addition to the huge bed and television, the room had a large armoire, a desk and office chair, a double-doored closet, and an open door that revealed an equally impressive bathroom.

"Guess what, Jasper?" Tony said.

Jasper bounced on the bed, fully awake. "What?"

"You and your mommy are staying here tonight. In this room."

Jasper's eyes widened. "We are?! Can I take a bath?"

Tony's eyebrows rose. "A bath? Wow. Never met a boy who voluntarily offered to bathe. My cousin's kids act like they're being asked to shovel manure anytime someone tells them to take a bath."

"What's manure?" Jasper asked.

"Animal poop," Tony replied, the response wildly hilarious to Jasper, who giggled with glee.

"You said poop," Jasper said.

Meanwhile, Jess was hung up on Jasper's request. She didn't realize until that moment how much her son missed his baths. Since losing their apartment, she'd worked very hard to make them as small as possible in the homes where they'd crashed, staying out until just before bedtime and not imposing by asking to use the shower. As such, they'd been forced to clean themselves by taking sponge baths, and sneaking quick showers at the motel on the weekends.

"Of course you can take a bath," Rhys replied.

Jasper hopped off the bed. "Can I get my toys?"

"Toys?" he asked.

"He has a few bath toys. They're in the trunk of the car." Jess enjoyed Jasper's enthusiasm, the boy practically dancing next to the bed. "I'll run down and grab them," she promised her son. "We need some clean clothes for you too. And I should probably repack our car tent cocoon."

Tony bent down and picked up Jasper's shoes from the floor, quietly bidding the boy to sit on the floor so he could help him put them on. Jess watched the simple, almost-fatherly act, overwhelmed by amazement and longing.

"Why don't we run down for your toys and clothes, Jasper, and your mom can get a hot shower in before you take over the bathroom?" Tony said, helping her son to his feet once his shoes were back on.

A hot shower? All to herself?

Jess was starting to wonder if she'd died and gone to heaven.

"You need anything from the car, Jess?" Tony asked.

"I should probably go down. Since everything is a mess."

"I'll take care of it. You don't need to go back out in the cold today."

Jess tried to remember a single time in her life when someone took care of her. Her mother, a cold woman, had never pretended Jess was anything more than a burden. So she hadn't been shocked when her mother had kicked her out after discovering Jess was pregnant, telling her she'd made her bed and she'd have to lie in it.

"Um...maybe just a clean shirt and some jeans?" Then she looked at Jasper. "Grab some of the library books too, buddy. For bedtime."

Jasper ran to the bedroom door, his expression matching the way she felt.

They'd both won the lottery.

Even if it was just for one night.

Chapter Five

"**A**re you sure you don't want any more garlic bread, Jess," Berta offered for the third time. "You're too skinny."

Tony sighed and shook his head. "You can't tell a woman she's skinny, Aunt Berta." Then he turned his attention to Jess. "See what I mean about that honest-to-a-fault thing?"

Jess just laughed. "It's okay. And truly, I couldn't eat another bite. It was all so good."

Jasper had already asked to be excused so he could go back to the guest room to watch *SpongeBob* on "the movie screen."

He'd been plugged in for most of the afternoon, but Jess didn't have the heart to tell him no. Neither of them had watched television the past few weeks, so she didn't want to deny him the treat of vegging out as much as he wanted. God only knew when he'd get the opportunity to do so again.

"Well, no matter," Berta said, rising from the table and picking up her plate and the basket of leftover bread. "I'll pack some of it and the lasagna for you and Jasper for your lunch tomorrow."

Jess rose. "That's very nice of you, but you don't need to do that. Here, let me help you clean up."

She picked up her plate and Jasper's as Rhys and Tony helped clear the table as well. The four of them made quick work of putting the kitchen back to rights, and despite Jess insisting it wasn't necessary, Berta did indeed pack her and Jasper enough leftovers to last them for days. Jess had been hungry enough this month that she'd had to blink back tears of relief at the thought of not having to worry about food for a little while.

"That's me for the night," Berta said as she hung up the tea towel to dry. "Going to slip down the hallway to say good night to Jasper before heading to my apartment to watch *Yellowstone*. I wouldn't kick that Kevin Costner out of bed for eating crackers." She hugged Jess. "Goodbye, lovely girl. I hope you'll come back to visit us again. And be sure to bring that sweet boy with you."

Jess nodded, sad to think she most likely wouldn't see Berta again.

Once Berta left the kitchen, Tony picked up a bottle of red wine from the counter. "Glass of wine before bed?"

She started to refuse, then reconsidered. This perfect night was dwindling down quickly. "That would be really nice."

Tony poured three glasses, and they all moved into the living room. She claimed one end of the couch, while Rhys took the other. Tony plopped down in the recliner next to her side of the couch.

"I can't thank the two of you enough for today. I...last night was probably one of the worst of my life, while today...well...it was one of the best."

Rhys took a sip of wine, then put his glass on the coaster on the end table next to him. "It was nice having you and Jasper here."

"Still planning to call social services tomorrow?" Tony asked.

She nodded, hoping to set his mind at ease, not wanting him to think she'd ever repeat last night's stupidity. "I am."

"Will you tell us if they don't have room immediately?" Rhys asked.

She hesitated, knowing why Rhys asked the question, and knowing she wouldn't impose on their generosity beyond tonight.

"Scratch that," Tony interjected when she was quiet too long. "You *will* tell us if they don't have room for you."

She raised one eyebrow, pretending to be annoyed. Not exactly an easy feat, given the giddy feeling that followed his alpha male proclamations. Jess had spent a lifetime fending for herself, so when Tony used that growling, demanding voice, she let herself loosen her grip on the reins for a second. It felt ridiculously freeing, even it if was fleeting.

Regardless, she wouldn't tell them if there wasn't room. She wouldn't continue to intrude on them that way. They'd already gone above and beyond.

"I wish you'd let us give you some money," Rhys said, but Jess quickly waved his words away.

"No. I would never take money from you. I just got knocked down for a little while. I'll find my way back up. I always do."

"You and Jasper have been on your own since he was born?" Tony asked.

She shook her head. "Not exactly. I got pregnant toward the end of my senior year of high school. I was the stupid girl who thought she'd found true love. You can probably guess how that turned out."

"Your boyfriend broke up with you?" Tony asked.

"Of course he did. My mom wanted me to get an abortion, but I refused. So she kicked me out right after graduation."

"Jesus," Rhys muttered. "What did you do?"

"One of my girlfriends from school, Danielle, had decided she wanted to move to Philadelphia, and she convinced me to come with her."

Tony took a sip of wine. "Where are you from originally?"

"Des Moines."

His brows rose. "That's quite the move for two eighteen-year-old girls to make on their own."

Jess shrugged. "Danielle's home life had been worse than mine. Her dad was a junkie, always in and out of jail. So we decided we both needed a clean break. We pooled our money, bought that crappy Honda parked outside, and drove halfway across the country to Philadelphia."

Rhys tossed a throw pillow to her. "Why Philadelphia?"

She placed the pillow against the arm of the couch and leaned against its softness. "Danielle was obsessed with *Rocky*. Like, insanely so. Which is silly, I know, but honestly, it didn't matter where we went as long as it was far enough away from our parents. So we found a shitty little apartment, got jobs waiting tables at a pizza place, and after Jasper was born, we took care of him together. We didn't have a lot, but we were making it work, and we had some great times."

"Where's Danielle now?"

"About a year ago, she started dating this guy, Ritchie. He was super nice and they fell in love. He got a job in New York in April, and she decided to go with him. It was already hard paying the rent with her salary *and* mine, so I found the second job as a housekeeper at Crossings Motel. Rocco is really cool about letting me bring Jasper along so I wouldn't have to pay for a babysitter."

Tony frowned, so she went ahead and answered his concern.

"I know the motel is sketchy, but I work there during the daylight hours, cleaning up after the guests have left, and Rocco is great about keeping an eye on me and the other girl who works there."

Tony merely grunted in reply, and she fought back the urge to laugh and call him a caveman. The description certainly seemed to fit. She'd never seen this protective side to him at the diner, but that made sense, considering the danger level at Paulie's was nil.

The majority of their customers were retired old men who'd meet up for coffee or the lunch special, while talking sports and politics with whoever else was around at the time. Tony, Rhys, and their friends brought the average age of the diner down to around seventy-three whenever they walked in.

"So Jasper's father isn't in the picture at all?" Tony asked.

"Nope. He's never even seen Jasper, not in person or in a picture. Jasper is a Monroe, and I only put my name on the birth certificate. The guy turned out to be a total dick, so it's better this way. Can I ask you guys a question?"

"Of course," Rhys responded.

"How old are you?" She and the girls at the diner had always been curious about their ages.

"Thirty-five," Tony said before nodding his head toward Rhys. "And that geriatric over there is thirty-eight."

"Thought I told you to take it easy on the old cracks, Moretti."

They all shared a laugh.

"How long have you been roommates?" she asked.

Tony leaned back, settling into his recliner, looking completely relaxed and at home, and she realized she felt the same way. Though it had only been about a month, it felt like ages since she'd been able to lower her guard. Tonight, she actually felt peaceful, calm. It was funny how quickly a person could forget those feelings when they lived in constant survival mode.

"Two years," Tony replied. "Two long, loooong years."

Rhys chuckled and rolled his eyes at Tony's jest. "I'm a better roommate than your brother, Joey, and you know it. That guy is a slob."

Tony didn't bother to deny it, grinning widely. "You're not kidding. If it had been him and me living in this apartment, Aunt Berta would have turn tail and run when we offered her the second-floor apartment."

"How did she come to be here with you?" Jess asked.

"Oh man," Rhys muttered. "Here we go." Jess frowned,

confused, until Rhys explained, "The Morettis prefer epic tales to simple answers. You might as well settle in, Jess, because I have a feeling we're going to be here awhile."

Tony clearly took no offense to Rhys's joke. If anything, he looked downright flattered.

"I was born in Philadelphia, but when I was in middle school, my dad got a good job offer in Maryland, which he took. We lived there for five years, then my family moved back to Philadelphia from Baltimore after my mother passed away from cancer."

"Oh. I'm sorry, Tony."

He nodded his head once, acknowledging her sympathy. "It was rough on my dad. After all, there were five of us kids, ranging in age from seventeen to twelve."

"You're the oldest?" She'd had a million questions rolling around in her head about Tony, Rhys, and all the guys they ate lunch with every Wednesday. It was cool to finally get some details.

"Yep. I'm the oldest, then Joey, then the twins, Gio and Luca, and Layla, the only girl, is the baby. She moved back to Baltimore a few years ago."

"And you were seventeen when your mom died?"

He nodded. "Obviously, Dad was overwhelmed, struggling to work and raise us kids on his own. Nonna, Aunt Berta, and Aunt Rose all convinced him to move back to Philly so they could help. We came back just before my senior year of high school. My uncle Renzo, Dad's brother—and Aunt Berta's husband—was a carpenter who'd been working as a contractor on his own for years. When we came back, he and my dad decided to open their own business. That's when Moretti Brothers Restorations began."

"Oh," Jess was surprised. "I assumed you and your brothers started the company."

"Nope," Tony said, crossing his feet where they were propped up on the raised foot of the recliner. "Moretti Brothers was the brainchild of Frank and Renzo Moretti. After I graduated, I joined them in the business. Then a year later, Joey hopped on board. Two years after that, Luca and Gio."

"And who are all the other guys who eat lunch with the two of you every week? Are they all Morettis too?"

Tony shook his head. "No, not all of them. My cousin Aldo usually joins us. He's a firefighter here in the city. Every now and again, Aldo's brother, Elio, comes along. He's not in town often."

"He's the hockey player, right?" Jess was very aware of who he was, even though he hadn't come for lunch more than a half dozen times. Whenever Elio walked in, the typically quiet diner erupted with a simmering excitement over the fact there was some big sports star in the room.

"Yep," Tony said. "You a hockey fan?"

She shook her head. "No. I mean, I've seen bits and pieces of games, but it's sort of boring. Bunch of men on skates pushing a puck back and forth."

Rhys laughed, while Tony looked at her like she'd just announced she was a vampire who fed on the blood of babies.

"Boring?" Tony repeated, completely aghast.

"You've done it now, Jess."

"Done what?"

Rhys winked at her. "Something tells me you're about to get schooled on why hockey is the greatest thing since sliced bread."

She turned her attention back to Tony and grinned. "If I take back what I just said, can I get the rest of the rundown on the lunch gang?"

Tony sighed heavily. "Pretty hard thing to take back. We can move on, but I'm reserving the right to teach you the error of your beliefs at a later time."

"So noted," Jess said with a playful salute. "Any other relatives at the table with you?"

Tony shook his head. "No. I've got a bunch of other

cousins, but they're not part of the lunch posse. The rest of the guys are just buddies, like Rhys. Kayden has been best friends with Aldo since they were in diapers, while Rafe and Gio played on the same hockey team all through high school. They've been thick as thieves ever since."

"You should probably start taking notes, Jess. There's going to be a test later," Rhys joked.

"Damn," she winced. "Wish I'd known that at the beginning of the lecture. Maybe you can sketch out a family tree later, Tony."

"Don't tempt him," Rhys said. "There's nothing this guy loves more than his family."

"What about you?" She turned toward Rhys. "Do you come from a big family too?"

Rhys shook his head. "Nope. Just me, my parents, and my kid sister, Penny, though we're all pretty tight. My dad texts me every night to check in, and I see my mom and sister at least once or twice a week."

"So they all live locally?" she asked.

Rhys nodded. "Yeah. My family moved down here from Connecticut shortly after I finished my undergrad. Once I completed my residency, I decided to set up a practice here to be close to them. Of course, our family of four is tiny when you put us next to the seventy-two thousand Morettis."

"Both of your families seem enormous compared to mine. By the way, you've met both of us already," she joked.

"Your family of two is awesome, Jess. You're doing a great job with Jasper. Never met such an easygoing kid," Tony said, and she smiled, wondering what it was about this man's praise that made her feel like a million bucks.

Jess gave Rhys a sideways glance and tucked her feet beneath her. "You weren't kidding about the epic tale. I still don't have the answer to my original question about Aunt Berta and why she lives here."

"Oh, Jess. We've got miles of ground left to cover." Rhys

laughed as he reached for a throw blanket hanging over the back of the couch. He unfolded it and tossed it over her lap. It was a simple, kind gesture that touched her more than she could say. All evening, the two of them had gone out of their way to make sure she was comfortable, something that felt completely foreign, but also totally wonderful.

Returning to reality tomorrow was really going to suck.

"Hilarious, Rhys," Tony deadpanned. "I would have gotten around to answering her already, but Miss Inquisitive has interrupted me with four thousand questions."

Jess closed her lips tightly, mimed locking them shut and tossing away the key.

"Around the time Rhys and I bought this building, Uncle Renzo had a heart attack and died."

"Oh no," Jess said. "Poor Berta."

"Yeah," Tony said. "She and Uncle Renzo had never been able to have kids of their own, so with him gone, it was just her in their big house, living alone, something she and the rest of the family hated. Nonna and Nonno were worried about her and invited her to live with them, but Uncle Renzo managed to marry a woman *exactly* like his mother. I suspect blood would have been shed within hours if Aunt Berta and Nonna had to share a kitchen. So Rhys and I came up with the idea to build her an apartment on the second floor. After all, half of Moretti Brothers Restorations—including the office space—was hers with Uncle Renzo gone. Not that she has a bit of interest in the business. Our original plan was that she'd be close by if she needed something, and if she wanted company during the day, all she'd have to do is step out of her apartment to visit me, Dad, and my brothers when we're at work."

"You say 'original plan' like that didn't happen," Jess pointed out.

"You were here all day, Jess, so you had to notice she was too," Tony said. "Aunt Berta is only happy when she has someone to take care of. So all that affection and attention she lavished on Uncle Renzo was transferred to me and, by extension, Rhys."

The smile on his face proved he didn't have a problem with that. Then she considered the fact that it wasn't just Tony filling a void in Berta's life. Because Tony had gained a mother figure as well, something that must feel pretty great, considering he'd lost his mom at such a young age.

"We couldn't live without Aunt Berta," Rhys added. "She's amazing."

"Yeah, she is," Tony agreed.

"Sounds like the perfect living arrangement." Unfortunately, saying those words reminded Jess just how dire and shitty her own situation was.

"I'm curious, Jess. How come you didn't just get another roommate after Danielle left? Wouldn't that have helped with the rent?" Rhys asked, changing the subject back to her.

"It was actually a one-bedroom apartment. Danielle and I had twin beds, and when Jasper outgrew the little bassinet we found at Goodwill, we exchanged it for a mattress that we put between us on the floor. When she moved out, Jasper graduated to the other twin bed."

"I see. So what changed for you financially? The two jobs weren't enough to cover the rent?"

"Oh no, we were doing fine for a while, but then Jasper fell and broke his arm on the playground at school. I don't have health insurance, and the hospital bills started stacking up. I got way behind on everything, so the landlord evicted us. I guess I just kept thinking... I don't know *what* I thought actually. Last night, I hit rock bottom. And you guys...you picked me up."

"I have a feeling you would have picked yourself up if we hadn't come along," Tony said, looking at her with something that felt a lot like admiration.

Jess shook her head. "I'd like to think so, but I haven't been getting a lot of sleep the past month. The fuzzier I got, the more mistakes I made."

She felt both Tony and Rhys's gazes, knew they were studying her face, looking for lingering traces of exhaustion.

"I feel better now." For some reason, it seemed as if they needed that reassurance. She was flattered by their interest in her life and touched by their concern. If the girls at the diner could see her now, they'd be green with envy.

"I'm glad," Rhys said, lifting his wine glass and tapping it against hers. "Here's to clear heads."

"And warm beds," Tony added.

"I'll drink to that." She took a sip of wine, then tried to stifle a yawn.

"You need more rest," Rhys mused.

"After that nine-hour nap, you'd think I would be wide awake."

Rhys considered that. "I suspect it'll take more than that to catch up for all the sleep you've lost lately."

"Yeah. You're probably right. I've basically been sleeping with one eye open to look after Jasper the past few nights. It all caught up with me today."

She didn't say aloud how grateful she was that her exhaustion had taken her down *here*, where Jasper had been safe and sound and protected by Tony and Rhys and Aunt Berta.

"Anyway, I'll call social services tomorrow, I'll find a new sitter for Jasper, and I'll keep saving until I have enough for a new apartment for us. Everything will be fine."

Rhys gave her an encouraging grin. "Well, my money's on you. I have a feeling there's nothing you can't do once you've set your mind to it."

Jess let Rhys's words soak deep, let them strengthen her. Then she yawned again. "I think I'm going to turn in for the night. The wine is making me extra sleepy. Besides, I promised to read Jasper a bedtime story."

The three of them stood, no one moving for a moment. Jess needed to be up and out early tomorrow so she could stop by Rocco's office to apologize for missing work today.

She smiled when she realized how tranquil she felt. For weeks—no, months—she'd been in a perpetual state of motion, her body and mind never stopping as she fought to drag herself and Jasper away from one disaster after another.

In just one day, Rhys and Tony had given her a chance to reboot—with sleep and warmth and food. Now she had a concrete way to move forward from here.

There was no way she'd ever be able to express to them exactly how much today had meant to her. So Jess followed her instincts, stepping toward Rhys and giving him a hug. "Thank you so much for taking care of me this morning."

Rhys wrapped his arms around her, returning the hug. He smelled good...and for a moment, she allowed herself to wonder what it would be like to kiss him.

"Any time. And the next time Jasper gets hurt, you call me. From now on, I'm your doctor. Got it?"

She stepped away and smiled when he playfully bopped her nose with his finger. "Got it, Dr. Beaumont."

She turned toward Tony but hesitated, suddenly feeling shy—something he wasn't having. He held his arms out, impatiently demanding his own hug. She grinned as she stepped into his embrace, his height and broad shoulders enveloping her, making her feel as small as Jasper.

He held her tightly, his large hand running up and down her back. He probably meant his embrace to be comforting, but it sent her mind straight to a dirtier place, and again, she dreamed of kissing him.

Kissing *them*.

Her loneliness was getting the better of her. Time to get a grip.

She stepped away from him, shoving her growing attraction to these two men back into the fantasy land category, forcing herself to accept nothing would ever happen between her or either man, the two of them so far out of her league it wasn't even funny.

They were both older, well established in their careers, and more experienced—both in life and definitely sexually. She'd lost her virginity to the asshole sperm donor and she hadn't slept with anyone since. Jess was nowhere near getting her shit together yet, the words *hot mess* drifting through her mind. She was a walking, talking dumpster fire, something Tony and Rhys had seen up close and personal.

Tomorrow, she would go back to just being their waitress and she'd try not to overindulge in naughty fantasies about them, though that was going to be difficult after today.

She glanced up at Tony's face and frowned. She'd grown used to his alternating smiles and overprotective scowls today, so she wasn't sure what to make of his grave expression.

"You're acting like this goodbye is forever," he mused.

"Oh, I know I'll see you at the diner. It's just...I wanted to say thanks. So, thank you."

He nodded, but his features didn't lighten.

"Good night," she said, deciding she would be smart to cut this farewell short before she did something stupid, like try to kiss one—or both—of these men. Her arousal was off the charts and she really needed to get control of her libido. She wasn't much of a wine drinker, but she'd had two glasses tonight, so that wasn't helping her current state either.

It was one thing to indulge in this perfect night, where she could pretend she wasn't homeless, wasn't broke. But it would be another thing to allow herself to think she could ever change her fantasies about Rhys and Tony into a reality.

To make matters worse, she was seriously thinking about *both* of them, not one or the other. As if that would ever happen.

Jess walked away, though she felt both their gazes following her as she left the room.

Jasper was still awake when she entered the guest room but just barely. She turned the television off and grabbed a book.

She hadn't read more than a few pages before he was snoring softly.

She rolled over and turned out the light, closing her eyes... then mentally deciding to hell with it.

She'd just keep breaking all the rules for this one night.

She drifted deeper into her mind, letting her fantasy out to play. She was sleeping on a bed soft as a cloud in a gorgeous bedroom.

Jess imagined Tony coming into the room and gently shaking her shoulder, his finger pressed to his lips, bidding her to be quiet and follow him. She'd let him take her to his bedroom, where Rhys would be waiting. They'd take turns kissing her before pressing her down on the bed. She imagined their lips and hands touching, stroking, caressing her until she cried out, demanding they take her.

Rhys would claim her first, his lovemaking romantic, building her orgasm slowly with soft kisses and sweet nothings whispered in her ear. They'd come together—and then Tony would take his place.

Unlike her sexy doctor, Tony would push her to her limits, with firm, strong hands, rough thrusts, and dirty talk. Her orgasm would hit her like a freight train, but Tony wouldn't care. He'd demand another and then another. Rhys would return, adding his own fuel to passion, sucking on her nipples, stroking her clit as Tony fucked her into oblivion and beyond.

"Stay with us, always," Tony murmured as she drifted to sleep in their arms.

Overheated, Jess jerked awake, her fingers on her clit, her pussy wet but unfulfilled. She instantly—foolishly—missed arms that had never been there to begin with.

She kicked off the thick duvet, then stood up, making her way to the bathroom, grateful she hadn't woken Jasper.

God, what was she doing?

She shut the door behind her and turned on the light,

looking at her flushed reflection in the mirror and forcing herself to accept the truth, to see what was really there.

She was a woman on her own, alone, with no one to depend on but herself.

And that was when she realized the danger of allowing herself to dream.

Because those beautiful fantasies drove in even deeper how terribly lonely and scared she really was.

Chapter Six

Rhys ignored the hockey game playing on the big screen, his gaze lingering on the handmade card resting on the coffee table. Tony was sprawled out in his recliner, but Rhys didn't think his friend was paying any more attention to the game than he was.

He and Tony had awoken to find Jess gone this morning, the card—complete with a picture Jasper had drawn—waiting for them on the coffee table. It was of two stick figures, clearly representing Jasper and his mother, standing by their car and waving. There were some jagged lines above them that Rhys assumed were birds, or maybe planes.

Jess had written "Thank You" on the inside, along with a note that she would repay Tony for the tank of gas on Wednesday at the diner.

Since finding her and Jasper gone, Tony had walked around the house like a bear with a thorn in his paw, quiet and sullen.

Rhys hadn't made an attempt to cheer up his friend because, in truth, he felt just as grumpy. Jess and Jasper had only been in their house one day, but the wake they left behind felt huge. As the day progressed, Rhys drifted deeper and deeper into himself, trying to figure out why the apartment he'd loved two days ago suddenly felt empty, devoid of life.

Somewhere along the line, he'd become complacent with his workaholic days and his empty bed nights. When he wanted female companionship, he asked a woman out on a date, and if they were compatible and the woman willing, he'd invite her to his bed. He'd accepted that as his lot in life because it was all he had time for.

It was one of the few things he and Tony had in common, both of them eschewing relationships, placing more value on their work.

Then Jess, with her quiet strength and cutting wit, and Jasper, with his energy, bubbling enthusiasm, and constant questions, crash-landed in front of the building and showed him just how empty his life was.

Jess said she planned to seek help through social services, after learning about a local family shelter they ran—a place designed to help women get back on their feet. And while he knew she'd be safer there than in one of the countless homeless shelters in the city, the idea of it still didn't sit right with him. She was a young, intelligent, beautiful woman who'd been dealt a shitty hand.

When he'd listened to her story last night and considered how she'd taken blow after blow, yet continued to get up and keep going, he felt slightly guilty about all that he'd taken for granted in his life. He'd been raised in a loving, upper middle-class home by two adoring parents.

While he had worked hard to earn a scholarship to college and then to get into medical school, he hadn't ever truly struggled. Not in the ways Jess had.

She had encountered more hardships in her twenty-five years than he was likely to ever face in a lifetime. He'd never gone to bed hungry, never had to worry that there wouldn't be a roof over his head, or that his family wouldn't always support him, no matter what.

"Fuck," Tony muttered.

Rhys glanced toward the television, assuming the Penguins had lost the puck. Then he realized Tony wasn't even looking at the game.

"Jess has no business living in any kind of shelter. I don't like it. Don't like... Well, I just don't fucking like it." Tony spoke the exact words Rhys had been thinking.

"You're right. She shouldn't."

"I don't like her working at that motel either. That place is dangerous, and I don't give a shit about her being there during the daytime or Rocco watching over her. I've heard some of the stories Rocco tells about the people who stay there—couples meeting up to cheat on spouses, hookers entertaining client after client, drunks stumbling over from the bar across the street, too wasted to drive home. Rocco says his housekeeping staff has had to clean up everything from used needles to broken beer bottles to discarded condoms. She can't really think that's a safe place for her or Jasper."

Rhys nodded, then played devil's advocate. Not because he wanted to but because he wanted to make sure Tony wasn't on the verge of making one of his impulsive decisions. "Jess has been on her own since she was eighteen, Tony. I know what she did the other night was ill-advised, but she owned up to that mistake. I don't get the impression she's reckless by nature. She's a savvy woman, capable of taking care of herself and her son."

Tony grunted, not bothering to reply. The two of them remained silent for a full ten minutes as Rhys considered what they could do. One option was to loan her money to rent her own place—but she'd already refused that twice, and he didn't think there was anything they could say to persuade her otherwise.

At breakfast this morning, Aunt Berta—who'd been disappointed to discover Jess and Jasper gone—had offered giving her apartment up to them, claiming she could move in with her in-laws, Tony's nonna and nonno. It was a generous offer that all three of them knew would make Aunt Berta miserable.

Which left the most obvious answer.

They could offer Jess and Jasper their guest room.

However, Rhys wasn't sure how Tony would feel about bringing a woman and a six-year-old kid into their peaceful bachelor pad. The two of them were creatures of habit, both with well established ways of doing things.

Personally, Rhys would kick normalcy to the curb if it meant sharing a living space with Jess and Jasper, even for a short time. They'd brought life to a house he hadn't even realized needed it.

Finally, Rhys decided to take the bull by the horns. "So what are we going to do about them?" He prayed he and Tony were on the same page.

Tony looked at him, long and hard, studying his face.

Rhys recognized immediately that they both wanted the exact same thing. For two vastly different men, Rhys had found a kindred spirit, a best friend in Tony, and he'd been an idiot to think for one second that Tony wouldn't want Jess and Jasper here as much as he did.

"We offer them the guest room until she gets back on her feet."

Rhys grinned. "It'll be a change, a big adjustment."

A smile filled Tony's face for the first time this morning. "It'll be fun and you know it. Bring a little excitement, a little life to the place."

Rhys chuckled. "Yeah. It would." He glanced at the clock. "What time do you think her shift ends at the motel?"

Tony rose from his recliner. "Doesn't matter. We're going to go get them now."

Jess peered underneath the sheet she'd tossed over her housekeeping cart to check on Jasper. He'd been out of sorts all day and she could only assume that, like her, he was finding it hard to adjust back to their shitty reality after yesterday's brief venture into paradise.

"You doing okay, buddy?" she asked.

Jasper had declared himself too tired to be her assistant today, instead asking if she'd build him a spaceship. It was a game they'd started a few weeks ago, on another cold Sunday. The sheet provided him privacy as well as a barrier from the chilly wind, while he entertained himself with two little matchbox cars Rocco had given him for Christmas.

"Yeah. Can we leave?"

"Just a couple more rooms to clean, okay?"

"Can we go back to Tony and Rhys's after?" he asked earnestly.

She'd been anticipating that question all day. She shook her head. "No. We're going to sign up for a new shelter, remember? The one for people just like us. I bet there will even be kids for you to play with."

"Okay," Jasper mumbled, not bothering to hide his disappointment.

She'd bitten the bullet and picked up the phone to call social services this morning, inquiring about space in the local women's shelter. The woman on the phone hadn't exactly been warm and fuzzy. In fact, she'd been grumpy and sounded downright haggard. She'd told Jess she would need to fill out some paperwork tomorrow morning when the intake center was open, then she gave her the address of an after-hours place that might be able to set them up somewhere tonight.

The idea of returning to another homeless shelter left her with a sinking sensation in her stomach, and Jess prayed it would only be for one night. Tomorrow, with any luck, they could move into the special housing that meant she and Jasper would have their own room.

She was starting to regret agreeing to stay with Tony and Rhys last night. One night in their beautiful, safe home had ruined her. She'd lowered her guard too far and now she was struggling to pull her armor back on.

Jess checked her clipboard and sighed. She'd cleaned all the vacant rooms. All that was left was to check to see if the people remaining another night wanted their rooms tidied or fresh towels. She always left those rooms until the end of her day in hopes whoever was in them would go out. She hated cleaning rooms with people in them. Some of the men who got rooms here looked at her in ways that made her uncomfortable. She usually set Jasper up with Rocco in the check-in office with a dollar for the vending machine while she finished this part of her rounds. Unfortunately, she didn't have a dollar today.

"You stay under there, Jasper. Don't come out," she said. "Hopefully, these last rooms won't take long."

He mumbled something that could have been okay or go to hell, for all she knew. He was taking his grumpiness to the next level.

She knocked on the first door. "Housekeeping," she called out.

When no one replied, she knocked again, happy at the thought the room might be empty. Her pleasure was short-lived when a greasy-looking guy opened the door, shirtless. His beer belly hung over pants that were unbuttoned and unzipped, revealing far too much of his boxers beneath.

Wonderful.

The guy leered at her and smacked his lips like she was some juicy treat. There was no way she was cleaning this jerk's room.

"Do you need fresh towels?"

The guy belched loudly, and she swallowed down the bile rising in her throat as the smell of his rancid, boozing breath filled the air between them.

"No. But you can come in and scrub my back."

She shook her head and swallowed down the scathing reply she wanted to give him. Not that she thought Rocco would fire her for telling the guy off, but because what she wanted to say was littered with foul language Jasper shouldn't hear.

"If you don't need anything then," she started, turning, intent on getting away from the asshole as quickly as possible.

"I didn't say I didn't need nothin'."

The guy reached out with a quickness she wouldn't have thought him sober enough to manage, his hand squeezing tightly around her upper arm. "Come in and we'll have a party."

Jess struggled against him, shocked by the guy's brute strength, but far too cognizant of Jasper sitting under the cart just a few feet away. She kept her voice low so she wouldn't alarm her son.

"Let go," she spat out through gritted teeth.

The man gave her a grin that revealed yellow, rotten teeth that screamed meth head. Rather than answer, he used his grip to pull her even closer—and that was when Jess began to panic. She really couldn't break free of him.

Raising both hands, she pushed against him as hard as she could, but her actions only spurred him on.

"I like a bitch with fight." He tugged harder, dragging Jess into his room. She needed to get away, and she was terrified of what the guy would do if Jasper revealed himself.

Once he'd gotten her across the threshold, her panic and sense of self-preservation overrode everything else.

She screamed, just as the guy flung her into the room roughly and slammed the door behind them. She tripped on a torn piece of the filthy rug, landing hard on her hands and knees. Jess rose, twisting in time to watch him throw the latch. She rushed for the door, but he looped his arm around her waist and pushed her back across the room again.

She thought she heard Jasper call out her name and panic clawed at her chest. The man either didn't hear or didn't care, now that he had her trapped.

Jess opened her mouth to scream again, hoping Jasper would know to run downstairs to find Rocco, to get help. But before she could make a sound, the man moved, lifting his arm and backhanding her so hard, her teeth rattled and her vision went gray for a moment.

She shook her head, trying to regain her wits, tasting the coppery tang of blood from where her lip had split open.

When he reached for her again, she went into full fight mode, lashing out with her fists, scratching him with her fingernails, fighting like the devil to land a kick that might take him down and give her time to run.

"Stupid cunt!" the man yelled when she managed to land a hard blow against the side of his head. Unfortunately, she didn't hurt him as much as piss him off.

In retaliation, he showed her what a real punch felt like, his fist slamming into her face, just to the right side of her nose. If he'd landed the blow dead center, the force would have broken her nose. She cried out in pain, her hands flying to her face.

"That'll show you who's in charge. You're just like that whore wife of mine. Think you're too fucking good for me, don't you? Kick me out of my own fucking house. Fucking bitch."

Suddenly, Jess wasn't so sure the man even knew who she was as he stumbled back, muttering obscenities. She took a step to her left, hoping he was too distracted by his anger at his wife to notice, a calculated risk that didn't pay off as his gaze sharpened.

Once again, she heard Jasper yell, "Mommy!" through the door.

The man turned toward her son's voice—and he took a step that direction.

Sheer terror gave her renewed strength. Jess fought, managing to kick his knee out from the back. She connected with enough force that he went down hard, howling in pain and cursing her. She tried to use that time to escape, but he was quicker, gripping her ankle and pulling her leg out from under her. She fell, kicking to dislodge his grip. When his fingers slipped free, she didn't bother wasting time to rise. Instead, she quickly crawled toward the door.

She'd only made it a few feet before she was taken completely off guard by the man kicking her in the side, all the air whooshing out of her in a pained gasp. She hadn't even heard him stand.

Jess fought to take catch her breath when he grabbed her hair, her scalp stinging.

"Fucking cunt!" He roughly tossed her onto her back, clamoring over her before she could escape again. He slapped her once more, and while this blow wasn't any harder than the previous ones, the pain and panic were taking their toll, leaving her unable to offer more than weak resistance.

"I'm going to fucking kill you for that, bitch," he spit out. "Make you pay."

She screamed loudly until his fingers closed around her throat, tightening, cutting off her air. Jess clawed at his hands, his arms, desperate to dislodge him, but nothing helped. Her vision turned gray with the lack of oxygen, and tears slid down her face when she realized this was a fight she couldn't win.

Chapter Seven

Tony had just gotten out of the car, he and Rhys heading across the parking lot, when he spotted Jasper sprinting down the stairs, shouting Rocco's name. Tony ran in his direction, pulled forward by the terror in the boy's voice.

"Jasper," he called out.

As Jasper turned his attention toward them, Tony saw the tears streaming down the boy's face.

"The bad man! The bad man!" Jasper gasped through choking sobs.

Rhys knelt in front of him. "Breathe, Jasper. Breathe. What bad man?"

Rocco came out of his office, a cigarette dangling from his lips. "What's going on?"

"The bad man," Jasper said, breaking down, crying inconsolably.

"Where's your mommy?" Tony asked, his gaze flying along the outdoor corridors until he spotted a housekeeping cart on the second floor.

Jasper trembled as he pointed to where Tony was already looking. "The b-bad man took her."

Tony fought down his panic, trying not to upset Jasper anymore. "Took her where?"

"In the room!"

Tony and Rhys reacted like sprinters to the starter gun, both dashing for the stairs.

"Call the cops, Rocco," Tony yelled. At the same time Rhys said, "Watch Jasper."

Tony forcefully shoved the housekeeping cart out of the way, turning the doorknob and finding it locked.

"Stand back," he said to Rhys, when he heard a man's threatening voice say "make you pay."

Lifting his foot, Tony smashed it against the door with all the strength he had. The frame splintered but didn't give way. It took two more kicks to finally break in.

The scene inside the room sent him into a white-hot rage.

Jess was trapped beneath some prick on the floor, his hands around her throat.

The man actually had the nerve to look over his shoulder at the damaged door and say, "What the fuck, man? Get the fuck out!"

Tony crossed the room in two steps, gripped the back of the man's shirt, pulling up and twisting him so he could slam his fist into the dick's face.

The man's hands flew to his nose. "You fucking broke it!" he yelled, blood pouring down his chin.

Tony followed up the punch to his face with a hard right to his gut, the man doubling over in pain.

"Fuck!" The guy tried to straighten, his fists clenched in an attempt to retaliate. He never got the chance when Tony clipped his chin with so much force, the guy's head flew back, slamming against the wall behind him. He slowly slid down, landing on his ass, smart enough to stay on the ground.

Tony looked over his shoulder in time to see Jess scramble to her hands and knees, coughing and gasping for air. Rhys knelt, his gaze flying over her, no doubt checking all her injuries.

Tony saw red at the large dark mark on Jess's cheek and the finger-sized prints around her slender neck. He turned back to the fucker on the floor, kicking the guy in the thigh with all his might.

The man cursed loudly. "What the fuck is wrong with you? Bitch had it coming!"

Sirens sounded in the distance and the stupid prick tried to stand up in a panicked attempt to run away.

Tony shoved him back into the wall. "Stay the fuck down!" he shouted, almost hoping the guy wouldn't listen to him so he'd have another opportunity to take another swing. The man went limp, the fight kicked out of him.

As Tony watched, Rhys gently lifted Jess from the floor, placing her on the edge of the bed. Tony spotted her bloody lip, and there was no question she'd have a black eye by tomorrow.

Tony paced a few steps away from the man, keeping himself between the prick and door.

"Is she okay?" he murmured to Rhys.

Rhys nodded. "I think so."

"J-jasper?" Jess was trembling from head to toe, clearly terrified, and all she could think about was her son. This was the second day in a row they'd found her shaking uncontrollably, first from cold and now from fear.

Never. Fucking. Again.

His jaw was clenched too tightly, rage still coursing through his veins, so Rhys responded to her question.

"He's fine, Jess. He's downstairs with Rocco." As he spoke, Rhys took in her injuries with the practiced eye of a physician. He gently cupped her cheeks, peering closely at her eyes. "Your pupils are dilated," he murmured. "Did you hit your head?"

She shook her head in response. "No."

"Possibly just the adrenaline." Rhys released a long breath. "God, Jess. I just lost ten years off my life."

Tony had never seen Rhys so rattled, so shaken. His friend was a good doctor because he was calm under pressure.

Strangely, to hear Rhys upset made Tony feel better...because right now, his heart was racing a million beats per second, and he still felt the uncontrollable urge to beat the ever-loving fuck out of the man who'd hurt her.

The sirens grew louder, and Tony heard brakes squealing outside. He remained where he was, keeping a close eye on the man, still sprawled out on the floor. The asshole appeared to have accepted his fate.

He turned at the sound of someone entering the room.

"Jesus," the cop muttered.

"Kayden," Tony said, walking over to greet his friend, grateful he was the one who'd answered the call. He was part of their Wednesday lunch group, and Jess knew him. He hoped that would put her at ease, as Kayden would certainly need to get a statement from her.

"Tony? You okay?"

Tony nodded, aware he was still breathing heavily. There was blood—not his—on his knuckles, and his long hair was hanging in his face.

Kayden took in the rest of the room, his gaze sliding from Jess, who seemed to be curling into herself on the bed, slightly bent with her arms wrapped around her waist protectively, to Rhys, who stood beside her.

"Rhys." Kayden offered him a brief nod before turning his attention to the dick on the floor.

Another cop entered—Seth, Kayden's partner. Like Kayden, Seth was able to size up the situation without asking a single question. "I got a statement from Rocco. At least as much as he could tell me from what the kid said," he said to Kayden.

"Jasper?" Jess whispered.

Seth held up his hand to set her mind at ease. "He's with Rocco. Shaken up, but safe and sound. Hey, Tony," Seth added.

"Seth." Tony nodded his head just once in greeting.

"Looks like you did all the heavy lifting," Seth said in an attempt to lighten the tension filling the room.

Kayden started to walk over to Jess, but before Tony could consider his actions, he took a large step to the right, blocking his path.

Kayden's brows rose in surprise. "Like that, huh?"

Tony nodded, unable to respond. He was a bit shocked by his own reaction. He was an intense bastard at the best of times, overprotective as fuck when it came to his sister or female cousins, but those traits had never transferred over to any of the women he'd dated.

Regardless, for some reason, he couldn't let Kayden get any closer to Jess.

"You're Jess, right? You remember me?" Kayden asked softly.

For the first time since Kayden entered the room, Jess lifted her eyes to look at him. "From the diner," she said softly.

Kayden nodded. "I need to ask you a few questions, but first I need to know if you're okay?"

"I'm fine."

Tony felt a strange sense of pride over the strength in her voice. Jess was a fighter.

Kayden took in her bleeding lip and the darkening bruises on her face and around her neck. "Just in case, we're going to take you to the hospital, get you checked out, and then I'll—"

Jess cut him off. "I'm not going to the hospital."

Tony frowned. "Jess. You're going to the hospital."

She shook her head, and the stubbornness he'd only caught brief glimpses of yesterday emerged full force. "No. I'm. Not," she stressed.

Tony recalled that it was her lack of health insurance that had started her and Jasper on their downward spiral. If it was money she was worried about, he'd pay the damn bill. He put his hands on his hips, ignoring the pain in his knuckles, ready to set her straight and make the offer, but Rhys stepped in.

"I'll examine her."

Jess looked like she planned to argue that point as well, but Tony wasn't budging on this.

"Rhys or the hospital. Those are your only two options. Pick."

Jess narrowed her eyes. She probably would have thought him touched in the head if she realized how much that look relieved him. He loved the way she didn't back down, the way she challenged him. Her fighting spirit was one of her best attributes, and he was thrilled to know the asshole on the floor hadn't beaten it out of her.

"Rhys," she said shortly.

"Good," Tony said.

At the same time, Rhys reached out to her, saying, "Come with me."

Rhys led her to the bathroom in the motel room and Tony followed, standing in the doorway, disgusted by the filth. The asshole had obviously been holed up here a few days, given the number of empty liquor bottles and cigarette butts littering the sink and floor. There was a used needle in the basin. Every towel was in a wet, soppy pile in the corner, and there was urine all over the toilet and the floor surrounding it.

Jess had to clean up shit like this every weekend?

Yeah. That was over as of right now.

"Tony," Rhys said, drawing his attention. "Do you mind grabbing us a couple of clean towels from Jess's cart outside?"

Tony did as asked, while Kayden and Seth read the asshole his rights and cuffed him. Seth took the guy out, and Kayden hung back and stepped next to Tony. "I need to get a statement from Jess."

"Okay. Let Rhys check her out real quick and then we'll see if she's up for it."

"I need one from you too. You did a fucking number on that guy. We're going to have to take him to the hospital before

85

processing. Broken nose, maybe a few cracked ribs, possible concussion."

"He hit her, Kayden. Had her down on the floor, strangling her."

Kayden held his hands in the air. "I'm not saying you were wrong, Tony. Guys like that should be fucking castrated, then locked up for life."

Appeased, he nodded, aware his emotions were riding way too close to the surface. He needed to get a grip. "Let me get these to Rhys, then we can talk." Tony returned to the bathroom, handing Rhys the towels. He wet the corner of one and used it to gently wipe away the blood on her lip.

"Don't think you're going to need stitches," Rhys mused.

"How bad do I look?" Jess asked. "I don't want Jasper to..." She paused for a moment, blinking back tears, taking a few steadying breaths. "I don't want him to see this and get upset. Is he okay? I mean...I think this..." she started, needing more assurances about her son's safety. "I keep hurting him."

Tony hated hearing her beat herself up. "You didn't hurt him, Jess."

"I put us here, in a situation that wasn't safe," she fired back.

"You're working to provide for him," Rhys reassured her. "Put all the bad thoughts away for now, okay?"

"He'll be fine." Tony was going to make damn sure of that. It was going to take some time for Jess and Jasper to get over today. Fuck, the two of them needed time to get over the past few months, but he and Rhys were going to do whatever it took to make sure they got it.

Jesus, they weren't the only ones who needed time. He couldn't stop replaying the image of that guy on top of Jess, his hands around her throat, the sheer terror on her pale face.

"Your lip is cut and a little puffy, and I'm afraid you're probably going to have a black eye, a bruise on this cheek, and on your neck," Rhys barely grazed the red mark on her face before tilting her head back to look more closely at her throat.

"Makeup," she whispered. "I can hide it all."

Rhys nodded. "I think we should do the rest of this exam back at my office, Jess. This place is..." Rhys looked just as repulsed as Tony at the state of the bathroom.

"I want to get out of here," she said.

"Kayden needs to talk to you. Are you up for it now, or should I push him off until tomorrow?" Tony asked.

"I want to do it now," she replied. "And then I'm never talking about this again."

"Sounds like a plan," Tony said, intent on doing or saying or giving her whatever she needed.

Jess stepped out of the bathroom. "I'm ready," she announced to Kayden.

Kayden took out his notebook and a pen.

"You want to do this in here or step outside? In the fresh air?" Kayden Gallo was a good cop, and once again, Tony was glad that he'd been the one to show up.

"Here is fine," she said. "It's cold outside and I...don't want Jasper to see us talking. He might try to come up."

"Okay. Do you want to step me through what happened?"

Jess began to relate her story, and Tony felt his blood go cold as she described the man dragging her inside, her fear for Jasper's safety. He'd hit her, pulled her hair, kicked her, choked her. She mentioned he was angry at his wife for something, and that it felt like he was punishing Jess for it.

Rhys listened intently to every word, and Tony could imagine the doctor cataloging every single blow she described in preparation for her exam.

Kayden asked a couple follow-up questions, but overall, he simply let Jess tell it in her own way, in her own time.

"Okay." Kayden closed his notebook and tucked it in his back pocket. "That's good for now. If I have any more questions, I'll call. Is there a number where I can reach you?"

Jess hesitated, and Tony wondered if she even had a phone. He'd never seen her with one.

"You can call my cell," Tony interjected. "Jess is staying with me and Rhys."

Through his peripheral vision, he saw Jess turn toward him at his proclamation, but for once—or maybe just for now—she wasn't arguing.

"Let's get out of here, Jess." Tony put a steadying hand on her back as he guided her out of the room.

They'd all just reached the bottom of the stairs when Jasper came bounding out of the office, Rocco right behind him.

"Mommy!" Jasper raced toward her. Jess bent down somewhat gingerly, wincing when he leapt into her arms.

He and Rhys exchanged a glance, then Rhys stepped toward them, reaching for the small boy. "Hey, kiddo." He extracted Jasper from Jess's arms gently and took his hand. "It's time for us to go home."

Jasper's face fell. "Oh. Okay." He looked at Jess. "We're going to the other shelter now?"

Jess shook her head. "No. Not tonight. We're going to spend one more night with Tony and Rhys."

"We are?" Jasper's eyes lit up, but Tony noticed the little boy's fear wasn't completely forgotten.

"Yep," Tony said, reaching down to lift the boy, putting him on his shoulders, grinning when Jasper giggled with surprise and delight. Tony held out his hand, palm up. "Why don't you give me your car keys, Jess? Jasper and I will drive your car back to our place and you can ride with Rhys." Until Rhys had a chance to properly check her out, Tony thought it best she remain with a doctor.

Rocco held out Jess's huge tote bag and her coat. "Here you go, darlin'. I got these out of your locker."

She took them from him with a quiet word of thanks.

"I'm sorry, Jess," Rocco said, the deep lines in his face proof of his guilt, his misery.

"Not your fault," she said, reaching out to place her hand on Rocco's forearm.

"I should have been watching, keeping a better eye out."

"I'm okay, Rocco. Honest." She attempted to reassure the old guy with a smile but winced at the pull on her cut lip.

"Come on, Jess." Rhys helped her put on her coat. She rifled around in her huge bag for her car keys and handed them to Tony.

"See you at home," Tony said, giving her a wink, desperate to find anything to take the darkness out of her pretty blue eyes.

She nodded numbly, then walked with Rhys to the car.

"Come on, little man," he said, turning toward Jess's vehicle, Jasper still riding on his shoulders.

The trip from the motel to their apartment didn't take long, but it gave Tony too much time to think.

He sighed as they pulled up in front of their building, glad to be home, and relieved that Jess and Jasper were with them, out of the elements, in their protection. If he had his way, there wouldn't be any more talk of shelters.

Jasper had been uncharacteristically quiet during the drive, and Tony worried about the long-lasting effects today's attack might have not only on Jess but on Jasper as well.

He'd texted Aunt Berta before leaving the motel. Told her there'd been an incident and that Jess had been hurt, so he wasn't surprised to see her standing in the open front door as they approached the steps.

Jasper dropped Tony's hand when he saw her, running straight into her arms. She hugged him fiercely, her eyes filled with worry when she looked at Tony.

Rhys arrived a few minutes after, he and Jess joining them on the sidewalk. Aunt Berta took in Jess's battered face and offered her a comforting smile.

"Jasper. I was just about to make some chocolate chip cookies and I need a taste-tester. Think you're up to the task?" Aunt Berta asked. "There's a cup of hot cocoa in it for you."

Jasper nodded, excitement finally edging out the fear and confusion that had been too prevalent on the boy's face in the last hour. "Can I, Mommy?"

"Of course you can. I'm jealous Berta chose you and not me for the job." Jess's ability to speak so lightheartedly after what she'd just endured had Tony wondering if she'd had too much practice pretending things were okay for Jasper when they weren't.

"You can help us," Jasper said. "Can't she, Aunt Berta?"

Aunt Berta started to nod, until Rhys said, "I need your mom's help with something in my office first, Jasper. She'll be up in a few minutes."

Jasper's gaze lingered on Jess, and she turned her head slightly, trying to conceal the mark that was starting to bruise, her hand shielding her neck.

"Come on, Jasper." Aunt Berta took his hand. "We'll make a big platter of them and then we can all have cookies and cocoa later."

Jasper and Aunt Berta disappeared up the stairs as he, Rhys, and Jess followed, then paused outside the door to one of the examination rooms.

"I feel fine," Jess said. "This isn't necessary."

Tony had been waiting for those words, had expected her to dig her heels in. It was why he'd remained with them rather than going up with Aunt Berta and Jasper.

"I'm glad to hear you're okay," Rhys said, opening the door to the exam room. "But I'd like that confirmed with an examination. I know I said I'd do it, but, Jess...I have a female colleague I can call if you'd be more comfortable with her. She could be here within the hour."

"I don't need anyone to—"

"Do you want him or his colleague to check you out? Pick one, or I'm driving you to the hospital," Tony interjected when she continued doubling down on her refusal.

She whirled on him, her eyes flashing with anger. "You are

not in charge of me, Tony Moretti, and I'm getting sick of you constantly steamrolling over everything I say." As she spoke, she drove her finger into his chest. "I make my own decisions. *Me*. Just me."

"Well, you're in for a world of disappointment, Jess Monroe," he replied, leaning down but keeping his voice steady, even. After what she'd just gone through, he wasn't about to do anything that might scare her. "Because as of right now, *I'm* taking charge of you. And I'm telling you to get yourself in that office so Rhys can examine you, or let him call his friend. I'm trying very hard not to touch you, because I don't want to upset or scare you, but goddammit, if you keep fighting us on this, I promise I will pick you up, toss you over my shoulder, and drag you kicking and screaming all the way to the hospital."

Her mouth slammed shut, but he wasn't sure if he'd shocked her into silence or if his threat truly frightened her.

He tried to soften his tone, hating to think he may have gone too far. "We'd never hurt you, Jess. You know that, right? You're safe with us."

"I know that." His words had obviously taken the wind out of her sails. "I know you wouldn't hurt me. It's just...I've been on my own for so long, and you two keep..."

She paused just long enough that Tony decided to fill in the blanks for her. "Helping you. We're helping you."

Tony realized that his pronoun with Jess was different than with most other people. He rarely spoke in terms of what *he* wanted to do for her. Instead, he spoke as a *we*—Rhys as much a part of this...God...what was it? A bond? A connection? Attraction?

Tony shoved that thought away. Now wasn't the time or place.

"So what's it going to be? Rhys or his colleague?" he asked.

"Rhys," she whispered. "I don't want...a stranger."

"Very well," Rhys said.

"And you can touch me," she said, her gaze traveling from

Tony to Rhys and back, her words so low, he wasn't sure he'd heard them correctly. "I want... I need..."

Tony had never seen anyone look more lost, more alone. He lifted his arms, making sure she knew the choice was hers, and Jess stepped into them, clinging to him, as if she was adrift at sea and he was the life preserver.

"I was so scared," she said, the words muffled against his chest. "I thought he was going to kill me."

Tony knew her well enough to know how hard it was for her to admit that.

"I know. But you were brave. You fought back."

She shook her head. "It wasn't going to be enough. He was stronger."

Her words destroyed him, gutted him. "You're so brave, Jess. So strong. Everything is going to be okay. We're going to make it all okay."

She breathed out an airy laugh. "Stubborn pain in the ass."

He chuckled. "And don't you forget it."

Rhys moved closer, and Tony could see the pain in his friend's gaze. Knew he needed the chance to comfort her as well. Tony released her, turning her so that Rhys could offer his own embrace.

Like with him, Jess wrapped her arms around Rhys, soaking up his warmth, his strength.

"Let Rhys examine you," Tony said at last. "I'll be right out here, waiting. Okay?"

"I don't want you to wait out here."

Tony's heart fell, hating the feeling that she was pushing him away. He wanted—fuck, he *needed*—to stay close to her right now. Walking away after what had happened...he wasn't sure it was something he could do.

His hurt was short-lived when she said, "I want you to come in too."

92

Chapter Eight

J ess stepped into the exam room and looked around. It was typical of pretty much every doctor's office she'd ever been in, the room painted a bright, crisp white, the examination table covered with a paper sheet, a rolling chair pushed next to a small desk attached to the wall. The blood pressure cuff was hanging on a wall by the bed, and there were various charts and posters, talking about all sorts of medical ailments, including one listing the signs of a heart attack and another encouraging people to give blood.

However, along with all the usual doctor fare, Rhys had added colorful artwork by a local artist depicting the Philadelphia skyscape from different perspectives, which broke up all the white and gave the room a cheerful atmosphere.

Rhys pointed to the exam table. "Why don't you hop up and take a seat and we'll get started. Don't want to take too long because Aunt Berta's chocolate chips cookies are the greatest thing you've ever tasted when they're warm."

Jess climbed up on the table as Rhys washed his hands, then placed a stethoscope around his neck. Tony had moved with her, coming to stand next to the table, more behind than next to her.

"Are you sure—" Tony murmured.

"Please don't leave."

She didn't have a clue what it was about these men, but as long as she was with them, she could breathe.

With them, she was safe. Tony had said it. And she felt it.

After a lifetime alone, having them close made her feel things she'd never experienced. The deep-seated loneliness that never left her vanished in their presence.

Rhys stepped in front of her, placing his soft fingertips under her chin, tipping her face up so he could look at it. "There's bruising on the right side of your face." He probed that area completely. "But I don't think there are any broken bones. And your nose looks fine."

"His punch missed," she said. "I've never...no one's ever hit me like that before."

A quiet rumble sounded from behind her. She'd only caught a quick glimpse of Tony's face when he came charging into the motel room, looking for all the world like a Viking warrior. His unleashed fury had been the answer to a prayer—and the moment she saw him, all she could think was everything was going to be okay. She wasn't going to die. Wasn't going to leave Jasper an orphan.

That thought prompted a sob that she fought to choke down. Neither man missed the strangled cry.

"Jess," Tony said.

She shook her head. "I'm okay," she lied, the words too thin, thanks to the lump in her throat.

"I'm sorry he hit you," Rhys said. "And I agree, taking a punch to the face hurts like hell."

"You've been hit?" she asked, glad for the distraction from her own thoughts.

Rhys gave her a crooked grin. "I let *that* one," he lifted his chin in Tony's direction, "talk me into sparring with him in a boxing ring once."

Tony chuckled. "I told you to keep your hands up."

Rhys rolled his eyes. "Spent the next week trying to explain to my patients why their mild-mannered doctor had a shiner."

"I suggested he make up a story about getting into a bar fight, but I'm pretty sure he bored everyone with the truth."

Jess laughed with them as Rhys moved on to feeling the top of her head, his fingers threading through her hair, his probing touch feeling like a soothing massage. Her scalp was still tender from where the man had pulled her hair. "No lumps or bumps. Sore?"

"Yes. A little. He pulled it hard."

"I should have killed the motherfucker," Tony muttered.

Jess's heart fluttered—and the vengeful bitch part of her she usually held at bay smiled—at the pure venom in his tone and the thought that he would go that far to avenge someone who'd hurt her.

"Okay. Now for the hard part," Rhys said. "I need you to lift your shirt, Jess, and lay down. You told Kayden that the man kicked you. I want to check to make sure no ribs were broken or cracked. If I suspect they are, you're going to the hospital for X-rays, no matter what you say."

Jess sucked in a wobbly breath, and she felt Tony shift, got the feeling he was about to leave.

"Don't go," she whispered, just before she tugged her shirt over her head. She slowly lowered herself down, the paper crinkling beneath her. Then she caught Tony's gaze, which remained steadfastly on her face, and lifted her hand. He took it in his, his firm grip reassuring.

Rhys gently prodded her torso and chest, careful to avoid touching her breasts.

"Tell me if it hurts when I press down." He continued probing here or there, watching her face for any indication of pain. Aside from the bruising, she was certain nothing was broken and the pain was bearable. She shook her head each time he touched somewhere else.

Then he examined her neck, gently tilting her head one direction, then the other.

"Sore throat?" he asked.

"A little."

"Does anything else hurt?" While Rhys's tone was calm, she could see the emotions swirling in his eyes, and she was touched to know he cared so much about her.

"No. We fought and then Tony broke down the door and you guys stormed in. That was the end of it."

"Good." Rhys took her other hand, using it to help her sit up. Then he handed over her shirt, turning toward the desk while Tony took the shirt and pulled it back on her carefully.

Rhys lifted a penlight and checked her pupils one more time. "Not dilated anymore." He grabbed a bottle of pills from the counter. "Ibuprofen. I don't think you need more than this, but if you're still in pain after taking two of these, let me know and I'll give you something stronger."

Tony helped Jess stand. "Why don't you go on up, get a hot shower, and afterwards, we'll plow through that plate of cookies?"

"Okay."

Tony had told Jasper that the two of them would be spending the night here, and Jess was so grateful for one more night. She didn't have the mental or physical strength to fake her way through a night at another shelter with Jasper, pretending everything was okay when it wasn't.

With Aunt Berta, Rhys, and Tony around, she wouldn't have to work so hard to hide how fucked up she was right now. With other people around to distract Jasper...

"A shower," *and a long, hard cry,* "sounds great."

Rhys sat up in bed and sighed. He'd crawled into bed at eleven, sleep eluding him as he tossed and turned. Now it was well after one a.m. and he was finished trying to pretend sleep was going to come. He couldn't settle his mind, couldn't push away the dark thoughts swirling.

Jess had taken them up on the offer of a hot shower after the exam. She'd locked herself in the bathroom for well over an hour, and when she'd emerged, her red-rimmed eyes told him she'd been crying.

He hated the thought that she'd shed those tears alone, away from them.

Rhys had dedicated his life to helping people who were hurt. And while that meant he attempted to heal their bodies, with Jess...he wanted to offer more. To hold her as she cried. To comfort her. To be there for her.

Always.

That was a new emotion for him, one he wasn't quite sure how to handle. Not just because it wasn't something he had a lot of experience with—but because he knew Tony was struggling with his own budding feelings for her.

He and his roommate were both falling for the same woman.

He'd never felt so out of control. His kid sister, Penny, had teased him most of their lives, given him the nickname Tin Man because even throughout high school and college, he'd chosen his books and education over girls and love every single time. He'd told her countless times he'd been fortunate to know from a very young age what he wanted to be in life and that becoming a doctor came with certain sacrifices.

Of course, Penny had never let that excuse slide, pointing out that many doctors were married and had kids. Rhys knew that. Most of his colleagues fell into that category, but he also knew that their spouses were the ones carrying the family while the doctors were constantly on call.

Like with his practice, Rhys knew that if he ever proposed marriage, he'd want to be all-in. And in his mind, he couldn't see how working sixty, sometimes seventy, hours a week as a doctor would allow him to be a good husband and father.

Rhys rose, sliding his feet into his slippers, wondering if there were any of those cookies left. He wasn't getting any sleep tonight.

Quietly, he walked from his bedroom to the kitchen, but a soft sound from the living room caught his attention. Changing direction, he found Jess standing by the large window, looking down at the street below. The slight tremble in her shoulders told him she was crying.

"Jess," he whispered, not wanting to alarm her.

She turned to face him, quickly swiping at her eyes and sniffling, attempting to hide her tears. Again.

"I'm sorry if I woke you up."

"Don't," he said.

"Don't what?"

"There's no shame in crying. After what you went through, you need to shed those tears. Don't hold them back. And you didn't wake me up. I couldn't sleep. I was worried about you." As he spoke, he walked closer, but he didn't seek to touch her.

"About me?" she asked, her tone tinged with surprise.

Hadn't anyone ever worried about her before?

"Yes. I'm always going to worry about you," he confessed. It was a roundabout way to tell her that he cared, but the truth was...he did. And that fact probably shocked him as much as her. How had she managed to slip under his Tin Man veneer so quickly?

Jess didn't reply. Instead, she walked toward him. He opened his arms and her slight frame leaned into him, as she silently asked for another embrace like the one they'd shared downstairs. He rocked her slightly, letting the slow motion soothe her as she let her sadness free and cried against his chest. He ran his hand up and down her back.

"It's going to be okay," he whispered. "It's all going to be okay." He said those words over and over, but he didn't seek to pull away, determined to give her all the time she needed.

He didn't have a clue how long they stood there—minutes or hours could have passed—but finally, she cried herself out.

Steadier, she released him but didn't move away. She lifted her face, cheeks shimmering with the tears she'd shed. He cupped her cheeks and used his thumbs to brush away the dampness, the two of them looking at each other for a long time. He felt the undeniable need to kiss her, and there was something in her eyes that convinced him she wouldn't push him away if he did.

"Feel better?" he whispered.

She started to nod, but it morphed into a shrug instead. "Every time I think things can't get worse...it's like the universe takes it as a personal challenge." She tried to back her words up with a ghost of a smile, to sell her attempt at a joke, but failed. She sighed. "I'm just so tired, Rhys. All the time."

He knew that she wasn't talking about physical exhaustion. Jess had the weight of the world pushing down on her, and while she'd managed to carry it this far, this whole fucked-up weekend seemed to have delivered the KO punch.

"I know you are."

He led her to the couch, the two of them sitting down together, and she put her head on his shoulder. Then, before he could overthink it, he pulled her sideways onto his lap, nestling her as he would a sleeping child.

The impulsive action was out of character, the sort of thing Tony would do, not him. Regardless, he needed her close, needed to comfort her, and those feelings blotted out all common sense, all rational thought.

However, it was Jess's reaction that was more surprising. She went with the motion, completely, sinking onto his lap, as if they'd sat this way together every night for years. She rested her head on his shoulder once more and released a long, slow breath, all the tension flowing out of her with the air and words she clearly needed to speak.

"I know there are people who have it worse, so I hate to sound like I'm complaining."

She was homeless, penniless, and had just been badly beaten by a junkie this afternoon. She thought there were people who had it worse?

"I don't think you're complaining. I think you're justified to feel the way you do."

"It's just... I'm so frustrated I can't find a way out of this mess. I go to work every single day. I don't drink or do drugs. Jesus, I don't even *date*. I go to work and take care of Jasper, and I'm doing everything I know how to do to make a decent life for us, but...it's still not enough. I don't think it's ever going to be enough."

He wrapped his arms around her, tugging her even tighter to him, wanting this lonely, scared woman to know—for once, and even if only for tonight—that she wasn't alone. "It'll be enough, Jess. I think your problem is you're trying to do everything on your own. You need to ask for help."

She gave him a rueful grin. "My mother told me my pride would be my downfall. Maybe she was right."

He shook his head. "No. She wasn't right." Given what Jess had told them about her mother kicking out her eighteen-year-old, pregnant daughter, Rhys was struggling to understand how such a coldhearted woman could raise someone as wonderful as Jess.

"Do you think..." She paused and lifted her gaze to him, her eyes shimmering with fresh tears. "Do you think Jasper deserves better than me?" she whispered.

Her question broke his heart. She'd devoted her life to her son, loved him with everything she had. "Jesus, Jess," he murmured, his voice stern when he responded. "You are an amazing mother. That little boy is lucky to have you. Don't ever ask that question again. Don't even think it."

She wiped away a lone tear that had escaped and nodded. "Okay. I won't."

"Good." He placed a kiss on her forehead. It was meant to be a platonic gesture of comfort, but it stirred something foreign, something unexpected inside him. He'd been attracted to women in the past, but this felt like something...more. Much, much more.

"You smell good," she said, her nose brushing his shoulder.

He chuckled. "Probably just my body wash."

"This whole apartment smells good. I noticed it right away. It feels like most of the world stinks. My old apartment always stunk of cigarettes even though Danielle and I never smoked. The diner smells like grease. Lots of parts of the city smell like week-old garbage, and the motel...well, that place is just fucking gross. But you...you smell like..."

"An Irish spring?" he joked.

She laughed, and he was glad to hear the sound, the heaviness that had pervaded every corner of her face, lifting. In these too rare moments when Jess let her guard down, when she forgot to be worried or scared, she looked younger, pretty.

No. Not pretty. Gorgeous. She was one of the most beautiful women he'd ever met.

"I was going to another shelter after work today. I called the woman from social services, and she told me to go there. Said I'd have to fill out some paperwork at the intake offices tomorrow when they're open."

"Okay."

"I just wanted you to know I'm following through on what I said I'd do."

Neither Rhys nor Tony had broached the subject about Jess living with them yet. She'd been too rattled from the attack, and they didn't want to overwhelm her when she was so shaken up. They'd decided to discuss it with her together at breakfast, after a good night's sleep and some time had passed. He considered bringing it up now, but he didn't want to do so without Tony there.

Jess placed her head on his shoulder again, and he relished

the closeness. He was moved by her trust in him. They sat in companionable silence for a few minutes, until the peacefulness of the night was shattered by a cry.

"Mommy! Mommy!" Jasper yelled.

Jess sprang up from his lap quickly, the tension in her body back in an instant. The two of them rushed down the hallway, entering the guest room just a few steps behind Tony, who'd beaten them there.

Jasper launched himself into Tony's arms.

"It's okay, little man," Tony reassured him.

"The bad man got Mommy again!" Tears flowed down the young boy's cheeks, and it was obvious he'd woken up alone and panicked.

"Jasper," Jess said. "I'm here."

Jasper, who hadn't seen her, turned at the sound of her voice and pushed out of Tony's arms, desperate to get to her. She picked him up, clinging to him tightly.

"I'm here," she murmured. "I'm right here."

"I thought…" the boy started, choking on a sob.

"No," she whispered. "I know what you thought. I'm right here, baby. I'll always be right here."

Jess had let her guard down earlier, given Rhys a peek at the woman inside. The one who was scared and tired and who didn't feel good enough. But now, the walls were back up. Her spine stiff, her shoulders tight, her face determined.

She turned to him and Tony, her eyes dry once more. "I'm sorry we woke you both. We're fine now." Her words were a lie, but Jess only knew one way. Only knew how to take care of things on her own.

Tony's face darkened, his expression fierce. Rhys recognized it for what it was. His roommate was going into full-blown protector mode.

Which suited Rhys just fine. Because he was feeling the need to set Ms. Jess Monroe straight on a few things too.

There was about to be a new normal in her life. She might not realize it now, but things were changing.

Jasper still clung to Jess, his arms wrapped so tightly around her neck, Rhys wasn't sure how she was breathing. He considered the bruises left there after her attack and he walked over, gently loosening Jasper's grip.

"Be easy with your mommy," he said softly.

Jasper nodded just once and did as he said.

Jess cleared her throat. "I shouldn't have left the room. We'll be quiet the rest of the night," she said, as if they'd be angry and kick them out in the middle of the night. "We won't disturb you again, I promise."

"That's it," Tony said, the rumble in his voice betraying just how shaken up he was. "Get in bed, Jess."

She placed Jasper on the mattress but didn't join him. Instead, she looked at Tony as if waiting for him to leave.

"I said get in. Scoot to the middle," Tony said, one brow lifted, daring her to disobey him. "Both of you."

If Rhys wasn't riding the razor's edge of emotion right now, he might have been amused by Jess's confused response to his gruff roommate. Her independent spirit, the one that had learned to rely on no one, kept giving way to the woman who reacted instantly and on instinct to Tony's demands.

Jess joined Jasper on the bed, both of them shifting until they were in the middle.

Tony looked at Rhys and jerked his chin up, toward the opposite side of the bed. It spoke to the level of friendship they'd achieved that Rhys knew without words what Tony wanted him to do. Each of them moved, claiming a side of the bed, where they sat with their backs against the headboard, flanking Jasper and Jess.

"What are you doing?" Jess whispered, even as Jasper settled deeper into the pillow, his tears dry.

"Go to sleep, Jess." Tony, who was next to Jasper, placed his large hand on top of the little boy's head. Jasper looked at both him and Tony with such trust that Rhys's chest tightened painfully.

"We're here," Tony said. "No one is going to hurt you or your mommy. Ever again."

Jess frowned at the last, but her exhaustion rivaled Jasper's, and within a few minutes, they were both sound asleep, looking more peaceful than Rhys had ever seen the pair, and he was suddenly determined to keep those expressions there.

That was when Rhys realized that Jess and Jasper had done the impossible in just two days.

They'd claimed his heart.

Chapter Nine

Jess carefully made her way from the car to the sidewalk, trekking through the sleet that was making the ground too slick to allow her to walk quickly. She'd driven from the diner at a snail's pace, terrified of crashing the car. Ordinarily, she would have walked to work or taken the bus, but she'd left late this morning and she was unfamiliar with the bus stops on this side of town. So she'd foolishly hopped into her car, despite the weather forecast.

She paused when she reached the front door and sighed, her breath escaping in a huge, white puff of fog.

Once again, she was outside Tony and Rhys's building. Glancing up at the light shining from the top two floors, she tried to figure out how she kept ending up here. It was only a little before five p.m., but it was quickly growing dark—damn daylight savings time.

After what had been a rocky start to last night—Jess shaken by the attack in the motel and Jasper's terror over "the bad man"—she would have expected to suffer from a sleepless night.

Instead, the moment Tony and Rhys had claimed their places on the edges of the bed, promising to keep them safe, she'd slept like the dead. Slept so well, in fact, she'd *over*slept. Something she couldn't remember doing in years.

Tony and Rhys hadn't been in the bedroom when she woke up, and all day she'd caught herself wondering how long they'd sat sentry before returning to their own rooms.

She'd awoken with a start this morning, in a panic over being late, belatedly recalling she hadn't figured out the babysitting issue with Jasper and that she wasn't going to make it to the intake office before work.

With no other choice, she had planned to ask Paulie if she could leave work early, hating the idea of losing yet even more pay but not seeing a way around it. In her plan, she was going to pick Jasper up right after school, make the journey to the social services office, and hope the woman there could find a place for them to stay.

But that wasn't how her day had gone at all.

After planning out her schedule, she'd gotten herself and Jasper ready for the day, hastily packed up their things, bid a silent, sad goodbye to the gorgeous guest room, and headed to the kitchen to say thank you to her weekend saviors.

That was when her schedule had been shot to hell. She'd been met by Tony, Rhys, and Aunt Berta, who had their *own* ideas about her day. In their version, Aunt Berta picked up Jasper after school and watched him until Jess got "home" from work.

That had been the word they'd used.

Home.

Tony said they'd planned to talk to her about that—and a couple other things—over breakfast, but because of her sleepy start, whatever they'd planned to say would wait until after her shift.

So here she was...after her shift...hoping whatever they had to say wouldn't take too long. She'd called the woman at social services on her lunch break but hadn't had a chance to fill out the paperwork yet, which meant they were spending tonight in the shelter, something she wasn't looking forward to.

After a full day on her feet, she wanted to grab something for her and Jasper to eat, then get in line. She was looking forward to the time when she could just sit down and be done with the day. Unfortunately, she was several hours away from that, as she also needed to take her car back to Debbie's before making the trek to the shelter.

Walking in, she encountered Rhys leaving his office with an elderly gentleman, clearly a patient.

Rhys smiled when he saw her, and her heart pitter-pattered a little harder. She'd been shocked last night when he'd pulled her onto his lap. She'd been even more surprised by how much that simple, comforting gesture had actually aroused her, something she wouldn't have expected after being attacked by the asshole at the motel.

"There you are, Jess. Tony was just about to send out a search team," he said warmly before turning to the man next to him. "This is Oscar Reynolds, one of my worst patients. Oscar, this is Jess Monroe, another equally bad patient."

Jess grinned. "Nice to meet you."

"You too. And good for you, Jess." Oscar laughed heartily, slapping Rhys on the back. "We gotta keep Doc on his toes. Wouldn't want him to get bored, would we?"

"Mmm-hmm," Rhys murmured. "I could stand to be a lot less bored by you, Oscar."

Oscar sighed. "I hear you. Less smoking, less drinking, less bacon. You're a real buzzkill."

"And don't you forget it," Rhys said, walking the man to the door. "I'll call you as soon as the results of the blood work are in."

The two men said goodbye, then Rhys locked the front door. "That was my last patient for the night." He gestured toward the stairs. "Let me get the lights and I'll walk up with you."

MARI CARR

Jess waited, her nipples budding when Rhys placed his hand on her lower back and guided her upstairs. Thank God she still had her winter coat on.

"How are you feeling today? Any pain?"

She shook her head. "No. The ibuprofen you gave me is doing the trick. Keeping the soreness away."

When they reached the landing just outside the apartment, he turned her toward him, his fingers on her chin. He studied her face, then her neck.

"I've been adding cover-up all day. How awful does it look?"

"You did a good job with the makeup, but I'd like you to wash it off when we get inside. Let me see how bad the bruising really is."

She shook her head. "It's not that bad. And you should know that bruises always look worse when they're getting better. Besides, I'm afraid we can't stay long. I still have a few errands to run before—" She stopped herself from saying the word "shelter" because of the scowl that word provoked whenever she uttered it. "Before bedtime," she amended.

Rhys nodded. "Come on."

He opened the door, and Jess was immediately assaulted by the smell of pizza. Her stomach growled loudly.

"Hungry?" Rhys asked.

She shook her head but stopped when Rhys tilted his head impatiently. Instead, she kept her mouth shut. If she said she was starving—which she was—they'd invite her to eat, and she really didn't have time for that. She'd learned her lesson the hard way Friday night about not queuing up in time, and she would move heaven and earth to make sure she and Jasper never had to spend another night outside.

"Mommy!" Jasper yelled, darting out of the kitchen to greet her.

She smiled as he jumped into her arms, giving her a hug before squirming to get down.

"Aunt Berta got me from school."

"I know," she said. Rhys reached for her coat, helping her take it off. She started to tell him not to bother, but Jasper kept talking, preventing that opportunity.

"We went to Terminal Market and got a pretzel and lemonade and looked at all the food," he said excitedly.

"That sounds great."

Jasper barely took a breath as he continued recounting his afternoon. "Then we bought stuff to make pizza for dinner. And a cheesecake that's this big." He held his arms out wide, clearly exaggerating about what he considered the greatest dessert he'd ever seen. "And then Aunt Berta helped me with my homework and read *Curious George Goes Camping* to me because she'd never heard the story, and then she let me watch *SpongeBob*."

Aunt Berta walked out of the kitchen, grinning as widely as Jasper. "The boy is easy to entertain," she said. "He loves everything."

Jess nodded, though she had to clear her throat before responding. She knew Jasper was a bright, inquisitive kid. His teachers—both in kindergarten and this year in first grade—had told her the same, claiming he was always the first to finish his work and always looking to learn more. She'd tried to expose him to new experiences and places as much as she could, but that wasn't always easy, given the fact she worked long hours, seven days a week. Too often, she was too tired to explore the city with him. Something she vowed to rectify after seeing his excitement right now.

"It sounds like you had an amazing day, Jasper. I can't thank you enough, Berta."

"Aunt Berta," Tony's aunt corrected.

Jess smiled. "Aunt Berta."

"Am I late to the party?" Tony asked as he entered the apartment.

"Nope," Rhys replied. "We just got home too. Jasper was

regaling us with tales of his adventures with Aunt Berta this afternoon."

Jasper darted over to Tony and leapt into his arms. Tony tossed him in the air playfully a couple of times, much to Jasper's delight.

Growing up with just women, Jasper had very little experience with adult males, and absolutely none with guys willing to roughhouse and play with him. It was a huge turn-on for Jess, her ovaries practically doing flip-flops at the sight.

Tony dramatically sniffed the air. "Damn, Aunt Berta. Is that your homemade pizza? Smells like heaven in here."

"It is. Made an extra one tonight since you and Rhys barely leave enough for me to have a single slice, and I want to make sure there's plenty for Jasper and Jess."

"Oh," Jess said. "You didn't need to do that. Jasper and I can't stay for dinner."

"We can't have pizza?" Jasper asked, his demeanor going from elated to dejected in two seconds flat.

"Of course you're having pizza," Tony said.

Jess narrowed her eyes, aware that somewhere along the line, she must have given Tony Moretti the impression she was a pushover. "No, we're not," she said insistently.

Tony set Jasper down. "Why don't you go into the kitchen with Aunt Berta, little man? Help her finish dinner while Rhys and I have a chat with your mom."

Jasper looked from Tony to Jess and back again. She'd taught him to listen to adults, and it was clear Tony had earned the boy's respect and admiration quickly. Rhys had as well.

But her son also loved his food, so she didn't doubt for a second he wanted to remain until he whined his way into getting her to agree to stay for pizza.

"Go on, Jasper," she said. "This won't take long. Help Aunt Berta until it's time for us to leave."

He nodded sadly. "Okay."

Aunt Berta took his hand, the two of them returning to the kitchen as Tony gestured toward the living room.

Jess walked across the room, sitting down at what was becoming her usual place on the couch, Rhys and Tony claiming the same spots where they'd sat Saturday night as well.

"We can't stay for dinner," she said, wanting to end the argument before Tony picked it up again. "I have to get the car back to Debbie's, then get in line for the shelter before six. That doesn't leave me much time."

"The shelter?" Rhys asked. "What about social services?"

"We were slammed at work and another one of the waitresses called out sick. I couldn't leave Paulie shorthanded, so I didn't make it to the intake office. I'll go first thing tomorrow morning to fill out the paperwork. It's just one more night, so—"

"You're staying here," Tony said.

She huffed, exasperated. "Tony, *no*. Enough is enough. I can't keep doing this to you guys."

Rhys reached over and placed his hand on her shoulder. "Tony's right, Jess. You *are* staying here. But it would be nice if the three of us could engage in a civil conversation about it. I prefer that to watching you two butt heads."

"Rhys, I appreciate the offer, but—"

"Can I ask you a question?" He cut her off midsentence.

She paused for just a moment, then nodded. "Yes."

"How did you end up outside our house Friday night?"

Jess leaned back, his question catching her off guard. "What?"

"Feels like more than a coincidence," he said quietly.

She considered lying, insisting it had been by chance, but the moment she opened her mouth, she found the truth spilling out.

"I knew sleeping in the car was dangerous. Not just because of the cold but because it left us vulnerable to other things as well. I didn't know *where* I was going at first. I was just driving around, trying to keep us out of the elements and get us warm again. We'd been walking all over the city, looking for a place to stay prior to getting the car."

Tony grumbled something she didn't understand, but she didn't look his direction. She didn't need to see his face to know he didn't like what she was saying. So she kept her gaze locked on Rhys.

"I was trying to figure out how to feed Jasper with no money, feeling depressed about my empty wallet...then I remembered it wasn't *totally* empty."

She slid her eyes to Tony. "You put one of your business cards on the bulletin board at the diner a few months ago."

Tony nodded. "I remember."

"I took it. I don't know why, but...a couple days after you hung it up, I took it down and slid it into my wallet. I pulled it out Friday night, looked at the address, and drove here."

"Why not knock on the door?" Tony asked.

She snorted. "Yeah, right. I was just going to knock on the door with my kid in tow and say 'hey, remember me, your waitress from the diner? Can I crash here tonight?'"

She had thought those same words Friday night, dismissing them as utter nonsense. Now that she'd gotten to know Tony and Rhys, she realized they would have swung the door wide and invited them in.

"If you weren't going to knock, why come at all?" Tony pressed.

"I told you. We were going to be vulnerable. You guys seem like the kind of men who would come running if someone yelled for help." Then she gave them a rueful smile. "When I think about it now, I didn't even yell and you *still* came running."

"Stay in the guest room, Jess." Tony leaned forward, his elbows on his knees, a pose she'd seen him in before whenever he said something serious, something pressing. "And not just tonight. Rhys and I want you to move in here until you get your feet under you."

She shook her head, though she wasn't sure if she meant that as a rejection or if she was simply too shocked to believe their offer. "I can't...do that."

"Of course you can," Rhys said, sliding closer to her on the couch. "We've discussed it, and the offer is sincere."

"I...isn't there anyone in your lives who might not approve?" Jess asked.

"Like who?"

"I don't know...girlfriends?" She couldn't figure out how either man was still single.

"Neither one of us is dating anyone right now," Tony replied, as he moved from the recliner to perch on the coffee table in front of her. "Jasper wasn't the only one who had the greatest day ever. Aunt Berta texted me no less than six times, demanding that we convince you to stay. I think she intends to plead her own case on why you should let her be Jasper's new after-school babysitter."

"I..." Jess was too overwhelmed to respond.

Rhys scooted closer, the two of them so near, she could smell their cologne. "Think about it, Jess. Think about the other people standing in line at those shelters. I suspect you weren't the only woman. The only one with a child."

"I wasn't." Jess recalled another woman who, like her, had a young child in her arms. She'd recognized the desperation, the desolation in the woman's eyes, because they'd mirrored her own.

"You staying here would free up space for others who need a place out of the cold. But more than that, it's a way of providing Jasper a safe home. You're a good mom, and I know you recognize that as the truth."

She wasn't sure how Rhys had gotten her number so quickly, but he certainly knew the right way to plead his case.

Everything they offered her was the answer to a prayer. But

there was that damn pride issue she never seemed able to beat down completely. "I don't have a lot of money right now."

Tony frowned, confused. "So?"

"I would want to pay my own way. I mean, I *am* going to pay. The two of you for rent and groceries, and Aunt Berta, for the babysitting."

"She won't take your money," Tony said.

"Then I'll pay her with gifts. I'm not staying here otherwise."

"Jess—" Tony started.

"Nonnegotiable," she replied, throwing the same word he'd used with her a couple times back at him.

He grumbled and crossed his arms. "Listen, Jess—"

"Fine," Rhys said quickly, when it became obvious Tony was ready to keep fighting her. "We'll work out the money part later. Take a couple weeks to start rebuilding your coffers and we'll revisit it then."

She wanted to insist they do it now, but it really *had* been a long day, and she didn't have the energy. Besides, she was still trying to wrap her head around their offer, trying to believe it was real.

She and Jasper would be safe and warm. They'd have food. She'd spent every single minute for the past eight months—no, scratch that—she'd spent her entire adult life worrying about Jasper, their future, their survival.

Tony and Rhys, with their incredible offer, had taken all of that away. Even if only for a few months. She wouldn't have to worry about sleeping in shelters or trying to figure out where their next meal was coming from. Jasper would be well cared for by an attentive, loving babysitter who wouldn't just shove him in front of a television and yell at him to be quiet all the time.

The tension in her shoulders and the crushing pressure on her chest lifted—and she suddenly felt so light, she couldn't believe her feet were still touching the ground.

"We won't be a bother, I promise," she said, realizing Tony

and Rhys were both making a very big sacrifice, inviting her and a six-year-old into their home. It would be a big adjustment for men used to living in a quiet bachelor pad. "You won't even know we're here."

Tony shook his head. "You're not hiding in the guest room, Jess. This is going to be your home for as long as you need it to be. Besides, Rhys is boring as fuck. I'm looking forward to you and Jasper livening this place up."

Rhys snorted. "Boring as fuck, huh?"

"Hey, Jasper," Tony called out loudly. "Come here a minute."

Jess was immediately wise to his plan. "Tony," she warned.

He took her chin in his thumb and forefinger, pulling her face up to look at him fully. She flushed at the intense, sexy look on his face. Why did he have to be so freaking hot?

"I'm not giving you a chance to change your mind or back out."

"Yeah?" Jasper said, walking into the room. Jess noticed his excited bounce from earlier was gone, and she knew she'd taken that away from him. Her sweet son had been through the wringer this past month. He was just a kid, a great kid, and he deserved so much better than the hell they'd been living in.

It was that realization that kicked her pride to the curb once and for all. Because there was no way on earth she was denying him this. This safe, loving home, where he'd be surrounded by good people.

"Grab your coat, buddy," Jess said, rising.

Jasper's shoulders fell. "Okay."

"Jess," Tony said, standing, his hands on his hips. He clearly thought she'd changed her mind.

"We need to get our things out of the car," Jess added quickly.

"Our things?" Jasper asked.

Jess grinned. "*All* our things. Tony and Rhys have invited us to move into the guest room. And I've accepted. We're going to live here until we can afford a place of our own. Sound good?"

"We're going to live here?!" Jasper shouted so loudly, Aunt Berta rushed into the room.

"What's going on? Jasper, are you okay?" Aunt Berta asked.

"We're going to live here!" he proclaimed, running over to hug Aunt Berta.

She laughed with delight. "Oh my word! That's wonderful! I was hoping your mom would say yes," Aunt Berta said, her gaze drifting to Jess. "Bought a cheesecake to celebrate, just in case."

Jess smiled, fighting to blink back the tears suddenly blurring her vision. This was all too much, too wonderful. "Thank you. For everything."

"Did Tony and Rhys ask you about me taking care of Jasper after school?"

Jess nodded. "Yes, and I insist on paying you."

Aunt Berta waved her away, much like Tony had when she said she wanted to pay rent, but before she could persist, Jasper ran over to her.

"Aunt Berta is going to be my new babysitter?" he asked.

"Yes," Jess replied.

Jasper, in true dramatic form, shouted, "This is the best day of my life!"

They all laughed, then Tony and Rhys helped her and Jasper move in, and all of them plowed through four homemade pizzas, before watching *Toy Story* together.

When Jess crawled into bed later that night, next to a sleeping Jasper, she whispered the same words. "Best day of my life."

Chapter Ten

J ess looked up when she heard the front door to the apartment open. She was home alone, thanks to a small kitchen fire at the diner. It hadn't been particularly bad, but it had filled the place with enough smoke that Paulie had decided to close up for the rest of the day.

Aunt Berta had gone out earlier to run some errands, telling her she'd time it so she could be at the school to pick up Jasper at the end of his day. Then she'd insisted that Jess "put her feet up and relax."

Jess was trying, but a large part of her felt guilty, sitting on Tony and Rhys's couch in the middle of the afternoon, while they were working and Aunt Berta was taking care of her son. She should have insisted on picking Jasper up herself, but Aunt Berta had revealed herself as a force to be reckoned with these past two weeks. When the woman made her mind up about something, she fucking made it up. As such, Jess had yet to win a fight against her, and she'd tried...a lot.

"Hello?" Jess called out when no one revealed themselves.

A blonde head peered around the door to the living room. "Oh. Hey. Who are you?"

Jess was taken aback by the strange woman's sudden presence. In two weeks, the only other people to visit the apartment had been Tony's three brothers, Luca, Joey, and Gio, plus Kayden, who'd very sweetly swung by one day to check on her after the attack.

The front door had been locked, which indicated this woman was either a professional at picking locks or she had a key.

"I'm Jess."

Jess waited, expecting the woman to chime in and offer her name, but no such luck.

"Ooookay," the blonde said. "So that really didn't answer my question, but my family is forever giving me shit for asking too many questions. Of course," the woman looked around, "they're not here, so could I bother you for some more details?"

Jess couldn't help but grin. "I'm Jess Monroe. A friend of Tony and Rhys's. I'm..." She wasn't sure if she should tell the woman that she was living there. The guys had said neither of them had a girlfriend, but what if they'd fibbed, thinking she wouldn't move in if they did? She hated the thought that they'd lie.

God. What if they'd deceived her?

But why would they deceive her about something like that?

"You're what?" the blonde prompted, walking into the living room and plopping down on Tony's recliner like she owned the place.

The woman was...unique. Jess couldn't pinpoint her age at all, though if she had to guess, she'd say she was somewhere in her twenties. Jess thought she was pretty, in a quirky way. Her hair was braided double Dutch style, but she'd tied the ends up, creating Princess Leia-style loops that struck Jess as a strange fashion statement. Her face was devoid of makeup, so the smattering of zits on her chin were apparent, and she wore eyeglasses with huge black frames perched on her nose.

Her outfit was equally as...odd. She wore baggy mom jeans, a faded black T-shirt that was way too big on her, with some weird bird spurting flames that said "Good Mythical Morning," and a thick gray cardigan that was missing several buttons. Her black half boots were scuffed to hell and if Jess had to venture a guess, she'd say the woman had tried to conceal the damage with Sharpie marker.

"I'm staying here for a little while," Jess finally said, struggling to picture this woman with either Tony or Rhys. For some reason, she'd imagined the women they dated would be elegant, classy women with great jobs, perfect hair, white teeth, and manicured fingernails.

"Really?" the woman said. "Cool."

"May I ask who *you* are?"

"Oh!" The woman burst into such loud, joyful laughter that Jess couldn't help joining in. "Damn. I'm such an idiot. I'm Penny. Rhys's sister."

Jess would never have guessed that in a million years, though now that Penny had said it, she noticed she and Rhys shared the same bright blue eyes. Of course, the comparisons stopped there. Rhys's hair was dark brown, Penny's blonde. Rhys was tall, over six feet, while Penny didn't appear to be much taller than Jess, who was barely squeaking five-foot-five. Where Rhys was sophisticated, Penny came off as—for lack of a better word—nerdy.

"You look familiar to me," Penny mused, studying Jess's face closely.

"I wait tables at Paulie's diner."

"Oh. Gotcha. That must be it. I've gone in there a couple times on my lunch break. I probably saw you there."

"You work downtown?"

Penny nodded. "Yeah. I work in IT for Russo Enterprises."

Jess perked up. "Oh, wow. Small world. I just got offered a job there a few days ago. Nothing like you do, though. I'd be cleaning the offices at night. I just lost"—actually she'd quit —"my second job working at a motel. Matt Russo came into

Paulie's. We got to talking and he said there was a position available."

What Jess *didn't* say was that Matt, another regular at the diner, had noticed her bruises. The man was as relentless as Tony when he wanted information—something she was starting to think was an Italian trait—and he hadn't relented until she'd told him the whole sordid story about the attack at the motel. He'd asked why she'd taken a job there to begin with, and she'd admitted to needing the extra income. That was when he'd offered her the job cleaning the offices.

Jess had been thinking about it nonstop ever since, especially when Matt told her how much she'd be making. Working at Russo Enterprises would help her achieve her goal of moving out a hell of a lot faster. The problem was, she couldn't drag Jasper along with her. The weekday hours were late, and she couldn't keep him up until nearly midnight on school nights.

While she'd only been living here a couple of weeks, Jess had noticed neither Tony nor Rhys went out at night very often. Actually, they hadn't gone out at all, the two of them staying in every single night, inviting her to join them after Jasper went to bed, to watch hockey or a movie. The three of them had fallen into a peaceful, companionable routine. And as much as Jess loved those few hours to just kick back and relax with them, she couldn't let herself get too used to that.

She couldn't impose on the guys forever, and the job at Russo Enterprises would allow her to move out sooner.

Unfortunately, she hadn't been able to work up the nerve to ask if Jasper—who she would put to bed before she left—could stay with them while she worked the second job.

There was no way in hell she was asking Aunt Berta to do one thing more for her. She already did too much. But she was hoping the guys might not mind. Especially when she made it clear it would enable her to "get back on her feet," as they'd said, much quicker.

"Does Tony know Matt Russo offered you a job?" Penny asked.

Jess shook her head, curious about the question. "No. I didn't even know they knew each other." Matt didn't dine in at Paulie's, like Tony did. Instead, he typically stopped in and grabbed his lunch or dinner to go.

Penny's eyes widened dramatically. "Oh, believe me, the Russos and the Morettis know each other. They've had some sort of feud going on the last million or so years. You should have seen the way Tony reacted when I met him the first time and told him I worked for Russo Enterprises. Told me I could do better. Actually, I think his exact words were 'you need to get the hell out of there,' but the truth is, I love my job. And the Russos, like the Morettis, are not hard to look at. I work more with Matt's brother, Gage, who's the king of the playboys. God, he's ridiculously hot. Like, next-level gorgeous. He's Harry Styles, Ryan Reynolds, and Chris Evans all rolled into one. Not that he would ever notice geeky old me, of course. His type is supermodels, not gamer girls addicted to YouTube."

Jess filed away the information about the Russos, feeling even more nervous about requesting Tony and Rhys's help so she could take the second job. If Tony hated the Russos as much as Penny said, there was no way he'd be cool with her working for them.

But she really needed the job.

Maybe she'd just be a coward and ask Rhys when they were alone.

Unless...

"Does Rhys feel the same way about the Russos?"

Penny shook her head. "No. We Beaumonts are too boring to ever have arch enemies."

"Rhys isn't boring. And I wouldn't say you are either," Jess added, enjoying this conversation. Penny was open and funny, if a little eccentric.

Before Penny could argue the point, the door opened once

more and the sound of Jasper's voice, chatting away a mile a minute, reached them before he did.

Penny looked at Jess's son with a great deal of interest when Jasper burst into the room.

She had to stifle a laugh when Penny and Jasper both said in unison, "Who are you?"

Penny replied first. "I'm Rhys's sister, Penny."

"Cool! He gave me this," Jasper said, holding up a lollipop, clearly delighted to meet someone related to Rhys.

In the two weeks since they'd moved in, Jasper and Rhys had established a pattern where Jasper would stop by his office before coming upstairs to tell the kind doctor one thing he learned at school in exchange for a lollipop.

If Tony was in the office—a somewhat rare occurrence, as he spent the majority of his workday on various sites—Jasper would also stop in there. Rather than report what he'd learned, Tony was more interested in his behavior. If he was good, he and Tony exchanged high fives, according to Aunt Berta. So far, her sweet son hadn't been bad at school, so Jess was sort of curious what Tony would say if Jasper ever got into trouble.

Jasper adored both men, relishing their attention.

"This is Jasper, my son," Jess said, when Jasper forgot to introduce himself.

"Do you live here too?" Penny asked Jasper, who nodded in response.

"Wow. Seriously?" Penny posed *that* question to Jess.

"Oh, Penny," Aunt Berta said, coming into the living room. "I thought I heard your voice. Sorry I'm late. The cake is in the kitchen, all packed up and ready to go. Let me go grab it."

"Can I have a snack?" Jasper asked Aunt Berta.

"Of course you can." Aunt Berta and Jasper left together. Jess grinned at the tight bond her son was forming with the older woman. Aunt Berta was patient and kind, and while she was indulgent, she never went too far or spoiled Jasper.

After their hellish January, Jess still couldn't quite believe how good February was.

"Cake?" Jess asked.

"They're doing an office party for Valentine's Day tomorrow and everyone is supposed to bring something. I hate to bake...and cook...and be in a kitchen."

"Really?"

"Yeah. Well, I guess what I really hate is to stand."

Jess laughed. "Stand, as in up?"

"That's all you do in a kitchen. Stand there and wait for shit to get done. Blah blah blah. Give me a gaming chair and my computer and I can sit contentedly all day long."

"I've never thought of cooking that way, but I guess you're right."

Penny leaned back in the recliner, her gaze on Jess's face once again. "You know, you're the first woman to ever stay here. I mean, the guys have done the occasional sleepover," Penny accompanied that comment with a few pumps of the fists to make it clear sleepover was code for sex, "but no one has ever moved in."

Jess felt the immediate need to clarify a few facts to Rhys's sister. "I'm not here for a," Jess repeated Penny's motion, "sleepover. I had a bit of bad luck and needed a place to stay. Jasper and I sleep in the guest room. *Only* the guest room."

"Oh, I wasn't insinuating it was anything more than that. I'm just...surprised, I guess. Tony and Rhys are well-ensconced in their bachelorhood, creatures of habit. I mean, look at this place. Minimal decorations, no frills, no fuss, no mess."

"I think you can attribute the lack of mess to Aunt Berta," Jess added.

"Some, yeah, but have you ever seen Rhys's bedroom?"

Jess felt herself flush. "Of course not."

Penny laughed. "Sorry. I didn't mean it that way. I'm just saying it's spotless, and I know for a fact Aunt Berta doesn't go in there. Rhys likes order in his life, routine. Nothing that ever rocks the boat. So...you and Jasper living here has me stumped."

"It was a generous offer on Tony and Rhys's part. Nothing more," Jess felt compelled to explain, though she wasn't sure if it was for Penny's benefit or her own. She didn't know what to make of the knowledge that Rhys was stepping way out of his comfort zone to help her. "And it's short-term. Hopefully very short-term. No more than a month or two."

Of course, that time limit only worked if she took the second job. Which meant it was time for her to pull on her big girl panties and make the request. She couldn't keep taking advantage of Tony and Rhys, hanging out like some lady of leisure.

Then, because she couldn't help herself, she decided to ask a question that had been niggling in the back of her brain since moving in here. "So they don't date often?"

Penny shook her head. "I can't really speak for Tony, but I know Rhys doesn't. He never has. He says he's married to his career and his patients will always come first. I've tried to tell him doctors can have both—the job and the family—but Rhys has never been interested in that. I mean, he's great with kids, but he's never expressed any interest in having his own. In fact, he's said outright that he doesn't want them."

"That's a shame," Jess mused. "I think he'd be a great father."

Penny nodded in agreement. "Yeah, so do I."

"So no girlfriends *ever*?" Jess was struggling to wrap her head around that fact. Surely Rhys had been in love at some point in his life.

"No. He has a few female friends with benefits, I guess you'd call them. Whenever he gets horny, he asks out one of them. Rhys is not the falling-in-love type. He's not even the romantic type. I accepted a long time ago I'm never going to have nieces or nephews, which makes me sad."

"That *is* sad."

Penny nodded, then added, "I think it's the same for Tony. While I've never heard him swear off marriage and kids like Rhys, he's definitely not looking too hard. If you ask me, it would be a hell of a shame if Tony Moretti didn't reproduce. Genes like his need to be passed on to sons for future generations of women to enjoy."

Jess laughed, mainly to conceal how much Penny's comments bothered her. She needed to stop indulging her silly fantasies about Tony and Rhys. Night after night, she found herself dreaming of the two of them taking her, claiming her, making her theirs...forever.

The sexual aspects of those fantasies were off-the-charts hot, which meant she lived in a constant state of arousal, something that was getting harder and harder to control. As such, she found herself blushing more frequently around them, like a silly schoolgirl with her first crush.

Which, when she thought about it, probably wasn't exactly too far from the truth. They were both older and she was woefully inexperienced.

If only they weren't so charming and sexy and...

God, *enough*.

If they wanted to die childless bachelors, that was their decision to make, and it had no bearing on her future plans.

"Well, for what it's worth, I'm glad you're here. Maybe we could hang out one day, binge watch *Murder Mystery Makeup Mondays* on YouTube."

"I have no idea what that is."

Penny feigned a horrified gasp. "Ohmigod. It's only the greatest true crime show. Plus, the whole time the host, Bailey, is talking about the murder, she's putting on makeup. I swear one day I'm going to try her techniques and give myself a makeover."

"Makeup and murder?" Jess said. "I have to admit that sounds kind of awesome."

"So it's a date. You and me."

Jess nodded, thinking how nice the plan sounded, even if it would probably never happen. Days off with girlfriends weren't something she saw in her immediate future.

"Here you go," Aunt Berta said, walking in with a cake box, Jasper in tow, a half-eaten thick slice of home-baked bread and butter in his hand.

Penny stood up and tipped open the lid. Jess rose to look too.

"It's red velvet." Aunt Berta had created a masterpiece, the cake looking too good to eat, with fluffy cream cheese frosting and a crushed-pecans garnish.

"You're the best!" Penny gushed. "Okay. I gotta go. It was really nice to meet you, Jess."

"You too," Jess said.

"Stay cool, Jasper," Penny said, offering a fist bump.

Jasper giggled when their fists touched. "Okay, Penny."

"I like her," Jasper said after Penny left.

"So do I."

It had certainly been an enlightening visit. From arch enemies to confirmed bachelors...Penny had given Jess a lot to think about.

Chapter Eleven

Tony glanced at the time on his phone. Again.

"She's late."

It was pushing midnight, and typically he and Rhys would have already headed to bed. The fact Rhys was still up and hanging out proved his roommate was worried too.

Jess—thank God—had quit her weekend job at Crossings Motel. Tony had been prepared to raise holy hell if she'd tried to go back, but as Rhys had pointed out, Jess was savvy and not reckless. The attack had scared her, but Tony sensed the worst part of it hadn't been the bruises or the beating for Jess. It had been her fear for Jasper's safety.

So, she'd called Rocco the day after agreeing to live with them and quit.

However, because Jess was Jess, she'd found another second job, this one parttime and not particularly dangerous. Except that it meant she would be out late on weeknights and working for the Russo family. Something that pissed Tony off more than he cared to admit.

The Morettis and the Russos were the Philadelphia equivalent of the Hatfields and the McCoys. Every time the Russo name came up in the presence of Tony's dad or his uncle

Cesare, they'd slide the tips of their fingers forward under their chins aggressively and scowl, gesturing that they didn't give a fuck about the Russos and didn't want to hear the name.

Unfortunately, Philadelphia's Italian society wasn't so big that the Morettis and the Russos weren't forced to cross paths more often than either side enjoyed. The Moretti brothers were the same ages as the Russo boys, which meant they'd gone through school with Matt, Gage, and Conor. The Russos owned countless businesses in the city, and with the growing success of Moretti Brothers Restorations, that ensured he and Matt ran into each other at fundraisers and other local events as they both rubbed elbows and attempted to make connections.

The Russos were old-money, big-wealth, wimpy-white-collar types who'd never eaten anything that wasn't on a silver spoon. Meanwhile, the Morettis were men's men, proud of their blue-collar roots and not afraid to roll up their sleeves and do a solid day's work.

"We should have told her not to take that damn job," Tony grumbled.

"She only would have kept looking for something else, and at least the job isn't dangerous." Rhys had fielded this same complaint from Tony countless times, so his answer was delivered by rote, with very little inflection or emotion.

Jess had accepted the job cleaning the offices at Russo Enterprises three weeks ago. After doing her shift at the diner, she'd come home, eat dinner with them and Jasper, give her son a bath, read him a bedtime story, tuck him in, make sure he was asleep, then she'd leave to do job number two.

Typically, she could clean the entire floor in three hours, always home by eleven.

The clock hit midnight.

He stood up. "To hell with this. I'm driving over—"

Before Tony could finish telling Rhys he was going out to look for her, the door to their apartment opened.

Jess looked surprised when she found them both in the living room. "You're still up," she said tiredly.

"You're late," Tony said.

At the same time, Rhys rose and asked, "Is everything okay?"

"Sort of," she said. "Actually, not really. My car died at a stoplight when I was on my way home."

Tony frowned. "Where is it now?"

"Resting peacefully on a quiet city street. A couple of guys helped me push it to the curb and I left it there. I walked back to work because it was closer than here."

Rhys helped her take her coat off as Tony closed his eyes and counted to ten. She'd been in yet another dangerous situation.

"I swear to God I'm going to start dressing you in bubble wrap," he murmured. "Never met any woman so prone to bad shit happening."

Jess laughed. "I hardly think my car dying warrants bubble wrap."

Tony put his hands on his hips. "You were walking, alone, in the middle of the night. Why didn't you call us?"

Her exhaustion meant her temper was riding just as close to the surface as his. Never a good thing. "That's what I was *trying* to do. I was going to use the phone at the office."

"What's wrong with your cell?" Rhys asked as he led her to the couch.

She sank onto the middle cushion, sighing when he draped a thick fleece blanket over her lap. "The battery on my phone won't hold a damn charge, so it was dead when I got home from the diner. I plugged it in and then forgot to grab it before I left tonight."

Jess's phone was as crappy as her car. It was one of those pay-as-you-go types and old as shit.

"Besides," she added, "it's not like I was walking in the hood. The streets are well lit and it was only a few blocks."

Tony was aware of Jess's tendency to downplay things in an attempt to soothe him. "Define 'a few blocks.' Specifically."

She shot him a look that proved he was right. "Eleven blocks."

"Goddammit, Jess!"

"You said you were going to call us from the office," Rhys interjected before Tony could properly lose his shit. "Why didn't you?"

Jess looked in his direction nervously, and Tony's Spidey senses went on the alert. "Jess," he prompted.

"I was walking in as...someone was walking out, and they offered me a ride."

Tony's eyes narrowed. "Who gave you a ride home?"

"Listen, Tony—" she started, clearly hedging.

Tony raised his hands in exasperation. "Don't tell me you accepted a ride home with one of the Russos."

"Fine, then. I won't."

She was purposely trying to put him off.

"Which one?" he demanded.

Jess looked at Rhys. "Is there any answer I can give that will make him less pissed off?"

Rhys shook his head. "Nope."

"Matt Russo. And he was a perfect gentleman. Though I'll admit, he seemed pretty surprised when he found out I was living here. Asked me if you knew I was working for him."

Tony lifted his gaze heavenward. "I bet he did." He sighed and tried to shove his annoyance down. It was either that or raise holy hell, which wouldn't be rational. Primarily because it wasn't Jess he was mad at. He and Matt had a history, one that ensured he saw red every time he heard the fucker's name.

Once he managed to calm down, Tony said, "I'm glad you're home safe and sound. I have a couple extra cell phones downstairs in my office. Gio is hell on his phones. Breaks a couple a year, usually when we're out at construction sites. I'll grab one tomorrow and get it set up for you."

She shook her head, but Tony was tired of losing fights.

"I mean it, Jess. You're taking the damn phone. We were worried sick tonight."

"You were?"

Jess and Jasper had been living at the apartment for five weeks, and she still struggled with accepting their help, completely out of practice when it came to unconditional friendship. Hell, he wasn't sure she'd ever had any practice to begin with.

"Of course we were," Rhys answered.

While Jess had initially been apprehensive about she and Jasper invading their space or overstaying their welcome, she couldn't have been more wrong.

Having them here had been great. Amazing. Fun.

Jasper was hands-down the best kid Tony had ever known. He didn't whine or pout or act like a little shit when he didn't get his way. He had seen the occasional bouts of crankiness whenever he was overtired, but those were normal. Jess had raised a kid who was grateful for the little things, polite, and so damn smart, he'd actually taught Tony a few things.

And Jess was incredible. He and Rhys were no slouches when it came to hard work, but Jess left them in the dust. The woman never stopped, determined to pull her weight, to pay her own way.

While he admired that, it also drove Tony crazy. Because the truth was, he didn't want her money. He loved having her here, and as far as he was concerned, she was using a space neither he nor Rhys needed.

Regardless of that, she gave them money each week for rent and groceries, always apologizing that it wasn't what she considered "enough." She'd also paid him back for the tank of gas he put in her car, though he'd fought her on that. It was the first fight he'd lost to her about money, but it sure as hell hadn't been the last.

The only person who won the money fight against Jess was

Aunt Berta, who absolutely refused to take a dime for babysitting Jasper. Instead, she'd sat Jess down and explained why Jess was actually doing her a favor, giving her a reason to get out of bed each morning.

Tony had known his aunt was lonely after Uncle Renzo's death, but he didn't realize just how sad she'd been. He'd thought sharing dinners with him and Rhys, plus doing odd jobs, shopping and tidying, was filling her days and helping her move past her grief.

It had broken his heart to listen as she talked to Jess about her inability to have children—something she'd wanted desperately—and how her time spent with Jasper was giving her the chance to do some of that mothering she'd missed out on.

After that, Jess didn't try to pay Aunt Berta again, though she and Jasper had practically wallpapered his aunt's apartment with little thank-you notes and Jasper's artwork, all drawn specifically for her.

Jess leaned back against the cushions, her eyes drifting closed. He'd hoped living with them would make her life easier, and while he knew it had in a lot of ways, she still worked tirelessly and there were still dark circles under her eyes. She was up at dawn, getting Jasper ready for school, and she didn't stop until she put her head on the pillow, most nights after midnight.

Without her weekend job at the motel, he'd thought she would at least have a couple days to relax, but Jess wouldn't even allow herself those hours off, often taking extra shifts at the diner or cleaning the hell out of their apartment in yet another attempt to "earn her keep."

Rhys reached for Jess's feet. "Here. Take off your boots. You're home now. Try to relax a little and warm up." He helped Jess pull off her boots.

"I'll grab Luca tomorrow morning and we'll go check out your car. See if we can get it running. If not, we'll get the thing towed to my cousin Bruno's garage."

"You seem to have a cousin for every problem in the world."

Tony grinned. "Rhys wasn't exaggerating about the size of my family when he said there were thousands of us. In the meantime, I'll drive you to work tomorrow night. No more rides with the Russos," he said.

Jess shook her head. "That's okay. If the car's dead, I'll just get it towed to a junkyard or something. I can take the bus to work. I should have been doing that anyway, but I've gotten a bit complacent, living the good life here with you two. Not being as thrifty as I should. That needs to stop."

"There's nothing wrong with complacency, Jess," Rhys said. "Nothing wrong with feeling safe and comfortable."

Most people tossed the word complacent around like it was a bad thing, as if it indicated being stalled or bored. For Jess, it meant so much more, something positive, something good. And Tony was glad to know she felt that here, but hated that she thought she shouldn't.

He stepped next to her. "Rhys is right. There's nothing wrong with being complacent. In fact, I think I'm going to go out of my way to make sure you keep feeling that way. Which is why I'm driving you to work tomorrow *and* picking you up."

She shook her head, intent on starting a fight.

He ran a playful finger along her nose, shocking her into silence, before he said, "Nonnegotiable."

"You need to find a new word. You use that one way too much," she grumbled.

He chuckled. "But it works so well."

She narrowed her eyes, but he wasn't letting her win another argument. She was going to have to learn to pick her battles. He claimed the other end of the couch, leaning against the armrest and dragging Jess toward him until she was nestled between his outstretched legs, her back resting against his chest. Rhys reached for her feet, pulling them onto his lap.

She sighed, all the air in her body slowly slipping out as Rhys began to rub them.

"Your feet are freezing," he mused.

Tony heard the humor in her voice when she said, "I'm always cold."

Her inability to feel warmth had become a running joke between them. Though they had the heat on, the apartment usually a balmy seventy, Jess would still be bundled up in thick socks and sweatshirts, while he and Rhys walked around in T-shirts and shorts.

"You need to gain weight," Tony added, wrapping his arms around her tiny frame, tucking the blanket around both of them. "You're still too thin."

"Thought it was rude to tell a woman she was skinny," she teased. "Besides, I've gained five pounds since living here."

Rhys chuckled. "You've still got a ways to go. I call it the Aunt Berta fifteen. It's why Tony and I started running every morning. I'm not sure what that woman puts in her food, but I've yet to taste anything she's made that couldn't headline at a Michelin-star restaurant."

"You're not kidding." Jess groaned in delight when Rhys pressed his thumbs into the heel of her feet. "Oh God, Rhys, that feels like heaven." She settled deeper into Tony, the tension in her body waning. "Are you ever going to tell me why you hate the Russos so much?" Jess asked.

"Shit." Rhys chuckled. "Please, no. It's another one of those Moretti epic tales. Might take a while."

"Smart-ass," Tony groused. "I can make it short."

Rhys snorted. "Twenty bucks says you can't."

Jess laughed. "Just tell me the damn story already."

Tony tightened his arms around her waist, relishing the way she felt lying against him. "My great-grandfather Lorenzo Moretti immigrated here before the second World War."

"Great-grandfather?" Jess exchanged an amused look with Rhys. "He's gonna owe you twenty."

Tony tickled her, then continued his story. "The Russos came over around the same time, and my great-grandfather grew up with Mattia Russo. The two of them were best friends. They even started their own construction business together. Lorenzo was married to a beautiful woman, Isabella. According to my nonno, Lorenzo was desperately in love with his young wife, so he was devastated when he discovered she'd had an affair with Mattia."

"Oh no."

"Apparently Mattia had had his eye on Isabella for a long time, and one night, he was finally able to seduce her."

"What happened?" Jess asked.

"As you can imagine, Lorenzo was heartbroken. Isabella begged for his forgiveness, but Lorenzo was a proud man, angry. Afraid he'd never forgive her, Isabella killed herself."

Jess stirred. "Oh my God. That's a terrible story."

"Lorenzo was devastated by her death and furious with Mattia. So he cut all ties with his former best friend. Their business was dissolved and the two never spoke to each other again. Lorenzo continued to work as a master carpenter, while Mattia, who'd always run the business side of their company, ventured into other things, amassing wealth through less-than-scrupulous means."

Jess tilted her head. "What does that mean?"

"There weren't too many crooked politicians Mattia didn't have in his pocket, and there were rumors that he worked with the Italian Mafia."

"Mafia?" Jess's eyes widened.

"The Russos are crooked, cheating, greedy fuckers, always looking to steal what isn't theirs. That trait has been passed down from generation to generation."

Jess wasn't quite convinced. "How do you know that? Maybe it was just Mattia who was the asshole."

Tony bopped Jess on the nose playfully. "I know because history has repeated itself with each generation. Lorenzo married my great-grandmother, Juliette, a few years after Isabella's death, and together they had my nonno. When Nonno was in his twenties, he met my nonna, Domenica. Mattia's son, Riccardo, was the same age, and he and Nonno competed for Domenica's hand. When she chose Nonno, Riccardo—the sore fucking loser—vowed revenge. It took him decades, but as Riccardo's wealth and influence grew, he finally had the power to destroy my family's small but prosperous construction business.

"Riccardo used his connections with local policy makers and county administrators to make Nonno's life a living hell. Nonno fought for years to keep the business afloat amid countless inspections, audits, and fines for trumped-up violations, but in the end, his health suffered from the stress and he had a heart attack. That was when Nonna stepped in and said enough was enough. He closed the business and retired."

"That's terrible," Jess said. "But again, it's sort of ancient history. Two generations in the past."

"My brothers and I grew up with the Russo boys. They're just as competitive, believe me."

"The way I understand it," Rhys chimed in, having heard this story—or parts of it—retold countless times, "Matt Russo had been a big shot in high school until Tony and his family moved back from Baltimore."

"He'd had three years to run unopposed for class president, and no one dared try out for quarterback of the football team," Tony interjected.

"Let me guess. You did," Jess added.

Tony grinned. "I won both."

"What did Matt do?"

That was when Tony's smile faded. "I'd been dating this girl, Adriana, most of my senior year. She was my first love, first serious relationship. I caught her and Matt in the backseat of his BMW right after graduation. Asshole actually looked up in the middle of fucking my girl and laughed when he saw me. I'm pretty sure he set the whole thing up so I would find them."

"Shit," Jess murmured. "What did you do?"

"Pulled his ass out of the car and started a fight. The two of us pounded on each other pretty good, while my *ex* first love cried and begged us to stop. After a while, when we were both bleeding and breathing heavily, leaning on his car—which had a few dents, thanks to our fight—I decided neither she nor Matt was worth it. I told them they deserved each other and walked away."

"Wow," Jess whispered.

"Yeah, wow." Tony hadn't thought of that fight in years. He recalled how much it had hurt at the time, but now it was nothing more than a memory, one that evoked none of the piercing pain that accompanied that first broken heart.

Of course, the anger was still there, but that fire had been stoked by the history of their families and by Nonno's fierce bitterness over losing his business to the Russos' corruption.

"You can give me that twenty in the morning," Rhys joked. The three of them laughed, and then they sat in companionable silence for a few minutes. Tony thought perhaps Jess had drifted to sleep. He was surprised when she spoke again.

"How come you guys don't go out on dates?" she asked.

"We do," Rhys responded, his words the truth. Or at least, they had been until Jess moved in. Since then, neither of them had asked a woman out.

"Not while I've been here," she pointed out. "Is it because of my second job? If it's cutting into your social life—"

"It's not," Tony reassured her. She'd consulted with them before taking the job, asking if it would work for them and their schedules. They'd insisted it would be fine to leave Jasper in their care, that between the two of them and Aunt Berta, there would always be someone home to look after the little boy. Because she put him to bed before she left, watching Jasper essentially required zero work, as he'd never once woken up while she was gone.

"Why don't you have girlfriends?" she asked.

Tony chuckled. "Are you trying to figure out what's wrong with us?"

She grinned. "Oh, Tony. I can make that list all by myself without any help."

"Minx," he said, tickling her.

She batted his hands away, giggling.

Rhys rolled his eyes at their antics. "I think it's safe to say we're both workaholics. Besides, marriage and a family...they aren't really in the cards for me."

"Penny mentioned you felt that way, but I'm curious why not?" Jess asked.

"I'm committed to my practice, my patients. I'm on call twenty-four seven. You've seen that. It wouldn't be fair to ask a wife to spend so much time on her own."

It wasn't unusual for Rhys to receive a phone call or several each night from patients, and he spent at least two or three nights at the hospital after office hours, making the rounds of his patients there.

"I think that's a shame," Jess said. "You'd be a great dad. You both would."

Over the past month or so, Tony had come to acknowledge the pull he felt whenever he and Jess were in the same room. He was drawn to her like a moth to a flame, helpless to hold back when it came to touching her, either to offer a hand to help her stand, his palm on the small of her back when they walked beside each other, or a hug before bed. Or like right now...as he held her in his arms. She felt good there. Right.

He'd never been much for those casual, affectionate touches in the past.

Of course, like Rhys, he hadn't been looking for a serious relationship either, preferring to keep the women he went out with firmly in the "just dating" category. He'd jokingly declared the hunt for a wife a forty-year-old man's game, likening himself to George Clooney, claiming he had too many wild oats left to sow.

He was committed to putting Moretti Brothers Restorations on the map, working overtime to see the business's continued success, but lately—since Jess—he was questioning whether or not that should be his life's number one priority.

Before moving in together, he and Rhys discussed their future plans, in regards to relationships and women. It would have been impractical not to, since they were not only buying real estate together but a home as well. Both of them had stated outright that marriage wasn't in their immediate plans, and overnights spent with women wouldn't be unheard of, but it also wouldn't be a common occurrence. They'd decided to revisit the discussion when one of them renounced their single status. That hadn't happened.

They'd both brought lovers home from time to time, but it was always a one- or two-night thing. None of the women had ever stayed beyond breakfast on the second day.

Tony glanced at Rhys as he massaged Jess's feet and acknowledged he wasn't the only one who'd changed with Jess in their apartment. Rhys was upstairs for dinner much earlier than normal, typically coming up shortly after Jess returned home from the diner.

When neither of them replied to her assertion that they'd make good fathers, Jess let the subject drop, stirring in his arms and sighing contentedly once more. "You guys are spoiling me."

Tony liked the idea of that, aware that he would pamper her a hell of a lot more if she'd let him. "You're easy to spoil."

She glanced up at him, smiling so sweetly, she took his breath away. Before he could think about his actions, Tony placed a soft kiss on her forehead before letting his lips drift lower, drawing them over her cheek slowly, seductively. Tony felt Rhys's gaze on them, but he didn't stop. He couldn't.

The lack of surprise on Jess's face told him he wasn't alone in feeling this...connection. And it wasn't a connection just to Jess. Rhys was part of it as well.

He would have thought that idea completely ludicrous a

few years earlier, but since then, he'd watched his sister Layla meet and fall in love with two men. He'd been a witness to just how strong and true that relationship was.

When he'd first learned his sister was dating Finn and Miguel, he'd been fully prepared to kick the guys' asses, certain they were just using her for some sort of kinky threesome sex. Then he'd gotten to know them, seen the way they adored Layla, cared for her—and each other—and he couldn't hold on to his belief that what they were doing was wrong.

Because it wasn't.

For them, it was...perfect.

It was that thought that drove him forward.

Tony cupped Jess's cheek and placed his lips on hers.

Their first kiss.

And it packed a punch.

Jess's lips parted on a gasp, and he took advantage, running his tongue along the line of her mouth. Her tongue darted out to touch his, the two of them sharing each other's taste. She was delicious, and he wanted more. So fucking much more.

His hands drifted to her hair, his fingers closing around her long dark tresses. Typically she wore it up in a ponytail, but tonight it was down, loose. Jess didn't resist when he deepened the kiss even more, her own hands rising, mimicking his as her grip tightened around his hair.

He'd had long hair since high school, something he'd taken a lot of good-natured ribbing for from his dad and brothers. Not that he cared. He was used to it being long, and he was perfectly aware that a lot of women found it sexy.

He'd never been so fucking turned on by a kiss in his life. His cock thickened. There was no way Jess couldn't feel the hard length of it pressing against her ass.

Then Tony felt a shift lower down on the couch. He hadn't forgotten Rhys's presence. Not at all. Having his friend there was spurring him on, driving Tony to move them forward to where he knew they both wanted to be.

With Jess.

Tony broke the kiss, drawing the backs of his fingers along the soft skin of her face. He held Jess's gaze for a second, then looked over at Rhys.

Jess followed the direction of his stare, both of them recognizing the burning need in Rhys's expression. Jess sucked in a sharp intake of air.

Rhys still held her feet in his hands, so when their attention turned to him, he used that grip to his advantage, tugging at her feet with just enough force. Jess slid down the couch, losing her balance and falling to her back, her head resting on the cushion between Tony's outstretched knees.

Tony sat still as Rhys shifted, kneeling over Jess, caging her beneath him. Rhys lowered his head and stole his own kiss. The three of them were close, intimately close, as the temperature in the living room quickly rose.

Rhys remained above Jess, supporting his weight with his elbows and knees, holding himself above her. Jess's hands found their way to his shoulders, her fingers bunching into the material of his T-shirt.

Tony watched as the two of them kissed, his cock thickening even more as his best friend kissed her. He fought to clamor his way through the barrage of emotions sweeping through him. He'd kissed hundreds of women in his life, but none of them had ever moved him like Jess.

While he'd known of Rhys's shared interest in the woman, Tony had still been concerned that once they reached this place, once they crossed the line, he'd feel jealous.

What he hadn't anticipated was finding pleasure in observing his friend kiss the woman he wanted. Needed. Cared for.

Loved?

He was too old for such a romantic sentiment, love an emotion he'd never managed to perfect. He shook that thought away, focusing instead on the here and now.

Tony was a dominant, demanding son of a bitch, who preferred to control the play in the bedroom. Unable to remain apart, he placed his hand on Rhys's shoulder, pressing his friend back and up, wanting to join in.

Rhys allowed it, lifting his head and looking at Tony curiously. Tony didn't have a clue what kind of lover Rhys was in the bedroom, neither of them the type to fuck and tell. It occurred to Tony—belatedly—that they needed to have that conversation before they allowed things to go too far with Jess.

Shit, they needed to discuss a lot more than just the sexual mechanics.

Jess rose between them, her face flushed, her breathing shallow, rapid. Their kisses had just as powerful an impact on her.

"Jess." Tony reached for her, intent on having those kiss-swollen lips once more, but Jess moved unexpectedly, rising from the couch before either he or Rhys could touch her again.

"I'm sorry," she said.

"What?" Rhys asked. "Why?"

"I can't...we can't do this."

Tony scowled. "Of course we can."

She shook her head, backing away from the couch. Neither of them sought to pull her back, but Tony sensed Rhys wanted to do so as much as he did.

"No. We can't...dammit."

Jess dropped down on Tony's recliner, her elbows on her knees, her frustration tangible.

"Tell us what you're thinking, Jess." Rhys, as always, managed a calm, reasonable tone, something that was beyond Tony's abilities at the moment. All he could think about was dragging her back to the couch and kissing her for the rest of time.

"I'm attracted to you. *Both* of you."

"Good," Tony said, surprised when Rhys put a hand on his shoulder.

He shook his head subtly. "Let her talk."

"And while that's its own insane problem, and something I can't even begin to wrap my head around, that's actually not the reason we have to stop."

Tony frowned. "It's not?"

"I can't risk losing this." She lifted her hands, gesturing at the apartment. "Jasper is the most important thing in my life, and every decision I make impacts him. This is the first safe, good home he's ever had. I would never—*ever*—do anything that would take this away from him."

Tony opened his mouth to argue, to tell her she was wrong, but...she wasn't. He'd kissed her impulsively without thinking beyond his own desires and needs. And Rhys had broken character and followed that lead. Something he could see his friend was now regretting.

"I understand, Jess," Rhys said, reverting back to his practical, reasonable self.

She looked relieved, and she smiled at him gratefully. However, that look slipped when her gaze drifted to Tony.

He wanted to tell her he understood too. And he did. But understanding and accepting were two different beasts, and he wasn't able to give her the same assurances. Because he didn't want to.

Didn't want to walk away from this.

From her.

No.

From *them*.

When the silence drifted too long, Jess looked away, then slowly stood. Rhys did the same, while Tony remained motionless on the couch.

"I'm going to go to bed."

Rhys nodded. "Okay. Good night."

"I..." she started. Tony suspected she wanted to apologize again, feeling sorry for something that wasn't her fault, for something he'd initiated.

"Good night, Jess," Tony said, letting her off the hook, even though it was the last thing he wanted to do.

She swallowed and nodded before leaving the room.

Rhys dropped back down on the couch heavily. "Not exactly our finest moment."

"Would you have done it?" Tony asked.

Rhys didn't respond immediately, which told Tony he was really thinking about the question, searching for the truthful answer. Tony respected the hell out of his friend for seeking to give him that, instead of firing off some knee-jerk response out of frustration.

Rhys rubbed his jaw. "Tony, I've never shared a woman with another man."

"Neither have I."

Rhys studied his face, then nodded. "I'll admit I've wondered about it."

His roommate knew Layla, Finn, and Miguel, knew about their relationship.

Tony grinned. "You think ménages are hereditary?"

Rhys chuckled. "No, I don't. Listen...it's been clear from the beginning that we're both attracted to Jess. And having her here, living with us, it's blurred some lines that might have remained in focus if we weren't in such close quarters all the time."

"My focus is crystal clear," Tony asserted.

"Is it? Because I think we can both admit that kissing her like that was impulsive. We didn't think it through, didn't play it out."

Tony appreciated Rhys's willingness to share the blame for something he'd instigated. "We would never kick Jess out, never put her and Jasper back on the street. You know that."

Rhys nodded. "I do. But Jess has lived her entire life being let down by people. Every single person."

"We won't let her down."

Rhys sighed. "Those are just words. I'm afraid they don't

stack up against a lifetime of actions—she's watched everyone walk away, and those scars run deep. Jasper will always—as he should—come first. There's nothing she won't do, nothing she won't sacrifice for that kid. I respect the hell out of her for that."

Tony ran his hand through his hair, hating every word Rhys spoke, even though he knew his friend was right. "I do too, but—"

"There can't be a *but*, Tony," Rhys interjected.

There couldn't.

"Fuck," he muttered.

"Yeah," Rhys said. "Fuck."

Chapter Twelve

"Goddamn Flyers," Tony grumbled.

"Tell me about it," his brother Joey concurred. "What a shit season."

Tony's phone pinged. He glanced at the text and groaned.

"Let me guess," Luca said. "Gwendolyn Baxter."

Tony grunted in response.

Gio, Luca's twin, shook his head. "Not sure why you were so determined to take that job. You knew Gwendolyn Baxter was going to make your life a living hell."

"*We* took it," Tony made sure to stress the *we* part, "because she's a big player in Philadelphia. If she likes our work, she'll tell her other rich friends and it'll put Moretti Brothers Restorations on the map."

"You're already on the map," his cousin Aldo pointed out. "Hell, the business has been featured on HGTV a few times."

Kayden upended the almost-empty Doritos bag into his mouth, shaking out the last few broken pieces. "Tony's just looking to be a big shot like the Russos."

Tony chucked a beer cap at Kayden's head. "Asshole. As if I'd ever want to be like those uptight prigs."

"You gonna text her back?" Gio asked.

Tony shook his head. "Fuck no. The second I answer, she knows she has me on the hook and sends me three hundred follow-up texts. We have a meeting first thing in the morning and there is nothing she needs to know now that won't wait until then."

Joey grinned. "I think we all know she's less interested in the hammer you're swinging in her house and more interested in the one between your legs. That woman is hot for you."

Tony had spent the past month enduring Gwen's flirting and constant sexual innuendoes, using his brothers as a buffer as much as possible. The woman would not take no for an answer.

"I'd take a job with the Russos before I'd ever sleep with Gwen Baxter," Tony said, taking a swig of beer. He'd had plenty of experience with the Gwens of the world, women with money to blow, who believed it gave them access to whomever their heavily mascaraed eyes landed on.

Tony was aware that women were attracted to him and his brothers. Nonna insisted it was their good Italian genes, proclaiming them the most handsome men in Philadelphia. Even Finn's mother, Riley, had dubbed them the Italian Stallions. He laughed whenever she called them that, but the truth was, women came on to him...a lot.

However, few had ever truly caught his eye, and even fewer had held his attention for very long.

Jess was the exception.

"Jess still working for the Russos?" Gio asked. His brothers had all taken a shine to Jess and Jasper, which ensured they didn't like the fact she was working for the Russos any more than he did.

Tony scoffed. "Yeah. Bet it's driving Matt crazy too, now that he knows she lives here."

"How the hell did she even wind up working for the asshole?" Kayden asked.

That had been one of the first things he'd asked Jess after learning she'd gotten the job offer. "The Russos eat at Paulie's too. Apparently Matt stops in at least once a week and grabs the daily special as takeout. He stopped in the week after Jess was attacked at the motel and asked about her bruises. Jess explained what happened, then said she was short a second job, and he offered her the cleaning gig."

Luca chuckled. "Paranoid bastard probably thinks we sent her in to spy on him."

"When you put it that way, I'm not so sad about her keeping that job," Joey said, laughing. "Let him sweat it out, thinking she's feeding us all his sordid secrets."

It wasn't unusual for the guys to come over on Sunday afternoons in the winter to watch whatever sport was in season together. Today was a little quieter than usual, as Aunt Berta had taken Jasper to a birthday party for his cousin's son, Billy. Jasper had been living for the party, talking about little else all week. Tony was glad the day had finally come, not sure Jasper would have been able to contain his excitement a second longer.

The moment she'd discovered Jasper would be occupied all afternoon, Jess had taken an extra shift at Paulie's, despite his invitation to join them all to watch the game.

It had been three weeks since he and Rhys had kissed her.

Three long fucking weeks.

Since then, Jess had spent most of the time she was in the apartment with Jasper in their room or taking on more shifts at the diner.

She was working herself to the point of exhaustion, and Tony'd had enough of seeing the dark circles under her eyes. To make matters worse, she was losing weight again.

Something needed to give, and he intended to bring the subject up to Rhys as soon as the guys left.

Tony glanced up at the sound of Jasper's voice.

He bounded into the living room with a bit more energy than usual. Which was saying something, considering the kid bounced more than Tigger.

Tony grinned as Jasper made his way around the room, fist-bumping all the guys, something Kayden had taught him to do whenever their team scored. Since then, it was Jasper's favorite greeting.

"Hyped-up on birthday cake?" Rhys asked Aunt Berta, who followed him into the room, looking like she'd had a day and a half.

"Fifteen kids under the age of seven," she said exhaustedly. "All of them on sugar overload by the end of the party. Not sure who thought a pinata was a good idea."

Tony stood up and gave his aunt a kiss on the cheek. "Why don't you go on down to your apartment and relax for a little while? I'll call Jess and ask her to bring us all subs home from Paulie's for dinner."

The fact Aunt Berta was okay with takeout told him just how insane her afternoon had been. "Sounds perfect." Then she looked around the living room, giving every single man a very pointed look. "All of these beer bottles are going to be in the recycling bin when I come back up, right?"

"You can count on me to keep these slobs in line," Joey said, winking at Aunt Berta, who rolled her eyes at him.

"Joseph Moretti, you were the one I was talking to. Lord help the woman who agrees to marry you."

Joey had a well-earned reputation in their family for his messiness. It was one of the reasons Tony had been anxious to move into this apartment with Rhys. If he'd had to spend another month picking up his brother's smelly socks and dirty dishes, he would have lost his shit.

Aunt Berta left and Jasper climbed onto the couch, squeezing a spot for himself between Rhys and Aldo, the latter playfully ruffling the boy's hair. "How are you doing, Jasper?"

"Good." Jasper grinned, revealing a new gap left behind by the loss of his second front tooth. He loved hanging out with the guys on Sundays, and Jess had admitted a couple weeks earlier the best part about living with them was that Jasper had the opportunity to spend time with positive male role models.

"Did you have fun at the party?" Rhys asked him during a commercial break.

Jasper nodded enthusiastically. "We played games and had cake and ice cream and...oh!" He jumped off the couch. "I forgot. We got toys too!" He dashed out of the living room.

Two seconds later, Tony heard glass breaking.

He and Rhys rose quickly, following the sound.

Jasper stood by the front door, his coat in his hands. Next to him, in three broken pieces, was a pottery bowl Aunt Berta had found at a yard sale. She'd given it to them to put their keys in.

Jasper's eyes welled up with tears. "I bumped into the table." He held up his coat, retrieving a small plastic football from his pocket. "I wanted to show you my toy."

"That's okay," Tony said, bending down to pick up the broken bowl and keys scattered on the floor. "It was an accident."

"I'm sorry." The boy's voice quivered as he tried to hold back his tears.

"Jasper," Rhys said, putting a comforting hand on his head. "It's okay, buddy."

"Are you going to make us leave?" he asked miserably.

"What?" Tony asked, kneeling in front of Jasper. "What are you talking about?"

"I broke a lamp at Miss Brenda's and she told Mommy I couldn't come back anymore. Are you going to make us go back to the shelter?"

Tony placed the three pieces of pottery and keys on the table and hugged Jasper, his heart breaking that the kid was so afraid of being sent away. "Jasper. It was an accident. We would never send you away for breaking something. Hell—heck," he amended. "There's *nothing* you could do that would make us send you away."

Rhys reached over and tipped Jasper's face up with a gentle hand under the boy's chin. "You and your mommy will have a home here for as long as you want it. Nothing you do will change that. That's a promise. And I don't break promises."

Jasper nodded, but he still didn't look convinced.

Tony, desperate to ease the boy's mind, stood up, grabbed the biggest piece of the broken bowl, and threw it down, splintering it into five more pieces. "Besides, I broke the bowl way more than you."

Jasper looked up at him uncertainly, but finally a small smile appeared. "You broke it on purpose."

Tony nodded. "Yep. And that's way worse than doing it on accident. Why don't you and Rhys go back and watch the rest of the game while I clean up my mess?"

"I can help," Jasper offered. "Earn my keep."

He was mimicking Jess, and it occurred to Tony that while Jess may not have intended it, her inability to accept help easily was rubbing off on Jasper. He and Rhys clearly still had some work to do. To convince mother and son that this was their home, and they didn't have to walk around on eggshells in order to stay.

"Come on. You don't need to be messing around with those sharp edges," Rhys said, grabbing the plastic football Jasper had dropped on the floor. "Leave that to a grown-up. We'll go back, watch hockey, and play with this with the guys. They'll all be jealous you have such a cool ball."

Jasper allowed Rhys to lead him back to the living room, while Tony retrieved a broom and dustpan. Once the mess was cleaned up, he returned to watch the game, but his heart wasn't into it. He was too distracted by his new roommates, wishing he knew how he could set their minds at ease.

Jess had made several comments in passing over the past two months about her upbringing, and it was apparent she'd never truly lived in a home where she felt she belonged, where she didn't have to earn the right to remain there. She had also told them about her experiences with foster care, explaining that was why she'd been hesitant to call social services immediately. It killed him to know she'd been so terrified of losing Jasper. As far as he was concerned, there wasn't a more loving mother on the planet.

He was still sitting on the couch, long after the game ended and the guys left. The television was on, but he wasn't paying a damn bit of attention to it. Rhys had found some National Geographic thing about penguins, though Tony suspected his roommate wasn't really watching it either. Jasper had crashed pretty hard after his sugar rush, falling asleep on the couch. Rhys had carried him back to the bedroom an hour ago so he could finish his nap in peace.

"You've been quiet this afternoon," Rhys mused.

"Just thinking. Worried. Jess never stops. I thought living here would take some of the stress off her, but it hasn't."

Rhys nodded. "I had hoped for the same thing. Jess has had to work hard her entire life, only having herself to rely on, Tony. It's going to take more than a couple months of living here to break something that is so deeply ingrained inside her."

Tony knew all of that, even though it was hard for him to accept. But that wasn't the main thing bothering him. "She's holding herself back from us. Staying away."

"Those kisses..." Rhys started.

Tony wanted to regret kissing Jess the way he had. It had been impulsive and stupid and it had spooked her. But that kiss...it had solidified something he'd only suspected up until that point.

Jess belonged here. With them.

"I want her. Want to be with her." Tony hadn't spoken those words aloud. Doing so now felt...freeing.

Rhys studied his face, and Tony could almost imagine the wheels turning in his best friend's brain, seeking—as always—the truthful answer.

In the end, Rhys forced himself to admit what they both knew. "So do I. I've never felt an attraction like this. I've spent more hours this past month than I care to admit, trying to pinpoint what it is that makes Jess so different from other women. Honestly, I think it's everything. She's tenacious, brave, intelligent, stubborn as hell, and so fucking gorgeous, it's hard to look away from her. She's one of the most loving mothers I've ever met, and I know that because I have a pretty amazing mom myself. She works as hard as we do."

Tony shook his head. "No. She works harder."

Rhys nodded, accepting that correction. "You're right. She does."

"I want to take away her stress. Her fears. I just...don't know how to do that because she won't let me. Won't let *us*," Tony quickly amended.

"I know, but she's not wrong to hold herself back, Tony. To use caution. I'd bet my entire life savings she knows we want her. And she wants us too. But none of us has a clue how to morph those desires into...whatever comes next. We're just as inexperienced when it comes to relationships as she is, if you think about it."

Tony ran his hand through his hair, overwhelmed by the need to argue that fact. But he couldn't. And he didn't get the chance when they heard the front door open.

Jess walked into the living room with a large bag in her hands. "Dinner," she said, offering them the same tired smile that had taken up permanent residence on her face. "Where's the key bowl?"

"I broke it," Tony lied smoothly, rising to take the bag from her hands. "I'll text Aunt Berta and tell her dinner is here."

"Jasper in the bedroom?"

Rhys nodded, rising as well. "Yeah. Overstimulated by the party. He conked out about an hour ago. You look tired." He lifted his hand and ran his fingers along Jess's cheek affectionately.

"I'm fine."

"You don't need to keep working extra shifts, Jess."

"Or the second job with the Russos," Tony added.

"You know Matt Russo is a pretty nice guy these days, right? He's not eighteen anymore."

It was the worst thing she could have said, but he got the sense that was why she said it. Jess was scrambling to maintain her distance, using every weapon in her arsenal. "Stay away from Matt Russo. He's a fucking prick," he groused.

Jess rolled her eyes, and Tony itched to spank her ass for it. She had a very spankable ass. Something she probably would not like hearing.

"You don't have to work so hard all the time." Rhys said the words gently, but Jess's response was the same as always.

She bristled, her spine stiffening, the response her go-to. "I can't impose on you guys forever."

Tony's temper flared, but he forced himself to bite his tongue.

"I'll go wake Jasper for dinner," she said, obviously aware she was pushing their buttons and ready to make a quick escape.

* * *

The rest of the night passed somewhat peacefully, Aunt Berta and Jasper dominating the dinner conversation. He, Rhys, and Jess were more subdued, the tension between them simmering just below the surface. The string connecting them had been stretched too taut and they were quickly approaching a day of reckoning.

Though God only knew what the hell that would look like.

He and Rhys had retired to the living room to watch yet another a hockey game. Aunt Berta had returned to her apartment right after dinner, still worn out from the birthday party. Tony had listened as Jess and Jasper worked their way through their nightly routine of a bath and bedtime story. It had been quiet in their room for nearly an hour. Tony assumed Jess had given in to her own exhaustion and gone to bed with Jasper.

So he was surprised when she strolled into the living room a few minutes later. She was dressed in a long-sleeved T-shirt and lounge pants, fuzzy socks on her feet. She'd pinned her hair up in a ponytail. She looked completely adorable, and his cock—the asshole—responded instantly.

Jess tossed a twenty-dollar bill down on the coffee table.

"What's that for?" he asked, not bothering to mask his irritation. He was tired of her constantly trying to give them money they didn't want or ask for.

"Jasper told me he broke the bowl."

Tony waved at the money. "Take that back. It was an accident."

"Accident or not, I'm paying for it."

Tony rose, the frustration that had been simmering all day finally pushing its way out. "Take. The. Money. Back."

"You lied. You said you broke it."

Tony raised his hands, gesturing in aggravation, his Italian roots showing. "It was no big deal, Jess."

"I'm trying to teach Jasper responsibility. And if it was no big deal, why would you say you broke it?"

Tony leaned toward her, refusing to back down. "The kid was scared. He thought we were going to kick you both out."

Rhys stood as well. "Jess. Jasper was upset. We were simply trying to defuse the situation."

She turned to Rhys, her voice still raised. "By lying?"

Tony pointed to the twenty. "This conversation is over. Pick up that money and take it back."

She crossed her arms, her stubbornness shining through. "No."

"Goddammit, Jess. Take it back."

"No!" she shouted.

"Fuck. I'm done with this." Tony reacted before he could think. Spurred on by so many emotions, he didn't know which end was up.

ched out and grasped her upper arms, tugging her toward him.

Jess gasped in shock, but that sound was cut off the second he slammed his lips against hers, kissing her roughly.

He expected her to shove him back, his body already tensing, braced for her retaliation.

What he didn't anticipate was her returning the kiss tenfold, her hands going to his waist, pulling him toward her.

Tony released her arms, wrapping his own around her body, needing to feel her—every inch of her—pressed against to him. The kiss elevated to the next level, tongues and teeth fighting for domination. Jess gave as good as she got when she nipped his lower lip, drawing blood.

The kiss went on and on. Tony was afraid to stop. Terrified she'd pull away again.

Finally, he felt a hand on his shoulder, one that didn't belong to Jess.

He and Jess ended the kiss at the same time and when he opened his eyes, he realized Rhys had placed a hand on both of them. He and Jess were breathing heavily, gasping for air like horses who'd just run the Kentucky Derby.

They looked at each other, shell-shocked, dumbfounded.

"We need to move this to the bedroom," Rhys said. "Now."

Chapter Thirteen

Jess walked down the hall to Rhys's bedroom, both men flanking her. For weeks, her brain had been working on overdrive, whirling twenty-four seven over this inevitability.

She'd come up with a very long list of reasons why sleeping with Tony and Rhys was wrong—top of that list including she didn't want to fuck up her current living situation, as well as the fact Tony and Rhys were confirmed bachelors who restricted their relationships with the fairer sex to booty calls.

Sex wasn't just a physical thing for Jess. She wished she could separate sex and emotions, but she wasn't wired that way. God, Rhys and Tony had only kissed her so far, and already she felt her tenuous grip on her heart slipping.

Then she'd created an equally long list of ways to avoid this situation that included staying away from them as much as possible and cold showers. Lots of cold showers.

She'd also come up with a strict budget she thought would help her achieve her goal of getting her own place sooner so she wouldn't be around them constantly, tempted.

Jesus, the temptation had nearly driven her mad. She

counted her savings at least a dozen times a day, as if counting would increase it.

Every single second of every single day had been exhausting, yet not enough to keep her from tossing and turning all night until the next morning, when she stepped on the treadmill that never stopped moving again.

All that thinking, fighting, resisting.

And now?

It was gone. All of it.

There wasn't a single thought in her mind as she walked into Rhys's room and watched Tony close and lock the door.

Nothing except the bone-deep feeling that for the first time in her life, she was exactly where she wanted to be.

The impact of that realization was so overwhelming, she couldn't breathe.

Something Rhys clearly noticed.

He cupped her cheeks, his astute gaze missing nothing. "There's no point of no return. You say no or stop, and it all ends. You understand that?"

"I want you," she whispered. "I want both of you. So much it hurts."

Those words were the ones she'd shoved to the deepest recesses of her mind, refusing to allow them out in the light of day. She'd buried them in the back of the filing cabinet behind all her very logical lists and budgets.

Once they were spoken aloud, the corner turned, Rhys and Tony moved in unison. It was as if she'd unshackled invisible bonds, setting them both free.

Rhys lowered his head to kiss her, his lips softer but no less hungry than Tony's earlier. She'd obsessed over the kisses they'd shared a few weeks ago, the memory of them fueling the fantasies she couldn't stop playing over and over in her mind.

The other waitresses at work had remarked on her new habit of daydreaming, constantly asking her what on earth she could be thinking about. She hadn't told them about her new living situation, though she wasn't sure why.

In her mind, she kept thinking this couldn't be real. That tomorrow she'd wake up to discover she and Jasper were still in the shelters, still hungry, still fighting for a way out. No matter how many mornings she woke up in that soft, warm bed, she couldn't find a way to believe that it would last. Life had a way of pulling the rug out from under her whenever she least expected it. She'd crashed to the floor too many times to trust this.

The problem was...while she couldn't trust this reality to last, she did trust Rhys and Tony.

That contradiction was wreaking havoc on her, which was why her brain never—NEVER—turned off.

"Put it all away, Jess," Rhys murmured, his lips brushing the side of her mouth.

She closed her eyes and sighed. "I want to. I'm trying."

Tony stepped behind her, his hands on her waist as he kissed the top of her head. She was surrounded by their warmth, bolstered by their strength, their affection.

Tony tugged out the band gathering her hair in a ponytail so that her brunette waves fell over her shoulders. He shifted all of it to one side, granting himself unhindered access to the side of her neck. He kissed it, his tongue darting out to stroke her skin, to tease the spot behind her ear.

When he spoke, his words were hot against her skin. "This was inescapable, Jess. From the moment we found you shivering outside this apartment, the three of us have been hurtling toward this night. Right here. Right now."

Her head tilted to the side, silently inviting him to continue his ministrations. Rhys watched the two of them for a few seconds before drawing one hand down the front of her body. He started at her throat, dragging his fingers over her shirt, cupping one of her breasts. She'd gotten ready for bed, intent on going to sleep with Jasper. Yet another weak-willed attempt at avoiding Tony and Rhys. It was easier to resist them when she wasn't near them.

She was almost asleep when Jasper—clearly eaten up with guilt—admitted he'd broken the bowl. She'd thanked him for his honesty, kissed him good night, then let her sexual frustration find a new outlet—anger.

When she was certain Jasper was asleep, she'd put on a bra, grabbed the money, and sought them out, a powder keg set to explode.

Learning that Jasper had thought Tony and Rhys would send them away nearly killed her. Had she unwittingly transferred her own fears, her own inability to accept unconditional help, to her impressionable son?

"Lift your arms," Rhys said.

Jess did so without hesitation, allowing him to pull her shirt off. His gaze drifted down to her bra, his fingers returning, drawing a line along the edge of the lacy material, tickling the tops of her breasts. "So beautiful," he murmured.

She felt Tony's hands working to free the clasp on her bra, his lips still grazing her neck and shoulder as he did so. They weren't just undressing her. They were worshipping her.

The realization only served to increase her feverish arousal.

Tony slipped the straps of her bra over her shoulders and the material fell away, baring her to their gazes. They looked their fill as she stood there, marveling over the fact she felt no embarrassment, no shyness with them.

Rhys cupped one breast, his thumb toying with her taut nipple. Tony reached around to claim the other, squeezing it with just enough pressure to send tingles along her spine, straight to her pussy. She could feel the wetness growing between her thighs. She was so ready for what came next.

Her sexual experience was painfully limited, yet with them, it didn't matter. Her sense of self was driven by the way *they* viewed her, not the way she perceived herself.

They saw beauty, so she was beautiful. They saw confidence, so she was confident.

"I want to see you too." She reached for the hem of Rhys's shirt and he allowed her to tug it off. Despite their status as roommates, neither man had ever walked around the house shirtless, something she suspected they were doing in deference to her and Jasper's presence in the apartment.

She sucked in a breath at Rhys's bare chest. He and Tony ran every day, and there was an expensive set of weights in a makeshift gym in the basement of the building. They'd taken her there a few days after she and Jasper had moved in, giving her a grand tour not just of the apartment but of the offices below, telling her all the improvements they'd made after buying it.

Rhys must have spent more time in that gym than she realized. His arms were muscular, his chest well-defined, sexy as fuck. His doctor's coat hid a lot—too much—of him.

Like him, she longed to touch. She ran her hand over his chest, his soft skin encasing rock-hard pecs and abs. She sensed Tony watching.

"Have the two of you..." She stumbled slightly on her question. "Is this something..."

"Rhys and I have never shared a woman," Tony answered, saving her from trying to find the words. "I've never shared a woman with anyone."

"Oh." The idea that they were willing to share *her* filled her heart with so much joy, she feared it might explode.

"I know it's been a long time since you've been with a man, Jess," Rhys said. "We'll go slow, take our time."

She'd mentioned her lack of dates to Rhys the night of the attack, the first time she'd lowered her guard and opened up to him.

"How long?" Tony asked.

"I've only ever had sex with Jasper's father."

She wasn't sure how Tony would take that news. She feared

perhaps he'd pull away, the overprotective man emerging, armed with a determination to save her, even if it meant denying himself. She'd become accustomed to his overbearing demeanor, the way he texted to check up on her, how he always asked about her day's plans, his demands to drive her places he didn't want her going to alone.

She always pretended to be annoyed, but the truth was, no one had ever given a shit where she was or if she was safe. His protective nature filled an emptiness she hadn't known existed until he'd come into her life, and it was yet another reason why she'd struggled so hard to think of him as just a friend.

Tony took the news in stride, running his hand along her side. "We won't hurt you."

Jess wasn't the type of person to give her trust easily, but Tony and Rhys had claimed hers nearly from the start. They'd kept her and Jasper—two strangers—safe from that very first morning, proving themselves honest, caring, good men.

Tony reached behind his neck, pulling his own shirt off. Like Rhys, he was beautifully built, though Tony's frame was larger, bulkier. Where Rhys was muscular, Tony was stacked... and then some. His arm was larger than her thigh, and she recalled the way he'd carried her up three flights of stairs without even breathing heavy after pulling her from the freezing-cold car.

She twisted, placing a kiss on his pec, right above his heart. He felt like steel—pure, unmitigated power. And he was here. Hers. Even if only for this single night.

She sank her teeth into his pec until she heard his grunt—of surprise, of pain.

Jess lifted her eyes to Tony's face. "Maybe I want it to hurt." Then she glanced over her shoulder at Rhys. "And I definitely don't want it slow."

"Fuck," Tony breathed, fisting her hair in his large grip and twisting her face back in his direction. He kissed her hard as his other hand slid into her lounge pants. Jess gasped in pure pleasure when he stroked her clit, applying the perfect amount of pressure, giving her exactly what she wanted.

Rhys stepped closer, sliding her pants over her hips and down. Jess stepped out of them, jerking slightly when she felt Rhys's cock brush against her ass. He'd taken his pants off while Tony distracted her with his kisses, his fingers on her clit.

Rhys slid his cock between her legs, not entering her, just merely slipping it back and forth along her seam, teasing her entrance as Tony drove her out of her mind with his fingers.

"Yes," she hissed. It had been so long since she'd been touched by anyone other than herself. And Tony and Rhys knew exactly how to touch her, how to stoke the flames of her arousal.

"God," she said, as Tony's lips traveled along her neck, his fingers still working their magic on her clit. "Please."

Rhys pumped between her legs, coating his thick cock in her juices. "Are you on birth control?"

She shook her head. "No money. No need." She glanced at him over her shoulder. "I would like..."

"I'll give you the shot. Tomorrow."

Jess was pure static electricity, every part of her sparking with the need to come, so much so, concentrating on his words was hard.

She nodded. "Yes. Okay."

Rhys stepped away from her, opening his nightstand drawer. He pulled out two condoms, tossing one on the bed. She suspected they'd led her to Rhys's room rather than Tony's because it was farthest away from the guest room, making it unlikely Jasper would hear anything.

She loved how much they cared for her son, protected him, considered his needs. For two bachelors who had little experience with young children, they were both naturals when it came to...she went ahead and let herself think the word...fathering.

Rhys stretched his hand out to her and she took it, letting him guide her to the bed. She scooted to the middle of the mattress, lying down on her back as Rhys moved with her. He quickly slipped on the condom, then crawled over her.

The mattress sank a bit as Tony sat on the edge, facing them, watching.

They said they'd never shared a woman, but neither man gave any indication of unease with this situation. She'd never met two men so comfortable with each other, in the apartment and now here, in the bedroom.

She lifted her hands to Rhys's shoulders, her legs parting as he placed the head of his dick at her opening. She gave him an encouraging smile when he hesitated for just a moment.

"So beautiful," he whispered, then he gave her exactly what she'd asked for. He slammed into her with one strong, fast, hard, amazing thrust.

Jess's pussy clenched and she came instantly. She'd already been clinging to that ledge, pushed there by Tony stroking her clit.

"Did she just come?" Tony asked, his voice deep, almost guttural, betraying his need.

Rhys nodded, his jaw clenched. "She did. She's not making it easy to... Fuck it." She wasn't sure what Rhys's original intent had been, but for the first time ever, her calm, cool, and collected doctor lost control.

And she loved it.

He pounded inside her like a man possessed, taking her with such strength and speed, she found herself at the precipice again within minutes.

"Rhys," she called out. "Jesus. Yes!" She came again, her back arching, and Rhys joined her, pumping slower but with just as much power, once, twice, three times more. His eyes were closed, her name falling from her lips. Somehow, he managed to make it sound like a prayer.

"Jess," he whispered. "God, Jess."

She stilled beneath him, gasping for breath, her chest rising and falling rapidly, her heart racing so, so fast.

Regardless of all that, when Rhys withdrew and dropped down to the bed at her side, she instantly raised her hand, reaching out for Tony.

He'd donned the condom already, but he didn't immediately move over her as she expected. Instead, he took her hand and used it to pull her upright, until she was sitting next to him. He closed a fist around her hair—something she was learning was his preference—as he kissed her.

"Get on my lap, Jess. Straddle me."

She moved into position without delay, Tony's thick cock brushing his stomach where it pointed upwards between them.

She looked down at it, not surprised to find him extremely well-endowed. Tony was a big guy. Everywhere.

Rhys's dick had stretched her just beyond the limit to what was comfortable. She might not be a virgin, but with these two, she felt as good as.

"Change your mind on the slow and easy?" Tony asked, his smug smile telling her that he knew exactly where her thoughts had gone.

She shook her head. "Not a chance."

Jess lifted herself up, her knees on the mattress on either side of Tony's hips. She reached for his cock, guiding it toward her. Then, she showed him just how un-slow and un-easy she wanted him. She dropped all her weight back down, driving his dick to the hilt as she cried out. Partly in pain—the good kind—and partly in unadulterated pleasure.

Her actions took Tony off guard but only at first. His huge hands encased her hips, stopping her before she could lift herself to do the same again.

He held her down, his cock filling every inch of her. "Give yourself a second to adjust, angel. Because you're about to go for one hell of a ride."

Rhys hadn't spoken when he took her, the two of them lost in the sensations, the pleasure. Tony was a dirty talker. And Jess discovered something new about herself. Because

MARI CARR

hearing the words was just as potent as the feelings these men provoked.

"Is that right?" she taunted. There was something about Tony Moretti that made her want to push all his buttons, the same way he pushed hers. And it wasn't in a bad way. It was in a you-drive-me-so-fucking-crazy-and-I-want-more way.

"Don't poke the bear, angel," he warned, his eyes twinkling, the slight upturn of his lips telling her how much he liked playing with her too.

She wanted to respond, but she was hung up on the word angel. He'd never called her that before, and it occurred to her that no one had ever given her a nickname, a term of endearment. Now he'd said it twice, and each time she felt the flutter of butterflies in her stomach that told her she was going to—

Oh, fuck off, Jess, she thought.

She needed to at least be honest with herself.

There was no *going to*.

She'd already fallen head over heels in love with these men.

Both of them.

It was why she'd fought so hard to stay away. To avoid this.

Because as strong and independent as she liked to pride herself on being, she had not won the battle over her heart. She'd lost it to *them*. Probably the second Tony had pounded on her car window asking her what the hell she was doing outside on that freezing-cold morning.

However, tonight, she found it impossible to give a shit about that. Especially when Tony tightened his grip, using it to lift her up until just the head of his cock remained inside, stretching her pussy to the limit.

Then he used those oh-so-strong muscles to drive her back down with more force than she'd ever have managed on her own. Jess's head flew back as stars flashed behind her closed eyelids.

"Open," Tony demanded, even as he lifted her again. "Let

me see those pretty blue eyes, angel. Let me see how good this makes you feel."

"You're too big," she said, gasping out the words when he shoved her back down again.

"I want to see your pain too," he said, his gaze holding hers captive, his words stripping her down until she was even more naked before him.

Rhys had risen somewhere along the line and moved closer. He ran his knuckles along her bare arm, his soft touch in direct contrast to the rough, forceful way Tony was lifting and pounding her down on his cock.

It was all too much, especially when Rhys reached between them and found her clit. It hadn't taken them more than a few seconds to find her self-destruct button. Rhys stroked it, mimicking the same force and speed Tony was using to fuck her.

And he *was* fucking her. She might be on top, but there was no pretending she had any of the control here. Tony was taking her exactly how he wanted.

With the added pressure on her clit, Jess was helpless to stave off her third and most powerful orgasm. She came in a rush, her body jerking as if shocked by a live wire.

Tony didn't draw it out but instead gave in to his own climax, going down with her.

"Fuck, Jess. So fucking tight. God, angel. *Yes.*"

She loved the idea that she could bring these two incredible, sexy men to their knees, that she could make them feel the same pleasure, the same ecstasy they'd given her.

Tony stood, still buried inside her. The unexpected action had her clinging to him, her hands wrapped around his shoulders, her legs entwining his waist. He turned and gently placed her back on the bed, before sliding out of her.

Somewhere along the line, Rhys had disposed of his condom. She'd been too distracted by Tony to see how or when. Tony slipped to Rhys's bathroom to do the same.

She lay next to Rhys, who rolled over to face her. He kissed her, the touching of their lips light, soft.

"Okay?" he asked.

Her sweet, caring doctor.

Jess nodded. "So okay."

He grinned. "Me too."

Jess sat up when Tony reentered the room. She knew he was intent on joining them in the bed, but she couldn't let him do that. If she did, she'd sink into the soft mattress, nestled between their hard bodies, and never leave.

"I can't stay," she whispered. She wanted to with all her heart, but cuddling with them would take the intimacy to yet another level. It was going to be hard enough to convince herself that this was just sex, that it didn't mean anything.

And she *had* to convince herself. It was the only way she'd come out of this on the other side without being completely shattered when they moved on to the next woman.

She prepared her arguments, afraid she might have to fight them. But she didn't have to say a word—and that was when she realized after-sex cuddles probably weren't part of their repertoire.

This was a casual affair.

An *affair*.

She repeated that word over and over in her mind, hoping that at some point it would actually stick.

Tony reached for her T-shirt on the floor, drawing it back over her head. Then the two of them pulled their lounge pants back on. She picked up her bra, and Tony his shirt, but that was as much as they bothered to dress.

Jess turned toward Rhys, who sat on the edge of the bed, and kissed him one last time. "Good night," she whispered.

"Good night, love."

Another term of endearment. That was all it was. She wasn't his love. Regardless, Jess's heart skipped a beat and she smiled.

Tony placed his hand on the small of her back, the two of them leaving Rhys's room together.

"I'll see you get home safely," he joked.

A breathy laugh escaped as, five seconds later, they stood before the closed guest room door.

"Well," she whispered, adding to his joke. "This is me."

Tony kissed her, this one more like Rhys's. A kiss of affection rather than passion.

"Tonight was..." she started, failing to find a word powerful enough to explain just what it had meant to her.

"Yeah," he said. "It was."

He kissed her again, then opened her door. She stepped inside, giving him a little wave as she closed it behind her.

Jess leaned against the closed door, her eyes closed, her body and mind and heart all in perfect agreement for the first time in her life.

Tonight was perfect.

Chapter Fourteen

"Hey."

Rhys looked up from the desk in his office and smiled when he saw Jess standing in the doorway. "Hey yourself. How was work?"

She was still bundled up in her coat, hat, and gloves, her cheeks ruddy from her two-block trek from the bus stop to here. Tony and Luca had gotten her car towed to their cousin Bruno's garage the day after it broke down on her, but in the end, they'd all declared it was toast. Jess took the news in stride, claiming she'd been surprised it had run as long as it did.

Unfortunately, that meant Jess was taking the bus to the diner every day, which was fine. It was the second late-night job that had been a continual fight. So far, they'd reached an unspoken and tenuous compromise, which meant she borrowed either his car or Tony's. The new argument stemmed around the fact that she now insisted on giving them gas money. The woman never spent a damn dime on herself, every penny she earned either coming to them for rent, groceries, gas, and a bunch of other shit they didn't want to be paid for, or into savings. Jess had assured them she was working diligently to save enough for her own place.

Rhys hated every time the subject of her leaving came up, but he merely nodded and listened. Tony didn't enjoy those conversations either, but he was a lot worse at masking it, typically telling her to stop worrying, or scoffing and walking away.

Rhys wasn't a fan of confrontation, preferring calm discussions to lost tempers and yelling. However, he had to admit there was something about watching Tony and Jess go toe-to-toe that was a bit of a turn-on for him. Strange, but true. And given their fire-and-gasoline personalities, Rhys had been treated to quite a few shows during Jess's time with them.

"Work was fine. You finished for the day?" Jess asked.

He nodded. "Last patient was half an hour ago, Ginny left shortly after. She had a hair appointment. I'm just finishing up some paperwork."

Ginny Edwards had been his nurse since he'd opened his own practice, and he couldn't live without her. She was forty-two, happily married with two middle schoolers, and one of the nicest women he'd ever known. Her soft-spoken, kind demeanor put his patients at ease. She'd taken an immediate shine to Jess and Jasper, the latter of whom had developed quite a crush. Jasper seemed to make his way downstairs at least once a week with a boo-boo that needed a Band-Aid and kiss-to-make-it-better from Ginny. Rhys knew his nurse was beyond curious about his and Tony's new roommates, but so far, she hadn't worked up the courage to ask him about them.

Jess turned to walk away. "Oh. Okay. I'll let you get back to it."

Jess had never stopped by his office before, so he was curious. It was obvious she wanted something but was hedging.

"I'm not busy. Get in here. Tell me about your day."

She shrugged as she entered. "Work was work."

"I missed you last night," he said, loving the way her eyes lit up at his admission. No matter how long she stayed with them, Jess still seemed surprised whenever he or Tony told her they worried about her or missed her or cared about her. She struggled to believe those statements, which just made him more determined to say them until she did.

"I missed you too," she said, her cheeks flushing slightly.

Rhys had spent all day yesterday, lost in the memory of his night with Jess and Tony. He'd been completely consumed with it, and he couldn't help wondering what would happen next.

Unfortunately, they hadn't been able to discuss it—or repeat the amazing experience—last night because one of his patients had suffered a mild stroke, and Rhys had spent the majority of the night at the hospital. When he'd returned home well after one a.m., he'd found the house dark, everyone asleep in their own rooms.

He'd been physically exhausted, but the second his head hit the pillow, sleep deserted him and he tossed and turned, torn between waking Tony and Jess to drag them back to his room for round two, and stressing out over what the fuck they should do now.

"Jess, about Sunday night..."

"What about it?" she asked, her voice suddenly nervous.

"Are you okay with what we did?"

She smiled, nodding. "Yes. I am. I really am. That's sort of why I'm..." She paused and looked around his office.

Suddenly, the light came on. "I promised you a birth control shot, didn't I?" he said, rising from his chair.

Jess raised her hand. "You don't have to—"

Rhys reached for her, tugging her close, until his nose was practically touching hers. "Scared?" he teased.

The taunt landed. "No. Of course not. I was just going to say, if you're too busy—"

Rhys silenced her with a quick kiss. "I already told you I wasn't. When was your last period?"

She scrunched up her nose. "Ugh. This is super awkward."

He laughed. "That's not an answer."

"It ended Friday."

"Good. That means the shot will be effective immediately. Or, if you'd rather take the Pill, we can go that route too."

They spoke for a few minutes about her past experiences with medicines and allergies. Satisfied that she was a good candidate for the shot, they decided to go that way, even though Jess's face flushed more and more with each question he posed.

Finally, he took her hand. "Come on." He led her to one of his examination rooms, pointing to the table. "Stay here and take off your coat. Let me go grab what I need."

As he retrieved the shot, he heard the front door open. He'd locked it after Ginny left, so he knew that meant Tony was home. He stuck his head out of the medicine closet.

"Welcome home."

Tony stopped at the sound of his voice, turning to greet him. Like Rhys, it didn't appear Tony had slept any better than he had last night. His eyes were tired, his face weary. "Hey."

"Jess is in the exam room," Rhys said, pointing behind him.

Tony scowled. "Is she okay?"

Rhys held up what he'd come to find. "Birth control shot."

Tony's frown held. "Did you suggest that or—"

"She came to ask me for it."

Tony's expression cleared, but he still looked uneasy. "Okay. Good. I, uh, I've been thinking about Sunday night."

"So have I."

"In fact, I can't *stop* thinking about it," Tony admitted.

"Same."

Tony ran his hand over his five-o'clock shadow. "It was incredible, Rhys. I know neither one of us has ever done anything like that, but...I don't know how to explain what it meant to me. She's...fuck...she's amazing. And having you there..."

Rhys smiled, and the tightness in his chest he hadn't acknowledged since Tony and Jess had left his room Sunday night lifted. "She *is* amazing. And I get what you're saying because I feel it too. What we did...it felt right."

want to stop."

posed and locked the medicine closet, then started back to the exam room. "Come on. You can hold her hand while I give her the shot."

Jess looked up and smiled when Rhys returned with Tony in tow. She'd shed her coat, hat, and gloves and was sitting on the edge of the exam table in her long-sleeved shirt and jeans. She tilted her head curiously at Tony's arrival.

"Just got home," he said, crossing the room to give Jess a quick kiss, like the one Rhys had given her in his office. It was a familiar, affectionate gesture that seemed to come naturally, considering they'd only switched their status from friends to lovers two days ago. "Rhys said you're getting a shot. Thought I'd hold your hand."

Jess shot Rhys a look, one brow raised. "I told you I'm not scared."

Tony chuckled. "Roll up your sleeve, angel, and get the shot. Then..." He looked around the room. "I think the three of us should play doctor."

Jess quickly rolled up her sleeve, her hasty action telling them just how much she liked that idea.

Rhys grinned as he prepared the needle, his thoughts whirling over Tony's suggestion. Despite his occupation, he'd never actually "played doctor" with any of his previous lovers.

He gave Jess the shot and put a Band-Aid over the puncture spot. Then, because he couldn't resist, he bent down to give it the same kiss to make it better that Jasper always craved so much.

Jess laughed softly.

Tony walked across the room, throwing the lock on the exam room door. "Take off your clothes, Jess."

Rhys had noticed the way Tony's voice deepened on Sunday night as he made his sensual demands, the way he didn't shy away from asking for exactly what he wanted...in fine detail. Jess responded to his dirty talk...but what Rhys hadn't anticipated was how much it would increase *his* arousal as well.

Rhys had always been more of a doer in the bedroom. Less talk, more action. But he had to admit he liked the pictures Tony drew with his words.

"What about the two of you?" Jess asked, even as she pulled her shirt over her head.

Rhys took a moment to look at her, the bright light in the room allowing him to see her more fully than he had in his dark room the other night, the only light there provided by a lamp on the nightstand.

"I'm not sure what sort of doctors you've been going to," Tony said as he walked over to stand next to her. "But the ones I see keep their clothes on."

"So you're Dr. Moretti now?" she asked with a grin. "What if *I* want to be the doctor while you two are the patients?"

Tony reached out and cupped one of her breasts, squeezing it. "We'll keep that scenario in the bank...for next time."

"Next time?" Jess asked.

"Did you think Sunday was a one-night thing?" Tony drew the straps of her bra over her shoulders, tugging until the lace fell away, revealing her nipples.

"I wasn't sure what to think," Jess replied honestly.

"It wasn't a one-night stand, that's for damn sure," Tony said with total assurance, and perhaps the slightest bit of annoyance that Jess might believe that was all it had been to them. "This is more than that. A lot more."

Neither of them had discussed any solid future plans with Jess, Tony only saying he didn't want to stop, so his words were news to Rhys. Not that he disagreed. He had no intention of Jess falling into the one-night stand column.

Hell, a thousand nights with her wouldn't be enough.

Tony put a hand under her elbow and helped her stand. "Take off your clothes," he repeated, his hands going to the button on her jeans, intent on helping her get naked.

MARI CARR

"Don't I get one of those paper sheet thingies?" she asked.

God, the smile on her face, her teasing tone, her all-in attitude was nearly Rhys's undoing. His cock, which had been semi-erect since Jess arrived in his office, was now rock hard, thick, throbbing.

He let Tony help Jess undress, while he rummaged through one of the drawers in the desk. He retrieved a couple of things and placed them on the counter. As he turned back around, Jess was resuming her seat on the edge of his table, the paper crinkling beneath her.

With a flourish, Rhys whipped open a paper cape and drew it over Jess's head. She laughed at his joke, while Tony merely shook his head.

"You're hiding all the best parts," he pointed out.

"You have no imagination," Rhys teased, as he helped Jess lie down on her back on the table. "Should we start with the breast exam, Dr. Moretti?" He lifted one side of the sheet, cupping her breast, squeezing it. Her nipple was erect, betraying her obvious enjoyment of their game.

Tony walked to the other side of the table, claiming her other breast. Jess moaned in pleasure as they played with her. She lifted her arms to Rhys, pulling him down for a kiss.

"This is so hot," she whispered against his lips.

"Have a medical fetish, do you?" he joked.

She shook her head. "I have a *you and Tony* fetish."

He gave her a quick, hard kiss, marveling over how good she made him feel. Every time she lowered her shields, giving him a peek inside, what he found was refreshing honesty. Jess never pretended to be someone she wasn't. He'd dated a lot of women who carried a hell of a lot less baggage than Jess, yet none of them possessed the strength—or was it courage?—to reveal their true natures, always pretending to be someone other than who they truly were inside.

Tony moved to the end of the exam table, grasping Jess's thighs and tugging.

She giggled as she slid down the table. Once her pussy was right at the edge, Tony grabbed Rhys's rolling stool, plopped down, threw Jess's legs over his shoulders and lowered his head.

"No stirrups, huh?" Rhys teased.

Tony merely shook his head, too intent on his goal.

Jess jerked with surprise and delight as Tony drew his tongue along her slit.

"Holy shit," she breathed.

Rhys watched Tony for just a moment, then reached out to tear her paper robe down the middle, lowering his own head to feast on her nipples.

Jess writhed beneath them, their ministrations driving her to the point of climax within minutes. However, before she could come, Tony rose from the stool, kicking it away.

"Tony," she gasped. "Please. I'm so close."

"I know you are, but you're going to come on my dick, angel. Let me feel it." He reached into his back pocket and pulled out a condom. Sliding it on, he remained at the end of the table, teasing Jess's slit with the head of his cock, running it from clit to anus and back again as she begged. "Is this what you want?" he asked.

Jess's eyes were closed, her body primed, ready. "God yes. Please."

"Open your eyes, Jess. I need to see them."

Tony had made the same request the other night. Rhys stood next to them, not participating, enjoying his role as voyeur. He wouldn't have expected merely watching to be such a turn-on, to be a hot button for him, but after making that discovery Sunday night, he wasn't even certain he'd be able to return to sex with just him and a woman again. Sharing Jess with Tony had ruined him, as far as he was concerned.

But he didn't know if that was because of the physical act as much as who they were and how important they'd become to him. Probably both.

Jess shifted her legs, wrapping them around Tony's waist,

using them to try to draw him into her. Tony, the devil, merely grinned.

"You're a terrible patient," he murmured.

"Tell me about it," Rhys added with a grin.

"Shouldn't you still be examining my breasts?" Jess demanded.

Rhys laughed, even as Tony narrowed his eyes. It was clear his friend had dominant tendencies in the bedroom, something that wasn't completely surprising, considering those same traits existed outside the bedroom as well. Tony was a take-charge kind of guy, a born leader.

Jess, used to being the captain of her own ship, hadn't fully figured that out yet, still accustomed to taking care of her own needs.

A loud slap rang through the room, and Jess lurched up on to her elbows.

"Bad patient," Tony said, repeating the same smack on her other ass cheek.

"Tony—" she started.

"Lay back down, Jess," Tony commanded.

She hesitated, just long enough that Tony's face morphed from amused to determined. "Your only response right now is 'Yes, Dr. Moretti.'"

Jess sighed out a soft breath of enjoyment as she lowered herself back down. "Yes, Dr. Moretti. But bear in mind, payback is a bitch."

Tony laughed as he looked at Rhys. "She's always going to keep us on our toes."

Rhys ran his hand along the side of Jess's face. "I'm not complaining."

Tony lifted Jess's legs around his waist once more, lining his cock up with her pussy. "Me either," he said as he pressed in.

Jess groaned, so many emotions flickering over her face in such rapid succession, Rhys wasn't sure how she could feel so much in so short a time. There was the briefest wince of pain, something not unexpected, given her relative inexperience and Tony's girth. But that look was quickly replaced by one of pleasure and perhaps even disbelief.

Rhys could relate to that. Ever since Sunday, he'd been able to think of little else besides these two people and the unexpected bond the three of them had somehow formed. It was so overwhelming, he'd managed to do little more than revel in it. The old Rhys would have spent the past forty-eight hours over-analyzing everything, then developing a plan moving forward, but he'd managed none of that, too hung up on reliving the bliss, rolling around in the happiness, and longing for another opportunity to be alone with Jess and Tony, like a teenage boy with his first crush.

"Tony," Jess gasped, once he was buried to the hilt.

"Hold on, angel," he said, his words punctuated with a series of hard, fast thrusts. Rhys was spellbound for a moment, before he realized he wanted a piece of the action. He bent over her chest, sucking one of her nipples into his mouth.

Jess's hands flew to his head, her fingers tugging his hair until his scalp stung slightly. "God!"

Jess's vocabulary shrank to Tony's name and his. Nothing else as the two of them worked in tandem to drive her to one orgasm, then a second. On the third, Tony was panting like a thoroughbred horse, his own climax imminent.

Rhys lifted his head to observe.

"Jesus, Jess. *Fuck.*" Tony stilled as he came, his eyes clenched closed tightly. Jess was trembling beneath him, both of their bodies glistening with the slight sheen of sweat.

Rhys ran his hand over the front of his pants, his cock threatening to erupt from watching the two of them in the throes of their own pleasure. He startled when Jess reached over, knocked his hand away, and began to stroke him herself.

Tony stepped away from the table, pulled off the condom, then hitched up his pants. Two quick movements, and he was put completely back to rights.

Jess remained on the table, her fingers caressing Rhys's cock through his pants. "I want you," she whispered.

"Impatient woman," he said, no heat behind the words. He wanted her too. With a need that was almost painful. "We still haven't finished the exam."

Her brow furrowed, confused, until he reached toward the desk and lifted the tube of lubrication he'd grabbed from the same drawer as the paper robe.

Jess stilled but offered no words of complaint or concern.

"I'll give you a choice, Jess. You can roll over onto your stomach. Or I'll pull out the stirrups."

"Fucking hell." Tony's softly murmured curse had Rhys fighting not to grin.

Tony Moretti wasn't the only dominating bastard with an arsenal of kinky fantasies waiting to be played out.

Jess bit her lower lip, considering her options. "I..." she paused. "I think I want to roll over this time." Her gaze shifted from Rhys to Tony, then back to him. "But I want to put the stirrups option in that bank for future times."

Tony chuckled and tapped the side of this head. "It's on the list. Roll over for Rhys, angel. I'm interested in watching Dr. Beaumont work."

Chapter Fifteen

"You're not watching, Dr. Moretti," Rhys said, amusement lacing his tone. "You're assisting."

Tony didn't need to be told twice. He rose from where he'd dropped down onto Rhys's stool, working overtime to get control of his breathing, calm his heart, aware that those functions weren't struggling merely because of having sex with Jess.

It was more than that. His emotions had never been so...engaged.

"Maybe we should check your reflexes a bit more." Rhys had taken Tony's position at the end of the exam table, and he was ready to expand on the "playing doctor" roles.

Tony joined them, stepping next to Jess.

Rhys pressed a button on the table, lowering her head until she lay completely flat. The paper beneath Jess no longer crinkled, now softer from her exertions. He grinned at the sight.

Tony had dragged his ass home, weary from work, tired from a shitty night's sleep, and stressed over how Jess—and Rhys—might feel about their night spent together. While he'd known from the moment he'd kissed Jess that he wanted more, he was worried that Rhys and Jess would try to pull away, try to claim it was a heat-of-the-moment thing that couldn't continue. He was aware that he had a tendency to be impulsive, and he'd feared that perhaps Rhys would use that as an excuse to step away to "think" about things.

And God knew Jess was still struggling with their living arrangement, unable to believe they would never kick her out or leave her stranded on her own again. Regardless of what had happened, they still had a long road ahead of them, convincing their brunette beauty that they were sincere in their desire to have her stay.

Tony was ready to put in that time, that effort, so he'd fully intended to show both his lovers the errors of their fears.

However, all that fretting had been a complete waste of time. He'd walked in this evening, Rhys had met him at the door, and boom—he was right back where he wanted to be.

Jess jerked when Rhys placed a hard smack on her ass, though Tony suspected the response was based more on shock than pain. After all, Rhys, thus far, had proven himself to be the gentler lover.

Tony glanced at his friend, feeling that same surprise.

Rhys must have anticipated his response because he was already looking at Tony, smirking in a "gotcha" manner. He raised his hand again and this time brought it down with some force, three times in rapid succession. Jess attempted to wiggle away, and when she couldn't manage that, she threw her hands back, trying to cover her ass.

Rhys looked at Tony. "Restrain the patient."

Jesus.

Fuck.

Rhys was blowing Tony's mind. Though he'd never admit it to him, Tony had sort of expected Rhys to be a vanilla guy in the bedroom, all missionary and kisses. Rhys wouldn't thank him for those assumptions, but they'd felt accurate, given his friend's mild-mannered approach to life.

This guy.

Shit.

This guy was for real.

Tony reached for Jess's hands, tugging them above her head as she continued to fight. If her efforts had been stronger, he would have released her, but he could tell she was putting up a token resistance at best. Even so, there was something that needed to be handled before they proceeded.

"Jess," Tony said. "Hold still and look at me."

She stopped moving, shifting her face toward him. Tony released her wrists, pushing her long hair out of her face so he could see her eyes.

"If you say stop, we stop. No matter what. Do you understand?"

Jess's gaze locked with his, and that powerhouse attitude he was used to seeing on her face emerged. "I'm not going to say stop."

"That wasn't what I asked you. If anything hurts or scares you, you *will* say the word stop. Do you understand?" he enunciated, driving home the seriousness of his question.

"I understand."

"Good." Tony reached down and picked up Jess's long-sleeved T-shirt, using it to bind her hands above her head.

Jess didn't resist. In fact, given the way her eyes closed and she shuddered, he'd wage a year's pay, the bondage was turning her on.

Satisfied, Tony gave Rhys a quick nod and the not-so-mild-mannered doctor continued spanking her until Jess's adorable ass was painted pink. Then Rhys rubbed the tender flesh with firm strokes and squeezes as Jess sighed, her eyes still closed, a slight smile on her lips.

Rhys continued for several minutes, alternating between spanks and strokes, as Jess relaxed more and more. Tony watched the play, fascinated not just by his lovers but by himself. He wasn't consumed by his typical desire to take control. Instead, he was curious about what else Rhys had in mind and filled with the unassailable knowledge that whatever it was, it would drive Jess out of her mind.

So Tony waited—uncharacteristically patient—while running his fingertips along Jess's spine, from the nape of her neck to the small of her back, retracing the route over and over.

Jess didn't bother to open her eyes when Rhys stepped away from the exam table to the desk, but Tony followed his actions with great interest. Especially when Rhys picked up a tube of lubrication, holding it up for him to see.

Tony nodded.

The short interaction was completely missed by Jess, who still hadn't roused, too blissed out by the spanking and sensual massage.

"Open your legs," Rhys said, as he returned to the table, handing Tony the lube.

Jess moved lethargically, her eyelids slowly opening, blinking several times as she attempted to focus her vision.

Rhys pushed her thighs apart when she didn't do as he asked.

"Your response time is slow. Be sure to record that in her records, Dr. Moretti."

Tony grinned. Rhys wasn't finished playing his role yet.

"Your reflexes are good, Miss Monroe, but we might need to do more tests on that in the future."

Jess looked over her shoulder at them, laughing breathily, joining the game. "There's not a damn thing wrong with my reflexes, Dr. Beaumont."

"That's not for you to decide. I'm the doctor," Rhys said. "Now be a good patient or I'll do those tests now."

Tony studied Jess's face, saw the way Rhys's admonition impacted her. He wouldn't call Jess a submissive—not by a long shot—but she was definitely responding to Rhys's dominant tone, his words.

Sunday night, Rhys had been the quieter of the two of

them, letting his actions speak for him, while Tony engaged in dirty talk. The tide had turned today.

"I'll be good," Jess whispered.

Tony's cock heard her response, the fucker thickening, despite the fact he'd just come a few minutes earlier. Something told him he was going to have to get used to walking around with a hard-on whenever Jess was near.

Rhys, breaking character, bent forward, covering Jess's naked body with his fully dressed one. He kissed her on the cheek, stroking the soft skin with his nose affectionately. "You're beautiful, Jess. Ready for the next part?"

Jess nodded eagerly, and Tony knew she didn't have a clue what that next part was going to be. Obviously, she expected Rhys to fuck her, but they weren't there yet.

"Fine," Rhys said, straightening up once more. "Then we'll begin with the anal exam."

Jess pushed up onto her elbows instantly, drawing her still-bound hands beneath her in an attempt to lift herself off the table. Rhys halted the attempt with one hard slap to her ass.

"Lay back down, Jess," he directed.

Jess's eyes sought his.

"All you have to say is stop," he reminded her.

And just like that, Jess calmed. She was no longer responding to what they wanted. Rather, she was thinking about it.

"Untie my hands," she said.

Tony reached down and tugged the knot in the cotton free without delay.

He expected Jess to continue to rise, but instead she lowered herself back down, prostrate on the table.

"I'm ready," she announced. "I want everything you're willing to give me. Please."

Jess had been chipping away at Tony's heart since the day he'd lifted her out of that car and carried her into their home.

Day after day, she'd stolen piece after piece. But now, she'd claimed the whole damn thing.

He was completely in love with Jess Monroe.

Tony bent forward and placed a kiss on her shoulder. He couldn't resist her, wanting to shower her with kisses and hugs for the rest of her life so she never had to feel alone or lonely ever again.

Rhys must have felt the same way because he ran his hands over Jess's back almost reverently. "So perfect," he murmured.

Tony straightened and shifted, feeling as if everything he'd ever wanted was coming to life right here, in this room, in this moment.

Sunday night, they'd left too much—hell, they'd left everything—unsaid, but today, they'd come together willingly, without reservation, and with no intention of letting this end.

Moving toward Rhys, Tony ran his hand over Jess's ass, still warm from the spanking, and once again, Rhys pushed her legs open.

Jess watched them over her shoulder, but this was one time Tony didn't need to see her eyes.

He shook his head. "Face forward," he said sternly. Then added, "Miss Monroe," with a wink.

Jess laughed, but did as he said, shifting her gaze away from them, laying her head down, and closing her eyes once more.

Tony uncapped the lube as Rhys unzipped his pants and pulled out his erection, wrapping his hand around it, stroking. Tony admired his friend's restraint. While Tony had already succumbed to his climax, Rhys had been waiting patiently in the wings. His dick had to be chafed from being so hard for so long in those pants.

"We want you to relax, to pay attention to the way this makes you feel," Tony said.

Jess sighed in response, giving them her trust. That wasn't something Tony took lightly.

He squeezed some of the lubrication on her anus, and Jess

tensed for just a second before relaxing once more. Tony spread it around with one finger before slowly sliding it in. Rhys reached over and stroked Jess's ass with one hand while the other stroked his dick.

Tony worked his finger in with shallow thrusts that grew deeper with each return. He felt Jess trying to resist.

"Relax," Tony soothed again. Once his finger was buried completely inside, he turned his attention to Rhys, curious how he wanted to proceed.

Rhys reached for a condom and slid it on, then he stepped next to Tony, the two of them standing shoulder to shoulder. "You ready, love?" he asked as he pressed the head of his cock against the opening of her pussy. "Tony and I are going to take you together. This time, it'll be my cock and his finger. But one day soon, you're going to take both our cocks inside you at the same time."

"God. Yes, please," she whispered.

Rhys nudged Tony, bumping their shoulders together, a smile on his face. Then he thrust inside.

Tony could feel the same tightness Jess was experiencing as Rhys breached her. He let himself imagine what it would feel like if it was his dick filling her ass instead of his finger.

Rhys paused once he'd completed his journey, filling her to the brink.

"Ready?" he murmured.

Tony nodded, withdrawing his finger, pressing it in as Rhys pulled back. They took her in tandem, Tony thrusting into her ass every time Rhys retreated. Jess's breathing quickened and soon she was lifting her ass off the table, offering more, inviting them to go deeper, faster, harder.

Tony applied more lube so that he could up the ante, slipping a second finger in with the first.

Jess gasped, then groaned. "Too much."

"Is it?" he asked, because her words didn't match her

actions. She was still pressing back against them, silently demanding more.

Jess shook her head. "No. More. I want more."

"You're going to get more, angel. You're going to get it all. One night, Rhys and I are going to take you to bed, where I'll fuck your pussy and he claims your ass. You're going to take both of us inside this pretty body, and then you're going to know, without a shadow of a doubt, exactly who you belong to."

Jess pressed her forehead against the table, her pussy and ass clenching as he spoke.

Rhys muttered a curse in response. Neither of them had stopped thrusting and his friend was reaching the cliff quickly, though Tony wondered if it was just the fucking or if Rhys was as turned on by the idea of double penetration as he was.

Tony hadn't considered it before, but now that he had, now that they'd dipped their toe into this ocean, he wanted to dive in completely.

"I...want...that," Jess said, her words coming out in hard breaths. "Now."

Tony slammed a third finger into her, and Jess's back arched as she cried out, coming hard.

"God!" she yelled.

Her ass clenched down so tightly around his fingers, it hurt. The same must have been true for her pussy, because Rhys quickened his pace for a few thrusts more, then stilled, coming as well, his fingers gripping Jess's hips to hold her in place.

"Jesus," Rhys muttered, his eyes closed with a pleasure that looked like pain. Tony knew that feeling well. It was fucking amazing.

Tony withdrew his fingers slowly, Jess whimpering, even as she clenched against them, as if she wanted to hold them inside.

"Tony," she breathed. "Rhys." Her eyes were closed, and Tony suspected she could fall asleep right where she lay if they'd let her. They'd taken her hard, both of them greedy bastards when it came to Jess Monroe. And even as fucking hot as this had been, Tony knew they'd only just scratched the surface of their desires.

"You okay, angel?" he asked.

"Better than okay. Can we do that every day after work?"

Tony chuckled as Rhys pulled out of Jess, disposing of the condom.

"I'm game if Tony is," he said, breathing heavily himself.

"Fuck yeah. Come on, Jess." Tony quickly washed his hands, then helped Jess up from the table, dressing her as Rhys put the room back to rights, cleaning up all traces of their less-than-professional use of his exam table.

Jess stepped into Tony's arms once her clothes were back on, hugging him, burying her nose in his shirt. She was a good deal shorter than him, something that he failed to remember at times. In his mind, she was larger than life, a force of nature. It felt as if someone like that should be a hell of a lot taller. As it was, the top of her head came to his shoulders, so it was simple for him to add to his embrace, to drop a kiss against her soft hair.

"Aunt Berta and Jasper will be wondering where we are," Tony murmured, sorry he'd said anything at all when Jess instantly pulled away.

"Oh my God, you're right. I'm late. That's not fair. Poor Berta has been—"

"Jess," Tony said quickly. "She won't mind."

"Even so..." Jess didn't bother to finish that statement. Instead, she grabbed her coat and headed for the stairs.

Tony raised his hand when Rhys started to speak. "I know. I know. I shouldn't have said a damn thing. I know all about her issues with accepting help and constantly feeling like she's imposing on us. I wish to hell I could figure out a way to make her realize this is her home and she's not an unwanted guest."

"I wish the same thing," Rhys admitted. "But I'm pretty sure nothing but time is going to solve that problem."

He and Rhys left the room, climbing the two flights of stairs to the apartment together. Aunt Berta was happily humming in the kitchen, the smell of pot roast filling the air. Tony and Rhys walked toward the living room, where they could hear Jess and Jasper's voices.

Jess was looking into Jasper's mouth.

"Lose another tooth?" Tony asked.

Jess shook her head. "No. He said his throat hurts." She put a hand on his forehead. "He does feel a little warm."

"His throat hurts?" Aunt Berta walked into the living room behind them. She claimed the other side of the couch next to Jasper. "Why didn't you tell me, sweetheart?"

"I didn't want to bother you." Jasper swallowed, and it was apparent he was suffering.

"That wouldn't bother me," Aunt Berta cooed. "I have to admit he hasn't been acting like himself since school let out. Very quiet. He just wanted to watch TV. Not interested in doing much else. And he left half his snack. I should have realized."

Jess placed her hand on Aunt Berta's arm and gave it a gentle squeeze before looking at Jasper. "The next time you don't feel good, and I'm not here, you need to tell Aunt Berta, or Tony or Rhys, okay?"

"Your mommy's right," Rhys said, reaching down to pick up Jasper. "Come on. Let's head to the bathroom, so I can get a better look at that throat and take your temperature."

Jasper wrapped his arms around Rhys's neck, laying his head on his shoulder. "Okay. If I'm sick, can I eat in bed?"

Jess had read a book to Jasper about a child who'd gotten sick and had to stay home from school. He'd been completely fascinated by the concept of eating in bed, something Jess didn't realize he'd never done.

"Of course you can, sweetheart," Aunt Berta replied before Jess could say a word. "I'm going to make you some chicken noodle soup right now and put it on a tray."

Jess and Tony remained behind in the living room.

"When did I lose control?" she asked, amused.

Tony laughed. "About three seconds after I carried you in here, freezing cold from that damn night spent in the car. Does it bother you? Because I can talk to Aunt Berta if—"

"Don't you dare," Jess said, cutting him off. "She's wonderful and Jasper loves her. One of our favorite bedtime stories is *The Napping House*, and it talks about a granny taking a nap with her grandchild. Jasper asked me a few nights ago if it was okay if he pretended Aunt Berta was his granny. I didn't know whether to laugh—so happy he has such a loving caregiver—or cry that my mom is such a coldhearted..." Jess waved her hands, unwilling to finish her name-calling.

"Bitch. You can call her a bitch, Jess." Tony scowled every time he was reminded of just how cruel Jess's mother was, tossing her out, pregnant and penniless.

Jess shrugged but didn't say the word. "I'm grateful to Aunt Berta. And to you and Rhys, and the rest of your family. He lives for the Sundays when all your brothers and cousins come over. The way you all include him, watching sports, roughhousing with him the way uncles or," she paused a moment before forging through, "a dad would."

As soon as she said the word, Tony let himself imagine himself in that role. He'd pushed all thoughts of getting married, settling down, starting a family into that "far in the future" column. Not because he didn't want those things but because work had always taken precedence, and he'd never met a woman who had made him think *forever*.

That was when he realized it wasn't just Jess who'd claimed his heart. Jasper had as well. And suddenly, the idea of fatherhood appealed to him a great deal.

"The guys are crazy about Jasper," he said.

"You've all shown Jasper what a large, loving family looks like. I never got that, so I'm glad he's had this time."

Tony reached out and hugged her. "You've raised one hell of

a great kid."

"Thanks," she said, her voice muffled by his shirt.

He released her, wrapping his arm around her shoulder. "Come on. Let's go check on him. Get the diagnosis from Dr. Beaumont."

Jess's face flushed at Tony's use of Rhys's title, and he knew exactly where her thoughts had drifted because his had gone to the same place.

He leaned closer. "Save that thought for later," he murmured in her ear.

She playfully swatted his chest. "Down, boy. You're going to have to give me some time to recover from those last half dozen or so orgasms."

He slid his hand down her back, swatting her ass lightly. "No problem. How long do you need? Five, ten more minutes?"

She laughed. "Behave yourself, Dr. Moretti."

He tickled her, Aunt Berta shaking her head at them as they passed her in the hallway. "Rhys said he has a bit of a fever and his tonsils are inflamed. I'm going to finish making him the soup I promised."

"Oh no," Jess said, walking to her room. Rhys was tucking Jasper into bed.

He turned as they entered, raising his hand when he saw the look of concern on Jess's face. "Gave him children's Tylenol to bring down the fever. It's nothing serious. Likely a bug he picked up at school. Day or two of rest and he should be all better."

Jess perched on the edge of the bed and gently kissed Jasper's forehead. "I'm sorry you don't feel well. Aunt Berta is making you soup. She's going to put a tray together for you and bring it in here."

Even though the boy was obviously sick, he perked up at the idea of dinner in bed. "Can I watch TV too?"

Jess laughed. "Yeah, you can. Let me go make a couple of

calls and I'll come back and watch with you, okay?"

Jasper nodded, and while he was clearly excited about the idea, Tony didn't think the poor kid was going to manage to stay awake much longer.

Jess rose, and the three of them walked to the living room.

"I'm going to call in and tell them I can't work tonight. I don't want to leave Jasper alone while he's sick."

"Better yet, call Matt Russo and say you're quitting," Tony murmured, still hating the fact that Jess was working for the Russos.

Jess ignored him, used to the constant suggestion. "I'll see if I can get one of the girls to take my shift at the diner tomorrow. It's one thing to ask Aunt Berta to watch him for a few hours each afternoon after school. Asking her to babysit a sick child all day is too much. I'll make up the time this weekend."

Tony frowned. "Sunday is the party at Nonno and Nonna's house."

Joey had a big announcement he wanted to make to the entire family. As soon as he'd made that known, Nonna had flown into party mode—Moretti style—demanding everyone attend. No one was excused. Something made apparent by the fact Nonna was making her famous eggplant parmesan and had recruited all the aunts to help with the preparations.

The second she'd announced the old family recipe was on the menu, one that every member of the family would walk fifty miles barefoot across the desert to eat, they knew attendance was mandatory.

Tony had been looking forward to taking Jess and Jasper, introducing them to everyone. While they'd met most of the guys, she still hadn't met his grandparents or father. Nor had she met Tony's kid sister, Layla, and her men, Miguel and Finn, who were coming up from Baltimore.

"I know, but I can't afford to lose the pay," Jess said.

Tony crossed his arms and shook his head. "You're not working this weekend, Jess."

She narrowed her eyes. "I'm not listening to the caveman routine tonight, Tony. I know you like to think—"

"Stop." Tony placed his finger against her lips. "I've let you win every damn fight when it comes to money. Every. Single. One. I'm not losing this one."

Jess started to speak again, but he cut her off. "I mean it. I want you and Jasper to meet my family. You can afford to lose one goddamn day of work."

Jess glanced in Rhys's direction, no doubt hoping he'd step in to support her cause.

Tony shifted his gaze as well and knew immediately his roommate was on his side.

"Jess," Rhys started quietly, "Jasper has done nothing but talk about this party. I think he'd be just as disappointed as Tony if you weren't there. And I know I would be too."

Tony had to hand it to his roommate. He was the king of diplomacy and he had a knack for knowing how to appeal to Jess. Tony could probably learn a thing or two from him, but he decided he'd leave the peaceful discourse to his friend. Tony loved sparring with their stubborn beauty too much to play nice.

Jess sighed and rubbed her forehead. "Fine. I'll call in tonight and give my shift away tomorrow. I just—"

"You just nothing," Tony interjected. "You deserve a weekend off, Jess. Take it."

Jess shrugged. "Okay."

Rhys chuckled. "Great. And gird your loins because Tony's family parties last at least five hours, include thirty to forty people, and consist of appetizers, wine, salads, bread, wine, soup, wine, the main course, wine, dessert and then...more wine. It's an all-day affair."

"Oh my God," she said, with a smile that passed for either amused or horrified.

Tony smiled, then gave her a quick kiss. "You're going to love the Morettis. And they're going to adore you."

Chapter Sixteen

J ess grinned as Jasper and Billy Moretti giggled over some
silly videos they were watching together on Billy's tablet.
The two of them had become fast friends at the birthday
party last weekend. Jasper had introduced Billy to Jess as
his best buddy in the whole world.

She was delighted to see the way her son had blossomed the
past two months. She hadn't recognized just how big a toll their
homelessness had taken, the changes in him—and her—
happening gradually. But she knew she'd never seen him so
happy, so carefree as he was today, and it meant everything
to her.

They'd only been at the party an hour, but Jess had already
felt the need to find a quiet place away from the action, unused
to so many loud people in one place, all talking at the same time.
She'd been introduced to countless relatives, too many to keep
straight in her head, though she was trying.

"It's insane, right?"

Jess looked over and smiled at Layla. She'd taken an instant
liking to Tony's kid sister, who was here with her two—that
revelation had taken Jess a second to soak in—partners, Finn
and Miguel. Tony had mentioned his sister and her partners

once before, but she'd been too overwhelmed by other things to question what that meant. Today, she was seeing it for herself.

"What is?" Jess asked.

"Moretti family get-togethers. Too many Italians all talking and waving their hands, with nobody left to listen. Took Miguel a while to get used to."

"Just Miguel?"

Layla nodded. "Finn's family is just as big and just as loud, so he took to the Morettis like a fish to water. Only difference is his family is Irish. Less gesturing, but the same amount of drinking and volume."

They laughed together as Jess watched Tony talking to his brothers and dad, none of them managing to speak without some accompanying hand motion.

"It's like a language all unto itself," Jess remarked.

"Oh yeah. Definitely. So what's it like living with my brother and Rhys?"

Jess wasn't sure how to reply, wasn't sure what Tony had told Layla about her circumstances or their recent change in status from roommates to...whatever the hell they were now.

They hadn't had sex since the encounter in the examination room, stymied first by Jasper's illness, Tony having to work late on a project for some horrid woman who was driving him crazy, and a couple of medical emergencies that had Rhys driving to the hospital two different nights.

Jess wasn't sure if she was annoyed by or grateful for the distractions. She needed time to think about what she was doing, but every time she tried to sort through her thoughts regarding Tony and Rhys, her mind drifted away from the practical and straight to fantasyland. As such, she'd spent the last few days in a perpetual state of arousal, swimming in a sea of lust-filled dreams.

"Tony and Rhys are great. They were awesome to offer me and Jasper a place to stay."

"And you knew them from Paulie's?" Layla asked.

gnant.”

Layla shook her head. “What a dick.”

“Yeah. Things haven’t exactly been easy for me and Jasper on our own, but I don’t regret having him. He’s the greatest thing in my life.”

“Maybe having Jasper around will work a bit of magic on my big brother.”

“How so?”

Layla shrugged. “I’m ready for nieces and nephews. Sort of hoping one of my damn brothers will settle down sometime soon and make that happen. Right now, all four of the stubborn asses seem too committed to their bachelorhood.”

“You think Tony wants kids?” Jess asked.

“I don’t know. I assume he does. Of course, he’d have to date someone longer than five minutes first, and he hasn’t done that in...God...years. He says it’s because he’s never met the right woman, but I can’t believe he hasn’t met one nice woman in the past twenty years. Since he’s moved in with Rhys, he’s burrowed in even deeper. I’m starting to worry he’ll never stick his head out of his man cave and look around for that ‘perfect’ someone.”

Jess listened intently, every word out of Layla’s mouth cutting through her like a dagger. She knew they were confirmed bachelors, but having that fact confirmed again after everything they'd shared was harder to accept than she cared to admit.

Layla, thank God, didn't notice the distress this conversation had caused Jess. "Miguel and Finn have been dropping hints that they're ready for kids. I suspect I won't be able to hold them off much longer."

"You don't want kids?" Jess asked, grateful for the change of subject.

"Oh no, I didn't mean that. I'd love kids. I'd just like to work out the marriage issue first."

"What does that mean?"

Layla took a sip of her wine. "Well, it's not like I can marry both of them. Legally, anyway. Miguel and Finn say they're happy with me marrying either of them...or neither of them."

"Neither?"

"Hell, the two of *them* could be the married couple if they wanted. Or we could just live together without marriage as part of the equation."

Jess was fascinated, curious how Layla was handling a committed relationship with two men. She would have thought that impossible.

"I'm completely in love with both of them, and no piece of paper will ever change that. So...maybe it's just me being silly."

"You want a wedding," Jess said.

Layla grinned. "Hell yeah. But I want to marry both of them. Lately we've been discussing having a commitment ceremony, skipping the marriage certificate part altogether. I would say something small, but between my family and Finn's, small is not an option. Right now, we're really just trying to pick a date."

"That's wonderful. How exciting."

"Yeah. I can't wait, though it definitely won't happen before summer. But it should be easier, now that the family has accepted my relationship."

"They didn't at first?" Jess asked, somewhat surprised after watching the Morettis with Finn and Miguel. There was no question Layla's men had been welcomed into the fold completely.

"God, no. Tony nearly flipped his lid. Kept threatening to drive to Baltimore to drag my ass back home...after teaching Miguel and Finn a lesson."

"Really?"

"My big brother takes overprotectiveness to the next level. I think he thought Finn and Miguel were luring his sweet baby sister into some sordid, kinky affair," she said, laughing. "And I'm sure he's mostly fine with our relationship now...but I've caught him watching the three of us today when he doesn't think I'm looking. He's got that broody, scowling expression that's always on his face when he's unhappy. Not sure what to make of it, really."

Jess didn't know what to make of it either. She was happy for Layla, but it drove in even deeper how much she wanted what Tony's sister had. She'd learned early on that Tony and Rhys weren't looking for relationships or a family or...love.

And like a fool, she'd let herself believe—pretend—that perhaps they *would* want those things with her. So what the hell did she do now?

The sound of someone clinking a spoon against a glass quieted all conversation.

Tony stepped next to Jess. "Finally."

"You really don't know what this big announcement of his is?" Layla asked.

Tony shook his head. "Nope. He's been completely close-mouthed about it, which is something new for him."

When Jess looked at him curiously, Tony added, "Joey is the worst secret keeper in the family."

Layla agreed. "Bastard ruined every surprise birthday party ever thrown in our family. Got so bad, we stopped telling him about them. Not that he did it on purpose. He'd just blurt it out in the middle of a conversation and half the time, he wouldn't even realize he'd spoiled the surprise."

Joey raised his hands, grinning from ear to ear as everyone turned their attention to him.

"Whatever it is," Jess mused, "he's obviously happy about it."

"If I can have your attention for just a minute, I have some news I'd like to share."

"Let me guess," Aldo called out. "You're pregnant. And it's twins. Who's the father?"

That joke prompted lots of laughter that only faded when Elio yelled out over the noise, chiming in on the teasing.

"Nope. That's not it. He finally made the Olympic team for his figure skating talents. You're gonna look hot in those tights, Joey."

"Boys!" Nonna admonished. "Go on, *patatino*. Tell us your news."

"*Patatino*?" Jess whispered to Tony, who grinned, shaking his head in amusement.

"Nonna had been calling us little potatoes our whole lives."

Jess covered her mouth with her hand, trying not to laugh. There was absolutely nothing about the Moretti boys that said "little" anything, but definitely not a potato.

Joey raised his voice, unruffled by the interruptions. "A few weeks after Moretti Brothers Restorations was featured on HGTV last fall, a producer called and asked if I'd be interested in auditioning for a new show they're producing for the network. Found out a couple of weeks ago, I got the gig. You're now looking at the host of *ManPower*. We start filming in a month!"

"Hot damn!" Tony called out, he and his other brothers rushing over to congratulate Joey.

"Wow," Layla said. "How cool is that?"

Miguel and Finn came over, hugging and kissing Layla,

bragging about their famous future brother-in-law. Then they all walked over to congratulate him.

Jess shifted back, watching as the family rallied around Joey, the men slapping him on the back and shaking his hand, the women hugging him, kissing him on both cheeks, proclaiming they knew he was destined for great things. Nonna appeared to be wiping her eyes, pride evident in every line on her face.

So this was what it was like to have a real family. What would she give to be a part of something as wonderful as this?

Tony's dad, Frank, pulled out several bottles of wine, uncorking one after another until everyone had a glass. Rhys walked over to Jess and handed her one.

Then Frank lifted his glass, calling out, "Salute!"

Everyone cheered and sipped, and the party kicked into overdrive. Someone turned on music, and the noise level in the house rose at least twenty more decibels, something Jess wouldn't have thought possible. She could set firecrackers off in the living room and she wasn't sure anyone would even hear them.

Jasper and the other children were being swept away by the tide of excited adults, running and jumping, shouting loudly. Jess tried to catch her son's attention, to tell him he needed to slow down, but she was stopped by Liza Moretti, another of Tony's cousins.

"Leave him," she said with a kind smile. "He's having fun. And holding him back won't stop the rest of them from stampeding through the house. Overwhelmed yet?"

"Completely," Jess said, prompting Liza to laugh.

"And we haven't even gotten started yet. In a couple more hours, this party will be totally off the chain."

Jess wasn't sure whether to laugh or cry over that fact. "Hours?"

Liza giggled, clearly taking Jess's question as a joke. "Keep drinking," she said, pointing to the still-full glass of wine in

Jess's hand. "It'll help you later when my dad pulls out his accordion."

Jess's eyes widened. "I don't think I've ever heard anyone play the accordion."

Liza winked. "He's actually very good, learned from Nonno. Have you sorted out who's who in our sprawling family tree?"

"I'm trying, but...there are a lot of you."

Liza grinned. "Tell me about it. Let me see if I can break it down for you. Nonno and Nonna had four kids."

"Okay," Jess said, enjoying Liza's easygoing, friendly nature. She, like Layla, had welcomed Jess into their fold today with arms wide open. "I think I know who they are. Maybe. There was an Uncle Renzo, right? Who was married to Aunt Berta?"

Liza nodded. "He was the oldest. It's still hard for me to remember he isn't here anymore. He had a larger-than-life personality and a booming laugh you could hear from three states away."

"He'd have to, to keep up with Aunt Berta."

Liza linked her arm through Jess's. "Right? Uncle Renzo and Aunt Berta didn't have any kids."

Jess knew about that, her heart breaking when Aunt Berta confided how desperately they'd tried, and how devastated they'd been when they'd learned it wasn't possible.

"After Uncle Renzo," Liza continued, "came Uncle Frank."

"Tony's dad."

"Yep. Uncle Frank and Aunt Moira had five kids. You know all of them."

Jess knew Tony's branch on the tree the best, having spent quite a bit of time with him and his brothers. Meeting Layla today had put the last brick in place in terms of Frank's kids.

"After Frank came Aunt Rose. She married Uncle Tommy, and they have Holly and David, whose little hellions are currently tearing up the house, and Erin, who couldn't make it today. She lives in Baltimore like Layla. In fact, Erin is dating Finn's cousin."

"Sounds like the Moretti women have a thing for the Irish."

Liza snorted, the sound completely out of place, coming from such a stunningly beautiful woman. Tony confided that Liza, the youngest and only daughter in her family, kept her brothers on their toes. "If you'd ever seen the Collins men, you'd know why."

"So who's left?" Jess asked, grateful for Liza's concise list. She'd been totally confused about who was related to whom after she'd first arrived and been introduced to a constant stream of aunts, uncles, and cousins.

"Last but not least is my dad, Cesare, who married my mom, who is right over there." Liza pointed to an attractive woman, refilling her wineglass.

"I met her, but I can't remember…"

"Margaret," Liza said, before adding, "and Mom and Dad had Bruno, Aldo, Elio, and me."

"Wow. That's quite a list. I was an only child and I never knew my dad."

"Well, that's all the more reason you should stick with us," Liza said genially. "Because we have dads to spare in this room. Pick one," she joked.

"Liza," Nonna called out. "Come help me with the salad."

"Duty calls."

Jess took a sip of wine as Liza went to the kitchen to help her grandmother, who pinched her cheeks upon her arrival. Then she watched as Nonno, a gruff man, bent down to pick up the smallest of his great-grandchildren, a three-year-old girl who giggled when he tickled her. Her gaze shifted to Layla, who was talking to her partners. Finn had his arm wrapped around her waist, as Miguel nuzzled her cheek. Aldo caught them and jokingly told them to "get a room."

The Morettis were very open about their relationships,

affectionate, and completely unapologetic about who they loved, be it one person or two. It was...magnificent.

She glanced around the room and found Tony, still standing with his brothers, all of them talking very animatedly. Rhys had been shanghaied by Aunt Berta to help carry appetizers from the kitchen to a dining room table that was covered with large platters and food and looked like it was already at its maximum weight capacity.

The house actually had two kitchens, something Jess didn't know was even a thing, though Layla said it wasn't uncommon among large Italian families. According to Layla, the Morettis took their parties very seriously, remarking that Nonna had begun cooking for this one four days ago.

Jess couldn't wait to relate that fact to Penny, who would no doubt be horrified by the prospect of standing for four days straight.

Everyone had been incredibly nice and welcoming...and yet, Jess still couldn't help feeling like she didn't really belong here. She'd let herself go with the flow the past week, allowing herself to pretend that she could potentially build something real, something long-lasting with Tony and Rhys. Seeing Layla with her partners proved just how badly she wanted that.

But it wasn't going to happen. Tony and Rhys had both admitted they didn't date with an eye toward forever. They were focused on their careers, not seeking a relationship or starting a family, and that truth had been confirmed by both of their sisters.

Secondly, even if they were looking for relationships, Jess was pretty damn sure she wasn't the woman. She was a decade younger than Tony, thirteen years younger than Rhys, and they had very little in common, professionally and personally. Her baggage had baggage.

And then...there was Jasper. Neither man wanted to be a father, and she could never stay with any man who wouldn't love her son as much as her.

They'd admitted they'd never shared before, which told her what the three of them were doing wasn't the norm. It was the exception. And most likely not something they would continue for the long run.

Neither Tony nor Rhys had mentioned what happened next. What if that was because...*nothing* came next? They were simply indulging in some pretty amazing, hardcore, kinky fantasies and when that was done...it was all done.

Nothing lasted forever. Jess had had that lesson knocked into her head at least a thousand times in the past, so she was acting like a fool. Letting herself dream of something that couldn't be.

Unfortunately, that didn't help her figure out her next move. Mainly because while living the fantasy was great, reality still sucked. She'd been saving as much as she could, but she didn't have enough money for a security deposit on an apartment, at least not one that wasn't in a sketchy part of town. The old Jess might have said to hell with it, picked one she could afford for now, and moved in. That was certainly what she and Danielle had done when they'd first arrived in Philadelphia. She shuddered to think what Tony and Rhys would say if they'd seen the apartment she'd been evicted from.

However, being homeless had chiseled away at her courage slowly, the attack at the motel the knock-out punch. Since moving in with the guys, she'd been able to sleep soundly, knowing that Jasper was safe, protected.

And that wasn't because of her.

It was because of Tony and Rhys and Aunt Berta. When it had just been the two of them on their own, he had ended up in too many truly frightening, dangerous situations because of poor decisions she'd made or because there simply hadn't been any more options.

She'd never forgive herself for endangering him.

Never.

So moving out wasn't an option until she could be sure she

wasn't dragging him back into a bad place. There was no way she would yank Jasper from a safe, loving home just because she had made the mother of all mistakes and fallen in love with their saviors.

Which left her with just one choice. She'd have to harden her heart and try to rebuild the wall she'd let tumble.

If she stuck to her current budget—and barring any unforeseen expenses—they'd have enough to move out in a couple more months, three max.

"Mommy!" Jasper launched himself into her arms, his cheeks ruddy from playing so hard.

"Whoa, buddy. You need to calm down a little bit. And not so loud, okay?" It was a foolish thing to admonish him for, considering there wasn't a single soul in this house using their inside voices.

"Billy has Super Mario at home and he said maybe I could go over to his house for a sleepover and play it with him. He's going to ask his mommy."

Jasper had never spent a single night away from her, his request driving home just how quickly he was growing up. "That sounds great."

"Billy says this summer, Nonna is going to have another party for the Fourth of July and she has sparklers and ice cream cake and a blow-up pool we can swim in. And she gives full-size candy bars at Halloween, and Billy said she gave him five Snickers last time, but his mommy would only let him eat one a day. And at Christmas, we're gonna have a turkey this big!" Jasper spread his arms as wide as he could. "And a bunch of presents. Like a million gazillion that it takes hours and hours to open." Jasper's excitement hit critical mass and he feigned complete exhaustion as he described a future that wasn't going to happen.

And that was when the bottom fell out. Because Jess realized it wasn't just her heart she hadn't been guarding. It was Jasper's too.

Shit.

How could she have fucked this up so badly?

"That, um, sounds great," she said, but her words were wasted as Jasper had already turned, sprinting back to Billy and the other young cousins, all of whom were crowded around the table, helping themselves to the warm focaccia that Nonna had just brought out from the kitchen.

She'd been so worried about her own imminent broken heart, she hadn't realized Jasper's was about to get crushed too.

She blinked rapidly against the tears forming in her eyes. She couldn't cry here.

Jess took several deep breaths, trying to come up with a plan B.

"Jess!"

Jess looked up when Tony's cousin, Bruno, came over and gave her a huge bear hug. She'd met him a couple times as he'd tried to fix her piece-of-shit car.

She forced a smile. "Hey, Bruno."

"Viv here has been after me to introduce you. Vivian, this is Jasper's mom, Jess."

Bruno and Viv were Billy's parents. "It's nice to meet you," Jess said, offering her hand.

Vivian, who, according to Aunt Berta, owned her own hair salon, took her outstretched hand in hers, drawing Jess's attention to her long, hot-pink fingernails. "You too. All Billy's talked about since the birthday party is Jasper. Those two are thick as thieves already."

"It's been the same with Jasper."

"Billy is after me to set up a sleepover or something for them," Viv said. "We'd love to have Jasper stay over if that works for you."

"Jasper would love that. Thank you for the invitation."

"I'll call you tomorrow and we'll pick a day that works. Maybe next weekend." Vivian linked her arm through Jess's and leaned in, as if they were close confidants. "So, Bruno tells me you're living with Tony and Rhys."

"Dammit, Viv. Don't be such a nosy busybody," Bruno grumbled. "It's that hair salon," he directed toward Jess. "All she does all day is gossip."

Viv waved her husband away, unoffended. "Oh, go away, Bruno. Like you and the boys at the garage are any better." Viv tapped her fingers and thumbs together, in the universal gesture for talking. "Flapping gums and talk, talk, talk, that's all you men do."

Jess tried not to laugh, but they were a funny couple, close enough to give each other a hard time without taking offense. "Jasper and I are just staying with Tony and Rhys until I can save up enough for an apartment. I got behind on some bills after Jasper broke his arm last spring. I didn't have health insurance and—"

"Ohmigod," Viv said dramatically. "Do *not* getting me going about healthcare and how fucking expensive everything is. Pharmaceutical companies driving up prices. It's criminal."

Jess nodded in agreement. "Anyway, Tony and Rhys were nice enough to offer their guest room. I'm close to having enough money. It's just hard to find an affordable place in a part of the city where I would feel safe living alone with a small boy."

Viv elbowed her husband. "What about the apartment behind the garage, Bruno?"

"Haven't had time to clean or paint it yet. That last renter was a fucking slob."

"You have an apartment?" Jess asked.

"Yeah. It's out behind the garage, so it's not exactly quiet during work hours, but we close up shop by six. Last renter moved out a couple weeks ago, and Viv's been on me to paint it and get someone else in there, but we've been slammed at work. You've been to the garage, Jess. It's not a bad neighborhood."

It really wasn't. It wasn't even in a different school district, which meant Jasper wouldn't have to change schools.

"I'm not sure when I'll get around to cleaning it up and slapping a coat of paint on the walls, though," Bruno said.

"I can clean and paint it," she offered.

Plan B had just presented itself.

"Hey, that sounds good to me. You do something like that and I'll skip the security deposit. Let me and Viv talk about it and we'll be in touch, okay?"

Jess smiled. "Okay."

Viv and Bruno walked away, and Jess tried to feel relief, happiness, hope.

Instead, the weight crushing on her chest tripled, and the only emotion she could summon was the one she'd foolishly thought she could stave off.

Pain.

Chapter Seventeen

They opened the car doors as quietly as they could after arriving home. Jasper had fallen asleep within the first five minutes of the trip, too many hours of playing and too much food taking their toll on the little guy. Jess had also been quiet during the ride, sitting next to Jasper in the backseat as Rhys drove them home. He'd kept checking on her in the rearview mirror, wondering about the pensive expression on her face.

Tony opened the back door and gently extracted Jasper from the car. The kid never stirred, sleeping soundly in Tony's arms, and the four of them entered the building in silence.

Aunt Berta had remained at Nonna's to help with the last few remaining cleanup tasks. Most of the mess had been taken care of before they left. It was one of the best things about the Morettis—while they partied hard, they all did their part when it came to cleaning up the mess. Aunt Berta planned to stay in Nonno and Nonna's guest room tonight, returning home sometime tomorrow.

When they reached their apartment, Tony whispered, "I'll put him to bed. Coffee?"

Rhys and Jess nodded. "Sounds good. I'll stash the leftovers in the fridge." He held a Tupperware container filled with lasagna, mushroom ravioli, eggplant parmesan, and God only knew what else. Nonna had made enough food to feed the entire East Coast, so everyone had gotten a doggie bag.

"I'll make the coffee," Jess offered.

He and Jess continued to the kitchen, working together like an old married couple, with her filling the pot with water, him scooping out the grounds.

"Quite a party," he mused.

She nodded. "It really was. I've never been to anything like that."

"Are you okay?" Rhys asked, worried about her change in demeanor. She'd been as excited as Jasper when they left the house earlier, but that had definitely dimmed somewhere along the line.

Jess paused—for just a moment—but it was long enough to warn him whatever she said next would be a lie. He'd come to learn her "tells."

"I'm just tired. That was a lot."

He chuckled, deciding he was overreacting. Of course she was tired. Because it *was* a hell of a lot. "You'll get used to it."

She didn't reply to that. Instead, she turned toward the cabinet and pulled down three coffee mugs.

Rhys leaned against the counter, watching as Jess reached into the refrigerator, pulling out cream for her coffee, then pulling a spoon out of the drawer.

She fit in their space.

She fit here.

He'd felt the rightness of that almost since day one, but it had become even better in the past two weeks, since they'd moved from roommates to lovers. Rhys would never have described himself as lonely, always opting for the word loner. He'd walked through his life with a plan, never questioning if it was right or wrong.

Jess had shaken his foundation, revealing cracks he'd never noticed.

Rhys had also studied Layla with Miguel and Finn all afternoon, and for the first time in his life, he'd felt a definite twinge of...well, he could only describe it as jealousy. He was jealous of what Tony's sister had found.

The problem was, while he, Jess, and Tony had changed their status, holding back nothing—physically—in the bedroom, none of them had mentioned what came next.

Did something come next?

Did he want something else?

They couldn't live in this limbo land of lust forever, though he had to admit that wouldn't be a terrible thing. Sex with Jess and Tony was off-the-charts amazing, and he didn't see it ever getting old.

But sharing a woman in the bedroom was different from sharing a...

Fuck.

Rhys let himself think the word.

Avoiding it didn't mean it wasn't there.

A *wife*.

He was actually considering taking a wife, and he wanted it to be Jess. More than that, he wanted—no, he *needed*—Tony to be part of that relationship. His reasons for eschewing marriage still existed. He was still a committed physician, and he would continue to work long hours.

However, he wouldn't have to worry about all the nights he'd have to leave to go to the hospital because Tony would be there. The three of them—all workaholics—had already proven they could share the load so much better together. They'd been making it work for two months.

So...what if they made this permanent?

He and Tony would raise Jasper as their son, and they could even have children of their own.

Perhaps that was the most shocking discovery Rhys made.

He wanted to be a father, wanted to be *Jasper's* father. He loved the boy more than he could say.

Jess stepped next to him, reaching for the pot.

Rhys stopped her, twisting them until she was pressed against the counter. He lowered his head and kissed her.

Jess didn't move for a moment, and he wasn't sure if it was his sudden act of passion or something else that held her back.

However, it passed quickly, and she lifted her arms, wrapping them around his neck. The kiss grew hotter, their tongues touching, stroking, tasting. He jerked slightly when Jess dug her teeth into his lower lip.

Lifting her, he set her ass on the counter, shifting between her thighs. Jess's legs came around his waist and she pressed herself against him, showing him with actions rather than words just how much she wanted him.

He slipped his hands beneath her sweater, engulfing her breasts in his hands, squeezing them with more force than he usually did. He was hungry, starving for her. Ready to devour every single bit of her, and then demand more.

"What the hell?"

He and Jess stilled at the rumble of Tony's voice in the doorway.

Rhys frowned, confused by Tony's furrowed brows, his scowl.

He looked pissed.

Actually, he looked jealous.

"Tony—" Rhys started.

Jess, startled, jumped down from the counter, putting some space between herself and Rhys. She'd clearly seen the same thing.

"I...shit. I'm sorry. I don't want to come between the two of you."

Between them?

Rhys shook his head, trying to figure out what the fuck was going on, his arousal quickly dampened. It was as if Tony had dumped a bucket of water on the flames.

Jess's words seemed to have shaken something loose in Tony, because he sucked in a deep breath, his anger vanishing as quickly as it has flashed.

"No. Wait." Tony raised his hand when it was apparent Jess intended to escape to her room. "It was hot. Don't stop."

"Tony..." Jess said, clearly not convinced.

"I mean it." Tony crossed the room to them in three long strides. He placed his hand under Jess's chin, tilting her face up to his. "This is still new. I saw the two of you and for a split second, I was pissed you started without me. If I wasn't such an impulsive motherfucker, I would have kept my mouth shut and enjoyed the show because watching the two of you is the hottest thing I've ever fucking seen. So we're moving this to the bedroom. Right now. And you two are going to continue the show. Only with a twist."

"A twist?" Rhys asked, his cock thickening once more.

"Yeah. I'm going to direct." Tony turned toward the door, drawing Jess in front of him, smacking her ass. "Get moving, gorgeous."

Rhys followed Tony and Jess to his bedroom, shutting and locking the door behind him. With the exception of the exam room, they'd limited their sexual encounters to his bedroom because it was the farthest from the guest room, and Jasper would be less likely to hear them.

Rhys silently wished it was *their* bedroom, one that the three of them shared every night. Something was going to have to give soon. They couldn't continue this affair without discussing the future.

Tony stopped next to the bed and turned to face them. Jess stood between them, her flushed face and taut nipples betraying her obvious arousal.

Tony looked at Rhys. "Undress her."

Rhys wasted no time as he tugged her shirt over her head. Then he gripped her arm and twisted her until she faced Tony. He unfastened her bra, tugging it away from her body.

Tony began to undress as well, his gaze glued to Jess's body, as Rhys revealed more and more of it. Once Jess and Tony were both naked, Tony held his hand out to her. "Come here, angel."

Jess accepted his proffered hand, the two of them climbing onto the bed together. Tony propped a couple of pillows together, leaning back against them in a position halfway between sitting and reclining. He drew Jess between his legs, her back resting against his chest, and Rhys was reminded of the night the three of them had shared their first kiss.

Rhys shifted to the foot of the bed, taking off his own clothing as his lovers watched. Tony's hands rested on Jess's stomach without moving. He didn't seek to continue their play without Rhys, calmly waiting as he stripped off his pants and boxer briefs.

While Rhys felt no attraction toward Tony—and he knew the same to be true of his friend—he wasn't uncomfortable with his nudity in front of him. Neither of them had bothered to hide their desire for Jess from each other.

Rhys hadn't anticipated that. What's more, he could appreciate Tony's muscular physique as much as Jess did, but it didn't turn him on like it did her.

"Show Rhys how much you want him," Tony murmured, placing a kiss on Jess's bare shoulder.

She parted her legs in invitation.

"Are you wet, Jess?" Tony asked.

Jess nodded.

"Show me," he commanded.

Jess didn't hesitate for a moment. She slid her finger along her slit, lifting it to show Tony. He gripped her wrist and sucked her finger into his mouth.

Jess's head fell back on a sigh until Tony released her finger.

"Show Rhys."

1

Because Tony still retained his grip on her wrist, Jess lifted her other hand, intent on offering him the same.

Tony snatched it before she could touch herself, shaking his head. "Not that way."

Rhys knelt on the end of the bed, crawling toward Jess, wanting exactly what Tony was suggesting. As Tony held her wrists, Rhys lowered his head, sliding his tongue along the same path her finger had just taken.

"God," Jess breathed. "Rhys."

He took his time, stroking her opening, teasing her clit, tasting her. With his hands on her thighs, he pushed her legs farther apart so he could settle more fully between her legs.

"You like Rhys's mouth on you, angel?"

"Yes," Jess whispered.

"You want him to fuck you with his tongue?" he asked.

"Please," she pleaded.

Rhys was already there. He plunged his tongue inside her, thrusting in and out, forced to hold onto her thighs to keep Jess steady as she began to writhe.

"So good," she said.

Rhys glanced up along her body to see that Tony had released her wrists. One of his hands now rested at the base of Jess's throat, his thumb tilting her head backwards so he could steal a hard, hot kiss.

Rhys resumed his own more personal, intimate kiss.

For several moments, the three of them drove the heat higher, as Rhys added his fingers to the play, stroking her clit as he fucked her with his tongue. Tony's hands had drifted to her breasts, where he pinched and pulled her nipples.

Jess undulated, climbing quickly toward her orgasm. However, before she could fall over, Tony said, "Don't let her come."

Rhys lifted his head, even as Jess cried out a complaint.

"No," she said, attempting to push Rhys's head back down.

"I was there. So close." Her words were breathless, more air than sound.

Tony bit her shoulder, shocking her into silence when she continued to beg, still trying to drag Rhys back into place.

"And you're going to get even closer, angel." Tony sat up, his change in position shifting Jess as well. "Hands and knees," he directed her. "Take Rhys in your mouth."

Rhys had sunk to his haunches, but as Jess did as asked, he rose up on his knees, gathering her hair in his fist to hold it out of the way. He didn't want to miss a second of her taking his cock inside her mouth.

Jess wrapped her hand around the base of his dick, holding him as she lowered her head. At first, she merely teased, running her tongue around his head, toying with the tip in a way that tickled more than aroused.

"Suck him," Tony said. He had risen to his knees as well, kneeling between Jess's ankles, his thick cock brushing against the globes of her ass.

Jess took Rhys into her mouth slowly, pausing after just a few seconds. He was too focused on her actions to understand why she stopped.

"Birth control?" Tony said, drawing Rhys's attention back to him. Tony was drawing his cock up and down along the slit between Jess's legs, the head of his dick shiny from her arousal.

"It's safe," Rhys answered in response. "Jess?"

Tony held his breath as he awaited Jess's response. He'd never taken a woman without a condom, never experienced what it felt like to take a woman—*his* woman—bare. But he wanted that with Jess. Wanted to stake his claim in the most primitive way, filling her with his come and, God willing, someday with his baby.

Jess released Rhys's dick with a pop, looking over her shoulder at him. She was the most fearless, beautiful, confidant woman he'd ever seen. She gave him a sultry grin that would have dropped him to his knees if he wasn't already there.

"Do it," she demanded before turning her attention back to Rhys, taking him deep into her mouth.

"Jesus," Rhys muttered, his fist gripping her hair tighter, using it to draw her mouth up and down along his dick. Rhys was controlling the speed, the depth. And Jess was letting him. For now.

Tony knew that wouldn't remain the case, however. While Jess went along with Tony and Rhys's commands, she was no submissive, and during the course of their sexual encounters, she'd made more than a few demands of her own.

Tony fisted his own dick, drawing it up and down her slit once more, teasing himself as much as her. He paused when the head of it brushed against her ass.

Jess stilled but didn't release Rhys.

Rhys, whose eyes had been closed, must have sensed the change in the air. He opened his eyes, his gaze traveling to Tony's cock.

Their sex up until now had been very straightforward, and if they discounted the fact there were two men in the bed, downright vanilla. They took turns fucking her pussy, indulging mostly in missionary and doggie style. Apart from pinching her nipples and giving her a few smacks on her ass, they hadn't drifted into anything overly kinky or dirty in this bedroom.

The experience in the exam room had opened a door, left Tony wanting to test limits, to explore so much more with them.

Without speaking, he pushed his cock harder against her anus, not breaching it, just...giving her a glimpse of where he hoped to take them soon.

Jess lifted her head, but she didn't look back at Tony. What she did was a hell of a lot sexier.

She pressed back against him, a clear invitation, one that Rhys didn't miss either.

Tony stroked her ass. "Soon, angel," he promised. "But not tonight. Tonight we're all coming together. Same time."

Gripping his dick, he pressed downward and then, with one hard thrust, he claimed her pussy.

Jess gasped at his fast, rough entry, then joined the race. Lowering her head, she sucked Rhys into her mouth and, given the look on his roommate's face, he'd say she'd taken off the kid gloves. Rhys tugged her hair, though Tony wasn't sure if it was to drive the rhythm or reclaim some control.

And he didn't care. All he knew was, he'd never felt anything more exquisite than the wet heat of Jess's body gloving his dick.

He gripped her hips and took them both for a ride, thrusting in and out, fucking her with a reckless abandon he'd never allowed himself. Control wasn't something he wanted here.

Not now. Not with her.

With them.

Tony wanted to lose himself completely in the wonder, the rightness.

The three of them moved together, a perfect tango, pounding together, as each of them gave and took, then took some more.

Rhys was the first to break. "Jesus, Jess. I'm going to—" It was all he said before he closed his eyes, grunting in pleasure as he came. Jess held him in her mouth, swallowing every drop. Tony slowed down as he watched, but he didn't stop. He couldn't.

As Rhys fell back onto his haunches, Jess lifted her head and looked back at Tony. "I'm close," she admitted.

He nodded. "I am too."

After that, words weren't necessary. Tony continued to

pump inside her, Jess meeting him blow for blow, adding more pressure, more force, more heat.

When she fell from her hands to her elbows, her face buried in the duvet, he knew she was there. She cried out as her orgasm crashed down on her, the tight pulsing of her pussy taking him down as well.

"Fuck," he groaned. "Goddammit!" Tony jerked inside her three more times before he couldn't hold back any longer. He came so hard, his teeth nearly rattled.

Jess moaned beneath him, her orgasm fading, her pussy quivering in the aftermath.

She trembled when he pulled out, her body limp as he and Rhys gently lifted her, placing her between them on the bed. She rested her arm around Rhys's waist, her head on his shoulder. Tony spooned her from behind, placing a soft kiss on her neck.

They lay there, still, fitting together like puzzle pieces, and again, Tony had a sense of coming home, of finally finding his place in the world.

It was these two people. And this room. This bed.

He'd just closed his eyes, the blissful exhaustion of his climax knocking him out, when Jess spoke.

"I need to go back to my room."

Tony longed to ask her to stay. But that wouldn't be kind to her. Jess was right to leave. She had Jasper to think of.

He kissed her shoulder again. "Okay."

Rhys gave her a kiss as well, his landing on her forehead. Then he shifted and sat up, allowing Jess to climb off the bed.

Tony lay there watching as Rhys helped her find her clothes in the dimness of the room, the only light provided by the streetlamp outside and the brightness of a full moon on a clear night.

Once she was dressed, she paused, her lips parting, as if she wanted to say something. He watched the words fade away, unspoken.

Then she kissed Rhys, smiled at Tony, offered them both an adorable finger wave at the door, and she was gone.

Tony forced himself to sit up then, aware he needed to go back to his own room as well. And equally aware that he didn't want to keep sleeping alone.

"We need to talk about this," Rhys said, breaking the silence.

Tony nodded. "I know we do."

"You feel it too, right?"

Tony stood and turned to face his friend, Rhys's words sending a wave of...utter relief through him. They were on the same page. Tony had suspected as much, but hearing it spoken aloud filled him with a hope that things were going to turn out just fine. "Yeah. I do."

"So we need to decide our next step," Rhys said, clearly ready to map out the next forty to fifty years of their lives tonight.

Tony stepped around the bed and reached for his pants. A conversation like this probably required some clothing.

Before they could continue, however, a buzzing from Tony's pocket caught his attention. He withdrew his phone and saw a text from Gio. "Shit. There's an alarm going off at the warehouse. We've had some problems with assholes trying to break in to steal the copper piping. I have to go."

Rhys nodded. "Lunch tomorrow? Meet somewhere downtown?"

"Sounds good. Text me in the morning and we'll figure out when and where."

Tony finished grabbing his clothes, dressing in the hallway.

As he walked toward the door, he paused outside Jess's room and grinned.

Tomorrow.

It was all changing tomorrow.

Chapter Eighteen

Jess sighed as she looked around her new kitchen, wishing she was more excited. She should be over the moon, thrilled.

She'd done it, accomplished what had seemed impossible back in January. She'd found a home for her and Jasper.

It just...didn't feel like a home. Not without Tony and Rhys.

She shoved that thought away and swallowed down the lump in her throat.

This was for the best.

She'd repeated those words over and over in her head a few thousand times this afternoon, wishing they would stick.

Today had been a whirlwind, starting with a morning phone call from Bruno, asking if she still wanted the apartment, then inviting her to come see the place when she said yes. She'd called Paulie's and taken the day off.

Her anxiety last night after leaving Rhys's room had been off the charts. She'd fallen recklessly, helplessly, completely in love with Tony and Rhys, and every second spent in their arms only made those feelings stronger.

Rhys was a compassionate, empathetic man, and an amazing doctor. Watching him interact with his patients moved her more than she could say. Falling in love with him was as easy as breathing.

Tony, meanwhile, was Rhys's polar opposite, passionate, impulsive, commanding. He only had to give her that look or use that tone and she felt her knees go weak with longing and desire. She loved the way he challenged her. They may not always agree, but she knew he was listening to her, taking her feelings and thoughts into consideration. They'd exchanged words countless times, yet it had never felt like arguing. It actually felt a lot like foreplay.

But neither of them had ever mentioned the three of them sharing a future, never offered her any insight into their feelings for her.

It had been on the tip of her tongue to say "I love you" last night before leaving Rhys's room. The words had been right there. Mercifully, she'd managed to hold them back because God only knew how they would have responded if she'd hit them with that.

She'd had a lifetime of experience watching people walk away—the father she never knew, Scott, her mother, even Danielle. While she and her friend had parted amicably, Danielle had moved on without giving them a second thought, never calling or having time to chat whenever Jess reached out to her.

Jess had also managed to move on, to accept losing those people in her life. But there was no way in hell she could watch Tony and Rhys walk away from her. It would cripple her, knock her down hard enough that she'd never manage to rise again.

So she'd made sure that this time...*she* was the one who did the walking.

She'd spent the past few weeks with the growing knowledge that leaving with her heart intact was no longer an option, so when Bruno unwittingly offered her a way to rip off the Band-Aid, she'd jumped at it.

Aunt Berta had offered to come see the place with her, and Jess had known in an instant it was perfect for her and Jasper. Bruno was obviously giving her a break on the rent, something she might have fought him on if, one, she could afford to, and two, she wasn't so determined to make a clean break.

Once she'd decided to move in, asking Bruno if she could do so immediately, Aunt Berta and Bruno had shifted into high gear, ready to help her in any way she'd needed. Aunt Berta had rallied her brothers, Frank and Cesare, to help, the two men gathering "extra" furniture from other relatives and delivering it to the apartment, while she and Aunt Berta had scrubbed the place from top to bottom. Bruno hadn't lied about the previous renter being a slob.

Bruno had loaned her a couple of air mattresses until she could afford to buy beds. Aunt Berta and Nonna had "thinned out" their kitchens, managing to almost fully stock Jess's with pots, pans, dishes, glasses, and silverware. Cesare had lugged an old dresser out of his attic for her bedroom, and Frank had an extra TV and stand he'd taken out of his guest room, claiming no one ever used it.

She'd been overwhelmed and more touched than she could say by their generosity. She was grateful she'd had the opportunity to get to know the Morettis and to be able to witness first-hand what it truly meant to be part of a family.

Because she and Aunt Berta been busy cleaning the apartment, Jess had texted Penny to ask if she could pick up Jasper and bring him home after school. Penny had become a friend, the two of them talking on the phone almost daily the past couple of weeks.

Penny had taken one look at the place and—after declaring herself an interior decorating genius, thanks to some Sims game she played constantly—immediately started discussing design plans and colors, even promising to help Jess with the painting.

Jess had expected Jasper to be delighted by the new apartment and the fact he would have his own room for the first time in his life. However, none of that excitement had been there. Instead, he'd followed her around as she gave him a quick tour, then asked if he could color a picture. She'd said yes, watching as he pulled a piece of paper and crayons out of his bag and started to draw.

She was concerned about his response, though she was aware he was most likely overwhelmed. She'd mentioned looking at an apartment today before he left for school, but she hadn't realized how quickly things would move. He'd need time to process the change, so she'd give it to him.

When Jasper finished his drawing and asked if he could give Tony and Rhys the picture he'd colored as a thank-you present, Jess realized she hadn't said thank you either.

She glanced at the time on her phone. It was just after five. They'd be getting home soon.

Aunt Berta was still fussing in the kitchen, the woman clearly in her element, delighted with setting it up. Penny was helping, but it was obvious the task was less fun for her, as she kept sneaking onto her phone to play a game.

"Do you all mind hanging out here for a little while? I need to go back to the apartment to pack up our clothes and toiletries, plus I want to talk to the guys and give them this." Jess held up Jasper's picture.

"Take your time, dear. Penny and I will take Jasper to the store to pick up some staples for your kitchen."

"You don't have to do that," she said, even though she knew the words would be wasted. Aunt Berta was tireless and having too much fun and not about to stop until she was done.

"I've already made a list," she insisted.

"Fine." Jess reached into her purse and pulled out her wallet, handing Aunt Berta all the cash she had on hand, hoping it would be enough to cover the bill. "Here. Don't spend more than this. I can go back to the store later this week to get the rest."

Aunt Berta took the cash, albeit reluctantly, and Jess suspected that list would be completely checked off regardless of how much it cost.

"I'll be back soon," she promised, borrowing Aunt Berta's car for the trip.

The drive back to Tony and Rhys's was just long enough to ensure her stomach was twisted in knots by the time she arrived.

Neither man was there, so Jess went to her room—the guest room, she supposed it would be again—and packed up her and Jasper's things. Then she walked around the apartment, seeking out little items that were scattered here and there—a pair of her shoes in the living room, Jasper's coloring books on the kitchen table.

She'd killed nearly an hour and still neither man had returned. She felt guilty leaving Penny and Aunt Berta for so long, so she sat down to write them a note.

It took her several minutes to figure out what she could say to them, because honestly, words would never be enough to tell them exactly how much they'd given her.

Once she finished, she reread it, sort of glad they weren't home. There was no way she would have been able to speak the words she'd written without falling apart completely, and crying in front of them was something she simply couldn't do. After all, it wasn't their fault she'd lost her heart.

Well, actually, it *was* their fault. Because they'd been wonderful, attentive, generous roommates...as well as gorgeous, sexy as fuck, and amazing lovers.

She'd let things go too far. She should have known better, should have protected not just her heart but Jasper's as well.

Jasper had instructed her to hang his picture up "somewhere special," so Jess hung it from the refrigerator with a magnet—front and center. She waited a few minutes more, then she placed the note, her key, and the last of the rent she still owed them in an envelope by the door, and left.

As she returned to the car with her bags, she felt equal parts relieved and disappointed that neither man had returned home while she'd been there.

She would still need to see them, talk to them.

Hopefully, when that time came, this piercing pain would have lessened, her agony less raw, her heart...

God, it didn't matter how much time passed.

She was a fool.

And her heart was irrevocably broken.

Tony walked into the diner a little after seven and spotted Rhys sitting in a booth by the front window, sipping his coffee. Rhys waved and he walked over, claiming the seat across from him.

The two of them hadn't managed to meet for lunch as planned, both of them dealing with unexpected emergencies at work.

The warehouse was robbed, so Tony had been knee-deep in police reports and insurance claims all damn day, trying to replace what was lost so they wouldn't fall behind on their schedule.

When Tony called an hour ago to set up this coffee meeting, Rhys confided that his day hadn't been much better. He'd been inundated by patients all suffering from a nasty stomach virus that was spreading like wildfire. Apparently, he'd spent the last three hours at the hospital, making rounds there.

Tony had heard the exhaustion in Rhys's tone and for a moment had been tempted to suggest they have this talk tomorrow. He couldn't make the offer, however, too ready, too desperate to move things to the next part.

"Can I get you something to drink, Tony?"

Tony looked up, recognizing their waitress as Debbie, the

friend who'd taken Jess in after she was evicted. He scowled when he spotted the black eye on her face, recalling how afraid Jasper had been of Debbie's brother-in-law, the bad man.

Tony lifted his chin, his temper rising. If there was one thing he wouldn't stand for, it was assholes who hit women. He still had moments of regret for not pummeling the fucker who'd attacked Jess more than he had. "Do I need to take care of somebody for that, or has it been handled?"

Debbie shook her head, clearly shocked by the offer. Apparently she and Jess had spent too much of their lives around people who didn't give a shit. "My husband took care of it. Kicked my brother-in-law out."

"Just kicked him out?"

"Mario has a drinking problem. Makes him a mean drunk."

"Don't give a shit. Sounds like he needed to be taught a lesson. Any chance your husband will let him come back?"

Debbie stood a bit taller, and Tony recognized the same spine of steel Jess possessed. "No. I told my husband it was me or Mario. He likes the way I cook too much to test me on that."

Tony smiled. "Good. I'll take coffee. Black."

"You guys need a menu?"

Rhys shook his head. "No. We're just having coffee tonight."

Debbie turned to fetch the coffeepot and a mug. They waited in silence as she returned and filled the cup for Tony.

Once she was out of earshot, he said, "So…"

"What are we doing with Jess, Tony?" Rhys leaned forward, not shying away from asking the million-dollar question.

Tony didn't hesitate. "I want to build a future with her."

"And in this future of yours…I'm there?"

Tony nodded. "Yeah. You are. I don't know how to explain why this works. God knows I never imagined this kind of relationship for myself. Marriage and kids was something that just kept getting pushed to the back burner. I've been blaming work for that, claiming my career came first, but I can see now, I just hadn't met the right woman."

Rhys ran his finger around the rim of his coffee cup. "I've been blaming my career too, so convinced that trying to have it all wouldn't be fair to whomever I married. With you there too...I don't know how to say it. It feels as if this is the answer to a prayer I wasn't praying. Jess and Jasper showed up on our doorstep and for the first time, I realized I wasn't the happy bachelor I thought I was. She shone a light on something I couldn't see. My loneliness."

Tony felt every single one of Rhys's words, though he never would have been able to speak them so succinctly. "It was the same for me."

"What we're thinking about doing," Rhys said. "It's not going to be easy. It's definitely uncharted waters for all of us. You and I have zero experience with committed relationships, and Jess has zero experience with...well...pretty much everything. She's younger than us."

"Do you think that's a problem?"

Rhys shook his head. "No. I don't. Life has forced her to grow up a lot quicker. She feels older than twenty-five."

"Yeah, she does," Tony agreed.

"Even so...a threesome," Rhys mused.

"It's not like we haven't seen the same type of relationship up close and personal. Layla is making this work with Finn and Miguel because they're all committed to the relationship, to each other."

Rhys glanced out the large plate-glass window, his gaze unfocused for a moment. "They are. But their relationship is different from ours."

Tony sighed. "Because Finn and Miguel are in love with each other, as well as Layla." Layla's lovers were bisexual, the three of them a true trinity. That didn't hold true for him and Rhys.

"I love you like a brother, Rhys," Tony said. "But I don't..." He waved his hands around, letting the gesture speak the words.

Rhys chuckled. "I don't either. Do you think that adds a wrinkle? Makes this harder?"

Tony considered that. "Do you feel jealous when I touch Jess?"

"Not at all. Which is something I've actually been struggling to understand. I would never have considered sharing lovers in the past. With you and Jess, it's hot, a turn-on. But Sunday night, after the party, when you came into the kitchen and saw me kissing Jess...were *you* jealous?"

Tony recalled that flash of anger when he caught them. "No. It was something dumber than that."

His response amused and confused Rhys. "Dumber?"

"I meant what I said. I felt left out. But the knee-jerk reaction passed quickly. If we move forward with this, I know there are going to be times I'll be with Jess alone. And times you'll be with her alone. I don't have a problem with that. I *really* don't," he stressed when Rhys looked slightly skeptical.

"The sex," Rhys started, not bothering to finish. It wasn't necessary. Tony figured his descriptions matched Rhys's perfectly.

Sex with Jess and Rhys was mind-blowing. Earth-shattering. Incredible.

Rhys had been a bit of a surprise in the bedroom, though Tony wouldn't admit that to his friend. He wasn't sure why he'd expected Rhys to be more vanilla, more straightforward missionary, but nothing could be further from the truth.

"I'm in love with her, Tony," Rhys admitted. "I'm committed to making this work between the three of us. I've never wanted anything more."

"Me either. I'm crazy about her. And Jasper."

Rhys smiled when Tony mentioned the little boy's name, the expression proving Jasper had laid claim to their hearts just as much as his mother had. "We'd be fathers."

Tony laughed. "God, how fucking cool would that be?"

"So tonight? We lay our cards on the table with Jess, tell her how we feel, what we want?"

Tony rose, opening his wallet to toss some cash on the table to cover the two coffees. "Yeah. Right now."

They'd just reached the exit when the door opened and Matt Russo walked in.

Tony was in too much of a good mood for even Russo to ruin it.

"Moretti," Matt muttered.

"Russo," Tony said darkly, peripherally catching sight of Rhys rolling his eyes. While his roommate had heard the stories, Rhys didn't feel the same passionate anger toward the Russos that Tony did. Hell, he didn't even blink an eye when his kid sister, Penny, told them she'd gotten an IT job with Russo Enterprises.

Tony started to walk by without saying more, but Matt turned toward him. "Still a possessive prick, I see."

Tony twisted to face him, confused. "What the fuck are you talking about?"

"Jess Monroe," Matt said, as if that should answer anything.

Hearing Jess's name coming from Matt had Tony's fists clenching.

Rhys put a hand on his shoulder. "What about Jess?"

"You expect me to believe you didn't play a part in her giving her two weeks' notice this afternoon?" Matt addressed to Tony, arms crossed.

"Jess quit her job with you?" Rhys asked.

While his friend's tone was calm, Tony could see the sudden concern in Rhys's eyes. Jess wouldn't just up and quit. She was still determined to make enough money to get her own place. The fact that she'd quit was...disquieting, and it left Tony with an uneasy feeling.

Matt nodded, his annoyance somewhat soothed when it became apparent neither he nor Rhys knew Jess had quit.

"Said she wouldn't be able to work the late hours anymore. Childcare concerns," Matt said to Rhys before shifting his attention back to Tony, his scowl shifting into something resembling a smirk. "I've figured out a way around that."

Rhys sighed. "Maybe you should just let her quit."

Matt shook his head. "She's confided her financial difficulties to me and I know about the attack in the motel. I want to help her."

Tony fought the urge to growl, unaware that Jess had shared so much with his sworn enemy.

"I'm going to change her hours, let her come in earlier, let her bring her son with her. I plan to call her tomorrow to discuss it with her."

Tony took a small step closer, his temper flaring at the thought of Jasper being anywhere near Matt. It was hard enough knowing Jess saw the asshole more than he was comfortable with. "Stay the fuck away from Jess...and Jasper."

"Yep. Still possessive." Matt chuckled, clearly not intimidated.

Before things got out of hand, Debbie called out, "Mr. Russo. Your take-out order is ready."

Matt shifted his gaze toward the waitress and the tension slowly faded. He nodded just once at Rhys. "Good evening, Dr. Beaumont," he said, ignoring Tony as he walked away from them.

Rhys gave Tony a slight nudge with his shoulder and the two of them left the diner. On the sidewalk, Tony reached for his car keys. "Jess quit her job."

Rhys already had his keys in hand. "Yeah. I don't like that. Meet you back home. We need to figure out what's going on."

Chapter Nineteen

"**C**ome on. Let's get upstairs and see what everyone is up to," Rhys said as they headed toward the stairs.

As soon as they entered the apartment, it was apparent no one was home. There was no noise from the television, no smell of dinner cooking, none of Jasper's sweet chatter.

Tony pulled his cell phone from his pocket to text, but Rhys held up his hand when his gaze landed on an envelope on the table by the front door. It was in Jess's writing and had both their names written on it.

Tony reached for it, ripping it open impatiently. Money fell out, and Rhys sighed. Jess was a stickler for paying her share. Something he intended to put a stop to after they'd settled this thing between them.

However, the money wasn't the worst thing in the envelope.

He spotted her apartment key.

Tony's eyes scanned the words of the note quickly before his fist closed around the paper, wrinkling it up. "Fuck!"

Rhys pried the paper from his grip, reading it with the same sense of...disappointment? Anger? Sadness?

Rhys couldn't sort out the emotions that hit him all at once.

. . .

Dear Tony and Rhys,

Mere words cannot express how much the past couple of months have meant to me. You found me at my lowest point and raised me up, helped me...saved me.

I've found a good apartment for Jasper and me, a safe home, something that wouldn't have been possible without your generous offer of a place to stay while we got our feet back under us.

Our time together was truly the happiest of my life. I'm not sure what the future holds, but please know that I wouldn't change a single second of what we shared. You are amazing men, and the best mistake I ever made was parking my car in front of your home that night.

Jasper and I will visit very soon, and I'll offer these same words of thanks in person. I didn't intend to leave without talking to you first, but this apartment came up quickly and I knew it was time to move on.

Enclosed is the rent I owe you. Jasper drew you a picture and insisted it be displayed. It's on the refrigerator.

With love,

Jess

Rhys turned and walked to the kitchen without saying a word. There, as promised, was the drawing. It reminded him of the drawing Jasper had given them the day after they'd first arrived. Jess had left that picture behind with a thank-you note as well. That drawing had depicted Jess and Jasper smiling and waving as they stood next to their car, intent on driving away.

In this one, the family had gotten larger. It was a picture of all of them standing before this building. Rhys stood next to Jess and Aunt Berta, while Jasper was on Tony's shoulders. All of them had big, wide, red crayon smiles.

Tony stepped up behind him, looking at the picture. "We're getting her back. They belong *here*."

Rhys appreciated the confidence in Tony's tone...and he hoped they managed to do just that.

"Why the fuck would she leave like this?" Tony asked.

Rhys knew why. Knew it the second he'd seen the envelope. "We never told her how we felt, Tony. Never even alluded to it. Sex and friendship. That's all we gave her. I watched her at your family's party. I've never seen such a longing to belong on some-one's face, such a strong desire to be a part of something like that. Jess has spent a lifetime being tossed aside. She left to protect herself, to ensure *she* was the one walking away this time. It's probably the bravest thing she's ever done."

Tony grunted, clearly unhappy with Rhys's observations. "We have to fix this."

Rhys pulled the picture from the refrigerator, smiling. "Quite the family portrait."

Tony looked at it again over his shoulder. "We're dragging her ass back here and tying her to the bed until we convince her this is real. This is forever."

Rhys chuckled. "Knowing our girl, she'll probably test us just so we *will* tie her to the bed."

"Come on. We have to find her." Tony opened his phone, but before he could send the text to Jess demanding an address, the door to the apartment opened.

"Jess?" Rhys called out, walking out of the kitchen, Tony following.

"Nope," Aunt Berta replied as they met her in the foyer. "Just me. Didn't you get Jess's note? She said she left one when you guys didn't show up after work."

"We got it," Tony growled. "Where is she? Why didn't you tell us she was leaving? How could you let her pack up and go like that? Where have you been?"

Aunt Berta narrowed her eyes, clearly displeased with

Tony's tone. "I was busy helping Jess move and set up her new place."

"How long have you known she was leaving?" This time Tony sounded less angry and more hurt.

Aunt Berta sighed and headed for the kitchen, the two of them following in her wake. "Bruno called this morning, right after you and Rhys left for work."

"Bruno?" Rhys asked, trying to figure out what Tony's cousin had to do with Jess's departure.

Aunt Berta pulled on her apron before she pushed a button on the oven to preheat it, then she pulled a pan of lasagna she had thawing out of the refrigerator. "He has that apartment behind his garage that he rents out. The last person moved out and Bruno said Jess could have it. He waved the security deposit because it needs a bit of painting and cleaning up. It really is ideal, because Jasper can continue at the same school, and it's in a safe part of the city. Plus, Bruno will be there during the day to keep an eye on them. I'm going to stay on as Jasper's babysitter, thank goodness. I told Jess the only way I'd help her move was if she promised me that. Sweet girl teared up and acted as if I'd given her a block of gold when really it's me who wins. I'm crazy about that sweet boy."

Aunt Berta had continued moving around the kitchen, preparing dinner as she spoke.

All that stopped when Tony erupted.

"Jesus Christ! What the hell is Bruno doing? Sticking his nose in where it doesn't belong!" Tony threw his hands up in frustration. While Rhys could see how Aunt Berta and Jess would think Bruno's offer was the answer to a prayer, all Tony had heard was that his aunt and cousin had taken Jess away from them.

"Excuse me? Why are you angry? This is what Jess has been working toward all this time. I thought you'd be happy for her."

"Happy?!" Tony's Italian temper was full-blown. "Happy?!" he repeated, even louder.

Aunt Berta picked up a wooden spoon, wielding it like a sword. Rhys was amused when Tony took a quick step back. Obviously, he was no stranger to Italian females waving wooden spoons.

"You have thirty seconds to explain yourself, Tony Moretti, or you're going to feel my wrath."

Rhys intervened quickly, placing a hand on his friend's shoulder. "Tony. Calm down. We're going to get her back."

Aunt Berta looked completely perplexed, lowering the spoon. "Get her back? Why?"

Tony blew out a long, slow breath. "We're in love with her, Aunt Berta."

"We?" Aunt Berta's gaze traveled from Tony to Rhys as recognition dawned. "You're both in love with her." There was no question. Just understanding. "Did you tell *her* that?"

"We were going to," Tony replied.

"When?"

"Tonight," Rhys explained. "We should have done it before this, but..." He raised his hands. "This isn't exactly normal."

Aunt Berta took off her apron and turned off the oven, scoffing. "If it's right, then it's normal. I think it's right. Do you?"

Rhys and Tony both nodded.

"And now I understand why Jess was so subdued today. I couldn't understand why she wasn't excited about the new apartment."

"She wasn't excited?" Rhys asked, Aunt Berta's words giving him hope.

"No. She looked almost sad." Aunt Berta smiled. "Get your keys, Tony. We're going to go get her."

"We?" Tony asked.

Aunt Berta rolled her eyes. "Don't make me pick that spoon back up to beat some sense into you. Yes, *we*. Someone has to take Jasper out so you two can tell her how you feel properly."

Aunt Berta left the kitchen, muttering something under her breath about men being idiots.

"Let's go get our girl." Tony slapped him on the shoulder, and Rhys smiled.

* * *

Jess scooped out a bowlful of macaroni and cheese—the orange stuff from the box, not the amazingly gooey goodness that Aunt Berta made from scratch—and handed it to her son. Not that Jasper noticed the quality of the food as he lifted the spoon and started shoveling it in.

She scooped out another bowlful and handed it to Penny, who followed Jasper to the living room.

Penny had remained after Aunt Berta left, something Jess was grateful for. She wasn't ready to be alone yet, and while Jasper was there, he was still quiet. No doubt her son was feeling the same heavy sadness as she.

Having Penny there to entertain him, distract him, was a gift because Jess couldn't summon any semblance of fake happiness right now.

She'd had to call Matt Russo earlier in the afternoon to quit her cleaning job. Without someone to watch him at night, she couldn't figure out a way to make it work. The hours were too late for her to take him along, and she refused to ask Aunt Berta to do anything more than she was doing—which in Jess's mind, was already too much.

So she would have to ask Paulie for more shifts until she could find another job to help her cover the rent. But that problem would have to be solved tomorrow. She was completely out of steam tonight.

"Sorry this isn't exactly a great dinner," Jess said, joining them in the living room, attempting to make conversation with Penny. Since returning from the guys' place, Jess had been too lost in her own head to be very good company.

Not that Penny seemed to mind. She and Jasper were sitting together on pillows on the floor—a couch was one of the first things Jess was going to have to save up for—chowing down on their bowls of mac and cheese, their heads touching as they played some game on Penny's phone.

"You're joking, right?" Penny said, looking up. "This is my favorite dinner. Seriously. I eat it once or twice a week myself. Easy to make—not a lot of standing—and if I can restrain myself from polishing it off in one sitting, it's good leftover for lunch the next day."

Jess grinned in amusement. Rhys's sister was truly funny.

Penny's outfit today was even more outrageous than the one she'd worn the day Jess first met her. She was in bib overalls, with a tatty orange sweater beneath. Her blonde hair was pinned up in a messy bun, and once again, she wore no makeup and the oversized glasses.

"Did you wear that to work?" Jess asked. "Or did you go home to change before picking up Jasper?"

Penny glanced down at her clothing. "Why? What's wrong with what I'm wearing?"

"Nothing. I was just wondering...don't you have to dress up for work?" Jess asked, attempting damage control when it appeared she'd inadvertently hurt her friend's feelings.

"Oh." Penny waved her hand. "No. I sit in a back room, surrounded by computers, plotting world domination and all that. No one cares what I wear. Hell, no one sees me at all. It's like I'm invisible."

Jess didn't miss the hint of sadness in Penny's voice and wondered if that was why she felt so close to Rhys's sister. Penny seemed like a lonely, lost soul too.

"I'm sure that's not true. You're hard not to notice," Jess said with a smile. "With your quirky, fun fashion style and gorgeous blonde hair."

Penny reached up to touch her hair. "You think my hair is gorgeous?"

Jess nodded. "Sure. Do you ever wear it down?"

Penny shook her head. "Not really. I'm afraid I'm not very good at styling it."

"I could show you some tricks sometime if you'd like." Jess and Danielle always used to try new hair and makeup techniques. She'd missed having a girl to hang out and to do girlie things with.

"That would be awesome," Penny said enthusiastically. "How about this weekend?"

Before Jess could reply, they were both startled by a loud knock on the door.

After two months of feeling safe and secure, Jess was forced to acknowledge it was going to take her some time to get used to being on "night guard duty" again. Until she got accustomed to the neighborhood, she was destined to spend more than a few sleepless nights, stressing out over every bump, creak, and car door slamming.

"Jess, open the door."

Tony.

Dammit.

She'd hoped to have more time before having to face him and Rhys. She'd taken the coward's way out, leaving a note behind, but she *had* waited for them. Even so, she should have expected they wouldn't accept it well.

She walked over to open the door. Her eyes widened when she discovered not just Tony on the threshold but Rhys and Aunt Berta as well.

For the first time since discovering they had a new home, Jasper bounded up excitedly, rushing into Tony's arms. "We got a new house," he said. "Do you all wanna come live with us? I have my own room. I can share it."

Tony grinned. "That's a nice offer. Tempting too."

Jasper wriggled, reaching out to Rhys. "You can share it too. But we don't have any beds yet, so we're sleeping on the floor."

"More camping?" Rhys asked, his gaze sliding to Jess, his

question reminding her of the last time she'd gone "camping" in her car.

"This time we have air mattresses," Jess said. "And blankets. And heat."

Rhys acknowledged her comments with a smile that didn't quite reach his eyes, while Tony scowled.

"What are you doing here?" she asked.

"We got your note," Rhys said.

"Did you see my picture?" Jasper was still holding on to Rhys tightly. She understood her son well enough to know he was unwilling to let go for fear they'd leave. That thought broke her heart even more.

"It's a great picture," Rhys said. "The perfect family portrait. We're going to buy a frame for it and hang it on the wall properly."

"Go on back to your room, Jasper," Aunt Berta said. "And grab your bag. The two of us are having a sleepover at my apartment."

Jasper released Rhys in an instant, excited by the prospect of returning to the home they'd just left. "We are?!"

"No—" Jess started.

"Yes, we are," Aunt Berta said, her hands on her hips, the pose one Jess was all too familiar with. It was Aunt Berta's I'm-getting-my-way stance.

Penny had risen at the arrival of her brother and Tony, but she'd been quiet thus far. She exchanged a look with her brother, a strange smile blooming before she said, "Come on, Jasper. I'll help you get your stuff."

"Wait," Jess said, but neither Penny nor Jasper stopped, so she turned back to Aunt Berta. "What's going on?"

Aunt Berta stepped next to her, placing a gentle hand on Jess's forearm. "The boys have something to say to you. I hope you'll hear them out. Either way, Jasper is staying with me the rest of the night and I'll get him to school tomorrow."

"But—"

Jasper raced back down the hall far too quickly, his bookbag slung over his shoulders, his pillow in his hands. Penny carried two of the duffel bags they'd lugged in from her car just an hour earlier, too tired to unpack.

"All ready," Penny announced. "I'll walk out with you, Aunt Berta."

"But—" Jess tried, only to be interrupted yet again.

"I'll call you this weekend, Jess," Penny said. "Get all the juicy details from you then."

"Juicy details?" she murmured, confused.

Rhys shouldered his sister affectionately. "You realize I'm going to be a part of those juicy details."

Penny shuddered. "Okay. Half of the details then."

Jess stood there dumbfounded, wondering where she'd missed a step or twenty.

Penny, Aunt Berta, and Jasper were all gone within seconds, leaving Jess alone in her new apartment with a scowling Tony and an amused Rhys.

"What the hell just happened?" she asked.

"Why did you move out?" Tony countered, ignoring her question and asking his own.

"Hasn't that been the plan all along? Your cousin, Bruno, called this morning and offered me this place. I can afford it, and it's in a great neighborhood. Jasper doesn't even have to change schools." Jess was rambling, over-justifying, when what she should have done was apologize for leaving without saying goodbye.

It was just...whenever Tony hit her with that tone, her back went up and the next thing she knew, she was talking back, rising to the challenge he presented. Probably not one of her better traits but something she didn't see changing in the future.

"Let me rephrase my question," Tony said, his arms crossed. "Why did you move out without telling us?"

She opened her mouth, searching for some response that

wouldn't reveal too much, but she couldn't come up with anything. "I liked the first question better."

"Fine. Then answer it properly," Tony said darkly.

"I couldn't keep impo—"

"If you say the word *imposing* to us one more time, I swear to God I will yank down those jeans of yours, toss you over my lap, and spank you until you can't sit comfortably for a week," Tony interjected, looking more than ready to follow through with that threat.

Rhys chuckled, sidling up next to her. Ever the peacemaker, he reached for her hand, drawing it up to place a soft kiss on her knuckles. "It's okay, Jess. You can tell us the truth. Answer his question."

"I was afraid..."

"Afraid of what?" Rhys asked gently.

God. She was afraid of so much. Where did she even begin?

"Afraid you'd ask me to stay longer, and I wouldn't find the strength to leave. Afraid of this damn future I've built up in my head that won't ever happen. Afraid that when everything we'd shared was over, you'd walk away. But most of all, I was afraid I'd break down in front of you and tell you...tell you..."

Tony stepped next to Rhys, tipping Jess's chin up to face him. "Tell us...?"

"I love you. Both of you. So much it hurts. And I'm sorry because I know that's not what you want, what you're looking for, but—"

"Jesus Christ, Jess." Tony expelled a huge breath of air, and she realized he must have been holding it the entire time. He wrapped his arms around her, embracing her tighter than she'd ever been held before. "Thank God!"

She pushed on his chest, frowning. "What?"

Rhys grasped her shoulders, pulling her against his chest as well, placing kiss after kiss on the top of her head. "We love you too. That's what we came here to tell you. We should have said it before. Should have made sure you knew that what the three of us have...it's a hell of a lot more than just physical."

"You love me?" Jess wanted to believe them. God, she knew she could trust them, that neither of them would lie, yet it was still so hard to truly believe. Good things didn't usually happen to her.

With the exception of Jasper, of course.

And them.

"Yes, goddammit," Tony said gruffly. "We love you. Both of us. And I know it's going to be hard for you to accept that fact, but just know we're going to tell you fifty times a day until it finally soaks into that stubborn, gorgeous head of yours."

"Only fifty?" she joked, her mind spinning so fast, she felt dizzy, giddy.

"A hundred and fifty," Tony amended.

"I didn't think you wanted a relationship." Jess took a deep breath and forced herself to add the words she really meant to say. "Marriage and kids."

"You've shown us the errors of our ways," Tony responded, not blinking an eye at what she longed for. "We want all of that...with you."

Rhys drew one hand down her arm, grasping her own. "Come home with us, Jess. Grab what you need for tonight and we'll clear the rest of this stuff out of here tomorrow. Move back to the apartment, not as our roommate but as *ours*."

"Yours?"

Tony reached for her other hand. "We have a lot to discuss, to figure out, but we're committed to making a life with you, and with Jasper. We'd like to be his fathers...if you'd let us."

Jess felt the first tear slide down her face. "You want to be his dads?"

She'd never heard anything more wonderful in her life.

"We're crazy about that boy," Rhys said. "We'd be proud to call him our son."

Jess didn't bother to hold in her sob. Her happiness was too big. "He'd love that so much."

"So you'll come home?" Rhys asked.

She nodded, certain she'd never heard a more beautiful word in her life.

Home.

Chapter Twenty

J ess stepped back into the apartment she'd just left, pausing over the threshold and smiling. She loved this place, loved the idea that Jasper would grow up here, with not just one amazing father but two.

Tony placed his hand on her lower back. "Keep walking," he said, pushing her gently toward the hallway. "Our room."

"Ours?" she whispered.

"Ours," Rhys repeated. "We can take it slow, Jess, give Jasper time to get used to what's happening here, but we *are* going to share a room, sleep together every night."

"I'd love that."

"And it's starting tonight," Tony said. "Aunt Berta has Jasper, so no more sneaking away after. I plan to hold you all night long."

They entered Rhys's—their—bedroom together.

"Take off your clothes," Tony demanded as he pulled his shirt over his head.

"Getting right down to business, I see," Jess joked, even as she took her sweater off, dropping it onto the floor next to Tony's shirt.

Tony reached for her, his large hands engulfing her waist.

He placed a fast, hard kiss on her lips. "You're lucky we're not punishing you for running away, for packing up and leaving without saying goodbye."

Jess's hand drifted to his hair, pulling the band out, the brown tresses falling over his shoulders. She gripped it, drawing his face back to hers, stealing her own rough kiss.

"I don't know if you should go easy on me," she murmured against his lips. "I *have* been a very bad girl. Imposing on you guys for so long."

The taunt had the desired effect.

Tony grasped her upper arm, dragging her to the bed. "I warned you about that word, didn't I?" He unfastened her jeans with expert fingers, drawing the denim—and her panties—over her hips but no farther.

Then he sat on the edge of the mattress and pulled her over his lap. She'd been wet ever since he'd made the threat to spank her earlier.

Jess grinned, even as she attempted to push herself back up. She wasn't going to make it too easy for him.

Rhys chuckled when he saw her face, but he didn't intervene. Instead, he stood before them, still fully dressed. As Tony pressed her head back down, Rhys ran his finger along her slit.

"Soaking wet," he murmured, proving her resistance was token at best.

Jess squirmed once more, though Tony kept a firm grip on her upper back. Her fake struggles ended when his hand came down on her ass, smacking her harder than she'd expected.

"Ouch!"

"Be still," Tony demanded, spanking her three more times on the same ass cheek in rapid succession.

"Tony," she said, but he didn't wait, refused to stop.

"Give it a second," he said instead, as he treated her other ass cheek and her upper thighs to the same smacks. "Feel the burn. Let it soak in."

Her ass was on fire, but she was no longer focused on the

pain. He'd been right to tell her to wait, as his actions sparked something she'd never experienced before.

She knew there were people who found pleasure in pain, but she'd never had the opportunity to explore that possibility herself.

Tony was giving her that chance now—and she fucking loved it.

Rhys knelt before her, grasping a handful of her hair, pulling it away from her face so he could see her more fully.

"Beautiful," he whispered.

Tony had paused, but after hearing Rhys's word, he continued the spanking, alternating his smacks with sensuous strokes of her slit, his fingers sliding through her arousal, teasing her until she thought she'd go mad.

"More," she begged.

"More what?" Rhys said, still kneeling next to her, watching her.

"More everything."

Tony chuckled. "I think we can handle everything."

He lifted his hand from her back, gripping her arm to help her rise. He remained perched on the edge of the bed, bending to help her remove her jeans and panties completely.

Rhys began to undress beside her.

She expected Tony to do the same, but he kept his jeans on when he stood.

Pushing her toward the bed, he instructed her to get on her hands and knees.

Jess loved the way they kept her on her toes, introducing her to new experiences, her guides in this sensual paradise, where she wanted to live forever.

She did as Tony asked, looking over her shoulder at the two of them, their gazes locked on her body, as if she was the most beautiful thing they'd ever seen.

She lowered her head to the mattress, drawing even more attention to her ass.

Tony groaned. "Fuck, Jess."

She listened as they moved behind her. She heard Tony's pants hit the floor. She needed them to take her. Now.

Fast. Hard. She was ready to get down and dirty.

She started to lift her head when she heard the nightstand drawer slide open. She looked over, curious about what they'd grabbed.

"No," Tony commanded. "Keep your head down."

She shivered in response, her orgasm hovering so close. So damn close. She suspected it wouldn't take more than a touch or two to push her over the edge.

Jess startled when she felt Rhys's hand on her ass, his gentle fingers caressing her still-heated flesh.

It took everything she had to obey Tony's command when she felt *his* hand on her ass as well.

"Open your legs, Jess." Tony's hand slid between her legs, pushing her thighs apart.

She was glad her flushed face was concealed in the duvet, as every single intimate part of her was laid bare to them.

Rhys took advantage of her new position, his fingers finding her clit, while Tony drew circles around the opening of her pussy.

"God," she breathed. "I'm going to come if you—" That was all she managed to say before her body erupted. She cried out as her orgasm took over.

Tony and Rhys stilled for a moment, letting her ride out the storm. The second it began to abate, they were back, resuming their previous strokes, as if they hadn't been interrupted at all.

"Please," she begged.

"Shh, angel," Tony soothed. "We're giving you everything, remember?"

She was suddenly regretting that request, uncertain she could withstand too many more orgasms as strong as that. She was quivery, shaky inside, not that her body gave a shit about that. It seemed to be operating on its own as she found herself

MARI CARR

thrusting back toward their fingers, silently demanding more. She needed Tony's fingers inside her, not merely teasing. And she wanted more friction, more speed from Rhys on her clit.

A long, blissful sigh flowed out when Tony slowly pushed two fingers deep inside her.

"Yes," she whispered. "So good."

Tony began to fuck her with his fingers, building the speed and the force. She followed that pace, moving frantically back toward him on each inward thrust. Rhys matched their rhythm, applying more pressure to her clit before pinching it, pulling it.

She came again, this orgasm sharper, harder. Her body started to collapse facedown on the mattress, her knees sliding away from her.

Tony halted her, gripping her hips tightly, keeping her on her knees. "We didn't say you could move." He backed that comment up with a hard slap on her ass.

She wanted to take offense at his arrogant tone, but fuck her if it didn't get her juices flowing even more.

"I can't take much more," she warned him.

Tony chuckled. "Tough. Because we haven't even scratched the surface on *everything*."

Jess jerked when she felt something cold on her ass. Glancing over her shoulder, she spotted the tube of lubrication in Rhys's hand. Now she knew what they'd gotten from the nightstand.

They'd introduced her to anal play in the exam room, and she'd been able to think of little else since then.

"You know what we want?" Rhys asked, spreading the lube around the rim of her ass without breaching her.

"Yes."

Rhys pressed the tip of one finger inside. "You can say no."

She smiled to herself, so in love with Rhys's caring nature. While Tony liked to bark demands, Rhys reminded her she would always have a choice in everything they did.

"I'm saying yes."

Rhys pushed his finger in completely, her back arching.

"Fuck," Tony muttered. "Hurry up and get her ready, Rhys. I need to be inside her. Now."

"That actually sounds like a good idea." Rhys removed his finger, and Jess whimpered in complaint. "Shift over, love," he said. "Let Tony lay down."

Jess did as he asked. Tony lay down on his back, then reached out to draw her over him.

"Ready to take another ride?" he asked with a wink, reminding her of the first time they'd had sex.

She nodded eagerly, gripping his thick cock and guiding it to her pussy. Tony was wider than Rhys, so she had to move slowly, her body needing time to acclimate to the stretch. She was glad it was Rhys who would initiate her ass this first time. She would have to work up to taking Tony there.

Once she'd fully taken him inside her, Tony reached for her, pulling her head to his chest.

Then Rhys climbed on the bed, kneeling next to them. He added more lube to her ass and his fingers, returning this time with two.

"God, Jess...Rhys, that feels so fucking good." Tony's hand rested on her hips, touching rather than holding, but Jess knew that would change if she attempted to move.

But damn if she didn't *need* to move.

Rhys, the patient, attentive lover, took his time, stretching her, helping her acclimate.

She needed less patience and more fucking.

A fact that had Tony and Rhys chuckling when she expressed it out loud. And one that had Rhys spanking her ass cheek in warning.

Not that it helped. Rhys had proven himself to be just as alpha as Tony in bed. It was a quieter, less demanding control, but he left no doubt that he'd do things in his way, in his time, and she would have to accept it.

"Please," she whispered, when Rhys had breached her ass

with three fingers, thrusting them in slowly, methodically, beautifully.

At last satisfied, Rhys withdrew his fingers...and she stiffened slightly when she felt the head of his cock brush against her ass.

"Let him in, angel," Tony said.

Jess relaxed, then closed her eyes as Rhys, who'd prepared her well, slid inside.

It was a tight fit, and there were definitely moments when the pain overrode the pleasure—just for a second or two.

Once he was seated to the hilt, Jess felt Tony's fingers beneath her chin, lifting her face up. "Open your eyes, Jess."

She was becoming accustomed to that request from him. She didn't mind because she loved looking into his gaze at times like this as well. Before tonight, she'd mistaken what she'd seen there, chalking his expression up to enjoyment, pleasure, desire.

Now she could see that she'd had it all wrong. It felt as if she could see all the way to the depths of his soul, and what she saw...blew her away.

Love.

How could she not have recognized it?

Tony smiled. "Say you belong to us. Say you're ours, and let that word sink deep. Because we're staking our claim, leaving our mark, making sure every single man in the world knows exactly who you belong to."

Rhys didn't move, but he was listening. She felt him run his fingers along her spine, the touch prompting her to shiver. "Say it," he prodded.

"I'm yours," she said to Tony before looking over her shoulder. "And yours."

"Always," Rhys added before he began the slow glide out.

Jess pressed her forehead to Tony's chest, gasping for air. Her heart was racing, but she wasn't sure if that was due to arousal...or affection.

Tony's fingers tightened around her hips, beginning to add his own strokes to the slow, easy tempo Rhys had found.

Of course, slow and easy soon gave way to faster, harder. Jess tried to add her own beat to the rhythm, but her lovers weren't relinquishing control. Tony's hands still had possession of her hips, while Rhys's fist was wrapped around her hair.

They pushed her to the edge once, twice, three times, each time backing away just before she could make that final leap.

The third time, she growled, bared her teeth. "Goddamn you."

"You're going to feel us all day tomorrow, angel. Gonna remember exactly who we are. Who *you* are to us." Tony backed up his proclamation, cupping her breasts, squeezing them. "Ours."

Rhys ran one hand over her ass, stroking the skin there before giving her another little smack.

Jess was amazed—and slightly overwhelmed—by their stamina, as neither man gave any indication of stopping.

"Please," she begged, aware that word was likely to become the most used one in her vocabulary. Not that it worked. They weren't swayed, weren't moved, determined to draw this night out...possibly forever.

Soon, the only sounds in the room were her whimpers, their groans and grunts, their panting breaths, and the slapping of their bodies coming together at an almost frantic pace.

The next time she reached the precipice, they didn't hold her back. Instead, they shoved her over roughly.

"God, yes," she cried out hoarsely, her body trembling violently, her pussy clenching tightly.

"Fuck!" Tony bellowed beneath her, still moving, still fucking her through her orgasm. It was animalistic, feral, savage.

It was everything...fucking *everything*.

Rhys used his grip on her hair to lift her, her back arching between them, his lips brushing against her shoulder before he sank his teeth in.

The sharp sting prolonged her orgasm. She scraped her nails down Tony's chest, scores of red welts rising. They weren't the only ones determined to leave a mark, to stake a claim.

Tony thrusted a handful of times more before he was there with her, his cock erupting inside her. Rhys fell only a second later, and she felt her name on his lips at her ear.

For several moments, they remained exactly as they were—a frozen tableau in a room so thick with humidity and steam and wet heat that it rivaled the rain forest.

Finally, they pulled themselves apart. Rhys reached for the nightstand, grabbing a handful of tissues, cleaning up the sticky evidence of their lovemaking from her thighs. Then the three of them lay on their backs, fighting to draw air into their lungs, words completely beyond them.

Jess reached for their hands, flanked by them, tucked between them. They clasped her hands in theirs.

"Jesus, Jess," Tony said, his voice thick, telling her he was on the verge of falling asleep. "Love you, angel. Love you so fucking much."

She smiled and offered him the words back. They came easy, and it felt good to be able to speak them without fear of rejection.

His response was the deep, even breathing of sleep.

Rhys squeezed her hand. "You okay?"

Her heart skipped a beat at his concerned question, his need to take care of her.

"I am," she whispered. "Very okay."

Rhys lifted their clasped hands and placed a kiss on hers. "You make me happy, Jess. So happy."

She nodded, blinking several times to beat back the tears.

Their hands dropped back to the bed, and soon Rhys followed Tony, sleeping peacefully next to her.

Jess had never truly belonged anywhere. Not until this moment.

For so long, she'd sought her place in the world, certain she would never find it.

And now she was here.

Home.

She'd found it at last.

Ready for more Italian Stallions? Book two (Penny's story) releases in June! You can preorder it now!

Hard and Fast

And be sure to be on the lookout for the rest of the Italian Stallions series releasing in the future.

Rough and Ready

Wild and Wicked

Hot and Heavy

Steady and Strong

Tempted and Taken

Kiss and Tell

Want to see how Layla Moretti found true love with Miguel and Finn? Want to see how the Moretti brothers got their Italian Stallions nickname? Check out these books, standalone within the Wilder Irish series!

Wild Side

Wild Dreams

Wild Chance

Calling all fans of Mari Carr AND Facebook! There's a group for you. Come join the Mari Carr's Facebook group for sneak peaks, cover reveals, contests and more! Join now.

. . .

And be sure to join Mari's mailing list to receive a **FREE** sexy novella, Midnight Wild.

About the Author

Virginia native Mari Carr is a New York Times and USA TODAY bestseller of contemporary romance novels. With over two million copies of her books sold, Mari was the winner of the Romance Writers of America's Passionate Plume award for her novella, Erotic Research. She has over a hundred published works, including her popular Wild Irish and Compass books, along with the Trinity Masters series she writes with Lila Dubois.

Follow Mari:
www.maricarr.com
mari@maricarr.com

Join her newsletter so you don't miss new releases and for exclusive subscriber-only content.

Made in the USA
Coppell, TX
15 January 2023

11146664R00152